RAFFAELLA BARKER

GREEN GRASS

B L O O M S B U R Y

LONDON · NEW DELHI · NEW YORK · SYDNEY

First published in Great Britain in 2002 by Headline Review
This paperback edition published in 2014

Bloomsbury Publishing Plc
50 Bedford Square
London
WC1B 3DP

www.bloomsbury.com

Bloomsbury is a trademark of Bloomsbury Publishing Plc

Bloomsbury Publishing, London, New Delhi, New York and Sydney

A CIP catalogue record for this book is
available from the British Library

ISBN 978 1 4088 5069 5

10 9 8 7 6 5 4 3 2 1

Typeset by Hewer Text UK Ltd, Edinburgh
Printed and bound in Great Britain by
CPI Group (UK) Ltd, Croydon CR0 4YY

GREEN GRASS

RAFFAELLA BARKER, daughter of the poet George Barker, was born and brought up in the Norfolk countryside. She is the author of seven other novels, *Come and Tell Me Some Lies*, *The Hook*, *Hens Dancing*, *Summertime*, *Poppyland*, *A Perfect Life* and *From a Distance*. She has also written a novel for young adults, *Phosphorescence*. She is a regular contributor to the *Sunday Times* and the *Sunday Telegraph* and teaches on the Literature and Creative Writing BA at the University of East Anglia and the *Guardian* UEA Novel Writing Masterclass. Raffaella Barker lives by the sea in north Norfolk.

Also by Raffaella Barker

Come and Tell Me Some Lies
The Hook
Hens Dancing
Summertime
Phosphorescence
Poppyland
A Perfect Life
From a Distance

For Roman with love from Mum

This is not a novel, it's an installation

CHAPTER 1

'Can you balance a spoon on your nose?'

Laura is grateful that Inigo does not demonstrate spoon balancing, but instead contents himself with arranging all the glasses and cutlery on the table into a gleaming circuit, with fork following knife following spoon, each one balanced on the rim of a glass.

'Everything has a point from which it can balance. The trick is finding it.' Inigo pushes back the sleeves of his shirt. His watch glitters and beeps, becoming a green screen for a second. He flexes his fingers and balances a cigarette packet on one corner, then flashes a grin at his audience. Laura has of course seen it all before, but she knows better than to roll her eyes and sigh; instead she beckons the circling waitress and whispers instructions. Manfred, an art collector who flew in this evening from Munich to dine with Laura and Inigo, claps his hands and laughs out loud.

'What a talent. What a talent,' he chortles, slapping Inigo on the back with a broad, well-manicured hand. Inigo, lost in contemplation of the menu, is caught off balance and lurches towards Laura. The apparently floating tableware crashes down, spilling water onto Manfred's soft black trousers and into his shoes. The flurry of napkins, the apologies and jangle of steel against glass and china goes unremarked in the roaring chatter and bustle of the restaurant. Laura takes a deep breath and exhales at length to stop herself saying something foul to Inigo. It is important to be supportive, she reminds herself, and anyway, there's no point in getting het up about his table arranging.

Unperturbed, Inigo pushes back his cuffs again with a big-armed gesture and begins to rebalance his place setting. A thin blade of a man slides into the fourth seat at the table, kissing Laura's cheek, winking at Inigo and shaking hands with Manfred, all in one smooth elision of movement and greeting.

'Manfred, it's good to see you again. Laura, Inigo, I'm sorry to keep you all waiting. Can I get any of you a drink or have you ordered a bottle?'

'You didn't keep us waiting, we were fine and we've ordered some wine.' On this occasion Laura can't quite suppress the bubble of irritation which blows up in her chest whenever she sees Jack Smack, Inigo's agent. Most of the time she has it well under control, and can meet his oily gaze with serenity, but this evening she is tense and tired, and determined to puncture the smug slickness of his arrival.

'Manfred wants to know more about Inigo's working methods,' she says untruthfully to Jack, who is painstakingly removing a fork and a knife from the suspension bridge Inigo has remade. 'Why don't you bring him along to the studio tomorrow morning, at about eleven, and we can show him something more substantial than these dinner tricks before he has to catch his plane?'

She smiles, her eyes demure, her hands folded in her lap. She knows that Jack is having a little more of his hair transplant done in the morning because his secretary Jenny told her so, and she can't resist trying to catch him out.

But Jack looks regretful, pours wine and says, 'What a wonderful idea – let's do it next time. I've already fixed Manfred up to see one of my young Turner Prize candidates for breakfast in a caravan underneath the Westway. They're being filmed for a documentary so we can't really cancel. Sorry, Laura.'

Laura has to bite her bottom lip hard to stop herself saying, 'Touché, Jack,' but she is diverted by Inigo leaning over to whisper loudly, 'Has Jack always had that scar on his head?'

Manfred and Jack are discussing something dreary: is it better to fly from Berlin to Gatwick or from Munich to Heathrow? Laura turns towards Inigo, putting her fingers up to his mouth and whispering in his ear, 'Sssshhhhh! He's halfway through having a hair transplant – haven't you noticed all those tufts that have started to appear? No, don't look now.'

But Inigo, to whom tact is a foreign language and subtlety another country, cranes past her to look, raising an eyebrow so it almost meets his own hairline.

Laura presses her fingers on his arm and shoots him a warning look; Inigo is quite capable of asking Jack about the transplant, but instead he squeezes Laura's hand back, and winks at her.

Manfred, watching them, beams approvingly. He likes to see a couple getting on well, and he likes it even more if they are attractive and are sitting with him. Inigo and Laura are striking, and although in a ideal world he would prefer to see a smaller nose on a woman, and perhaps long curly blonde tresses where Laura has an aquiline profile and auburn hair scooped up in a twist, he appreciates her creamy unlined skin, and her neat waist. His eyes linger for a moment on her stomach, or what he can see of it beneath the smooth fabric of her damson red skirt, then he coughs and asks Jack, 'Did you say that Laura and Inigo have children? How long have they been married?'

The food arrives, and conversation becomes general, Inigo answering Manfred as he hands him a fork he has inadvertently tucked into the breast pocket of his jacket, presumably to save for a bit of balancing later when the table is cleared.

'Yes, we've got two. Twins, in fact. They're called Fred and Dolly. They're thirteen now.' He pauses, fishing for his glasses and putting them on to survey his food. 'They're bastards,' he adds, scrutinising his plate, which must look very off-putting due to the green lenses in his glasses. 'I thought I ordered organic mushrooms, but this looks like excrement.' Inigo raises an arm to beckon the waitress.

Manfred looks shocked and cannot think what to say next. Laura places a soothing hand on his arm. 'Oh honestly, Inigo, you don't have to put it like that, do you? Sorry, Manfred. What he means is that we aren't married.'

Neither Inigo nor Manfred is listening. Both are gazing at Inigo's plate on which ooze some pieces of black slime. The waitress, her hands cupped in apparent supplication, is delivering an earnest lecture on organic methods of mushroom growing.

'Well, I think they do grow them in compost, but I'm sure it's well rotted and comes from completely organic cows, or sheep or whatever manure they use . . .'

'See? I said it was excrement,' mutters Inigo, lifting his plate up to examine it further.

'For heaven's sake, man, either eat it or send it back,' Jack interrupts testily, having wolfed half of his vivid red mound of steak tartare and pushed away the plate, indicating his readiness for the removal of this course and the arrival of the next.

'I'm going to eat it, I just want to know what's in it. After all, this place makes a great song and dance about being organic and pure. I bet your beef is untraumatised, so why shouldn't my mushrooms be serene?'

Laura eats her own, delicious salad, wishes she was thin enough for bread as well, and finds her glass is empty again. When Manfred fills it, Laura is faintly aware that this is the third time.

He asks her, 'Are you against marriage for any particular reason?'

5

Bemused for a moment, Laura stares at him, noticing the kind eyes, the large cheeks, the soft fold of his chin dolloping over his stiffened collar. 'Against marriage? What do you mean? Oh, us,' she laughs, sips her wine, and because Inigo and Jack are talking now, and because she has had two glasses of wine on a stomach empty of all save lettuce, she launches into explanation.

'No, I'd love to be married in some ways. Someone asked me once, but that was years ago, before I met Inigo.' She pauses, fiddling with her glass, gazing at nothing; Manfred nods sympathetically. He is having a lovely time looking at Laura's cleavage and hearing about her marriage, or rather her non-marriage. He hadn't planned to buy an Inigo Miller piece – the prices have become absurd – but really, Laura is enchanting. Perhaps there's something with an image of her on it. Or in it. He'll ask Jack to sort it out. It'll cost a bit, but what the hell. Maybe Laura could come along when Inigo instals it. He must make sure it's something big which needs installing. And it had better be fragile, so it will need restoring by the artist. Laura must come to watch the restoration, of course. Mmmm . . . splendid. Manfred pops a piece of bread in his mouth and chews.

Laura is talking again. 'Inigo and I had a commitment ceremony in New York. We'd been together a couple of years – longer, maybe – because Fred and Dolly were about two. We were all living in New York. It was fun, but hard work with small children . . .' Laura tails off, lost in memories of dragging her

6

double buggy up endless stairs to the apartment, of putting on and taking off toddler hats and gloves to keep the children from over- or under-heating. She loved her life then.

Manfred coughs gently, drawing Laura back. She smiles apologetically. 'Oh yes, anyway, the ceremony. We were all on the roof of the gallery where Inigo was having his show, and he'd put up a huge Möbius strip studded with sequins and it was snowing.'

Manfred raises a hand. 'Yes, yes,' he beams, 'I remember. I have seen a photograph of it in an auction catalogue. It is called *Perfect Moment*. I love that piece.'

Laura sighs, slumping her head on one hand. 'Well, it should have been a perfect moment, just Inigo and me and our children and this lovely priest we met out there, but then Inigo and Jack decided that it would make fantastic art so they invited all the critics and a few favoured clients and said it was an exclusive Private View. Inigo took photographs between vows, and released a limited edition of twenty prints. Some are called *Private View* and the others are called *Perfect Moment*, depending on whether the photograph has us kissing or not. They went for a fortune, but I would rather have had my ceremony to myself.'

'But Laura, my sweet, then I wouldn't have got my forty per cent.' Jack leans across to break up their conversation and Laura, her cheeks suddenly burning from the wine and the memories, pushes her chair back and crosses the restaurant towards the lavatories.

Inigo watches her move between the tables. She catches the heel of her shoe against the leg of someone's chair, stoops to apologise, and continues. Inigo grins to himself, unconsciously playing with a pen, threading it between his fingers, twirling it around the middle finger then balancing it on its point on his thumb. Laura is like that, so is Fred. At home, Inigo likes clear surfaces on which he can place objects, position them perfectly, move away and come back to look at them. He likes to suspend things – a compass perhaps or an ivory paper-knife, from invisible thread, so the object hovers just above the mantelpiece or the kitchen shelf. His daughter Dolly shares his fascination with the way things are in their space; she too finds it hard to walk past a pile of books or a bowl of fruit without rearranging it. But then Fred or Laura come in and the constructions are doomed. Fred throws a school bag on top of a pyramid of lemons and paperclips on the kitchen table, Laura, searching for her keys, which are never where she thought, elbows a hovering display of glass prisms above the mantelpiece so they swing and tangle in rainbow-lit abandon. It's not intentional; Laura and Fred are simply clumsy. Dolly finds it maddening, but Inigo has endless patience for recreating poise in their wake. Laura, in turn, finds this maddening.

Laura washes her hands in cold water and presses them to her cheeks to reduce the burning heat of alcohol. She drinks water from the tap then dries her face, feeling better, more controlled. A glance in the mirror above the wash basin confirms that her hair has come loose and her expression is glazed. Laura places her palm over her reflected face, wishing she could change into someone else. This evening is hard work. She feels heavy, dull and joyless. And old. Too old to gulp her wine and let Jack irritate her. And far too old to pour her heart out to Manfred. She must stop feeling sorry for herself; her face is definitely beginning to set in a downward droop. Not very becoming. Laura cranks a grin onto her face – it almost hurts, it feels so alien.

Unequal to dealing with her state of mind, Laura fiddles in her make-up bag for her lipstick. She smoothes it across her mouth, repins her hair and makes her mirror face, with eyes wide, chin down and what she hopes is a sophisticated and provocative small smile playing on her lips. Making the most of having got this look right, she pushes wide the door back into the restaurant and stalks out with determined grace. The plan is that she will skim back to the table, and will be admired by all she passes for her smiling chic. Inigo will be amazed. Laura holds her head high, pretends to be a swan, and steps straight into a pile of white polystyrene boxes which are lurching along from the kitchens.

'Ow! God, I'm sorry. Oh bugger. So much for being a swan, or indeed soignée,' she mutters, crouching to help pick up the flimsy boxes, thankful that she is hidden from the restaurant tables by a frosted-glass screen. The man behind the boxes still has two, but he lets them fall and holds out both hands to pull her up from where she scrabbles for a lid behind the lavatory door.

'I'm so sorry. Are you all right? I hope—' He breaks off as she faces him. He forgets his hands are still holding hers, tightening with amazement. 'You're Laura. How extraordinary. It's Guy. Do you remember me?'

Laura pulls back, breathless and flushing, madly convinced for a moment that she is naked.

'Guy,' she says and stops, unable to think of anything more to say. She stares at Guy who is taller than she is, even though her heels are so high she sways on them. The silence is a flash of time, but it is painful before Laura breaks it.

'What are these boxes for?'

Guy laughs, and Laura stops feeling naked although her throat is thudding with shock and a sense of peeled-back years. She was twenty when she last saw him.

'They're for my vegetables. I had to drive down with an extra delivery this evening. This place is getting through the stuff twice as fast as I anticipated.'

'What did you bring?' Laura asks, afraid that to ask anything less bland might bring back the naked feeling.

Guy grins, as if he knows what she is thinking. 'Mushrooms straight out of a compost heap and still steaming. But this is incredible – to see you again.' He pulls her away from the screen, back towards the tables and the lit restaurant. 'You've changed, and yet you haven't. You're looking lovely, Laura. Tell me, what are you doing here? How are you? I see your brother sometimes.'

Even though she doesn't, Laura says, 'I know.' The swirling roar of the restaurant hovers between them as they stand silent for a second. Laura has a sense of toppling, which she puts down to her heels. She hopes Guy doesn't put it down to drunkenness. Determined to get a grip on herself she holds out her hand, intending a businesslike shake. 'I must go back to Inigo and the others.'

Guy takes her hand and kisses it. 'I'm so glad to see you,' he says quietly. She turns and walks away.

Back at the their table, Inigo is discoursing on his favourite topic, loops, to an audience of only Manfred. Jack has vanished.

'You see, the Möbius strip is in essence a loop. It moves and changes, yet goes nowhere and stays the same. It is a metaphor for the absurdity of life. Take Samuel Beckett . . .'

Manfred, who is writing notes, leaning forward eagerly across the table, nods and scribbles 'Samuel Beckett' in his notebook.

'Take *Godot*, for example.' Manfred takes *Godot*. Inigo interlaces his fingers and straightens his arms over the table, stretching his palms towards Manfred's eager nose and face. 'In *Waiting for Godot*, nothing happens twice. It's brilliant. Superb.' Inigo stops, his expression arrested, gaze fixed on Manfred, waiting. Manfred chews his pencil, and looks blank.

Laura smiles encouragingly at him and kicks Inigo, muttering. 'Don't start, please. I don't think Manfred is a Beckett fan.'

But Inigo is warming to his theme, and he delves in his pocket to bring out a strip of black rubber which he passes to Manfred. Manfred shrinks back; it looks like something for taking blood pressure, or more likely an implement for kinky sex. He wants none of it.

Inigo's eyes are blazing enthusiasm as he changes gear and motors smoothly on with his theories. 'You see, the Möbius strip has no end and no beginning. Look at it. Look at life. We are born, we wake up each day, we eat, we go to sleep, and at some point we die and are replaced by the next generation. It is futile and wonderful, moving and petrifying.'

'It's just one of his strips,' Laura hisses to Manfred. 'Do you see? It looks like a link of a chain or a figure of eight, but actually it is a form with one side and one edge. It was invented by a German mathematician, in fact. August Ferdinand Möbius was his name.'

Manfred watches her run her finger along the whole of the black rubber thing, proving presumably that it has one side. This is lost on him, but he does like leaning towards Laura, breathing in the scent of her hair and her perfume as he looks over her shoulder at the strip.

'What's it for?' he asks.

'It's not so much that it's for anything, it's a physical manifestation of an idea,' Laura begins to explain.

She loves amassing, reconstituting and doling out information. Some people, including her older brother when they were children, and her own children now, interpret this as control freakery and appalling bossiness, but Laura sees it as a way of keeping some part of her brain alive. There have been times in the thirteen years that she has been a mother, when she has felt her brain beginning to sidle softly out of her head. Without a concerted effort to return it to position, Laura imagines her brain might just bob away to a peachy cloud where it will live in peace for ever, wallowing in the luxury of having continuous, uninterrupted thoughts whenever it wants to. She would then be left, lobotomised and dutiful, to meet her family's needs without ever complaining or thinking for herself. In many ways it would be a huge relief.

Jack reappears at the table, brushing a casual hand across the light down on his head then leaning over to kiss the crown of Laura's. 'I've got a taxi waiting outside. I'll take Manfred back to his hotel and we'll talk in the morning,' he says, folding the receipt ostentatiously into smaller and smaller rectangles, just in case anyone missed the fact that he has paid the bill.

Manfred rises and reluctantly bids Laura farewell. He would like to stay drinking coffee and schnapps and preening his intellect; he thinks it is a bit much of Jack to drag him away as if he is a schoolboy, but it is difficult to argue with someone who presents his own suggestions as a fait accompli.

Laura and Inigo, left alone at the table, are suddenly and simultaneously overwhelmed with a desire for sleep. He smiles and holds out a hand to her.

'Come on, let's go home, it's late.'

CHAPTER 2

The winter sun wakes Laura, and she opens her eyes to a dazzle of pink, glad for once of Inigo's belief that curtains would cut off his creative dynamic with the world. Buoyed by the roseate joy of the morning, she rises, determined to be serene today, and performs what should be a short but satisfying sequence of yoga stretches on the floor at the end of the bed. In fact it is nothing of the sort. Collapsing with a groan from the agony of doggy position, she decides to look for an alternative exercise programme. Inigo sleeps on. All she can see of him is the black slash of his hair on the pillow. In all the years they have been together, he has never woken up before her; even if his alarm clock is set, Inigo is incapable of being first out of bed. He likes someone else to pave his way.

Outside, sunbeams stretch across the street and the cars parked on each side of the road glitter and sparkle, coated with frost like the crystallised fruits Laura's mother always has in the house for Christmas.

Slapping her feet up the rubber-floored staircase Laura realises with horror that no thank you letters have been written to her mother for the Christmas presents she sent the children, and now it is almost March. She wonders whether to try and get them to do it this morning, but decides it will be easier to forge their handwriting herself and fake the letters. That way at least they might appear to be a tiny bit grateful for Dolly's flower press and Fred's mouth organ.

She opens the door to Dolly's room, but the bed is already empty, the curtains flung back to let in the light and a rap music station is pulsing from the radio next to the bed. Dolly is in the bathroom. The air is thick with her favourite ozone-killing body sprays and hair volumiser, and the floor is littered with towels, T-shirts and trainers. Clearly Dolly is choosing her outfit for the day. The scene in Fred's room is some-what different. A fug of dark, silent warmth greets Laura when she opens the door. She tries a school-mistress approach first.

'Good morning, Fred. It's a lovely, lovely day – do look.'

Her son does not move or make a sound, despite the rude crack of his blinds pinging up and the search-light of morning sun falling onto his pillow and his turned-away face. Laura tugs at the duvet, and the visible part of Fred vanishes under the covers accom-panied by a low groaning sound.

'Come on, I'm making breakfast.' She turns to leave the room, trying not to look at the heaped clothes, the sliding piles of books and hurled odd socks. Picking her way out, Laura stands on something soft and yielding yet crunchy.

'Urgh, gross. It's something alive, I think!' she shrieks.

Fred is out of bed in a flash. 'Where? Let's see.' He kneels next to her, scrabbling on the rug, then sighs. 'Mum, you've trodden on my owl pellet. That's so annoying, I was going to dissect it.'

Laura shudders. 'Why was it on the floor then? What's in it anyway?'

Both of them crouch on the floor, examining the desiccated mess of mangled feather and bone. Fred picks up part of a tiny skull.

'Look, this is a shrew, I think. I didn't know London owls ate shrews.'

'Where did you find the pellet?'

'Under the oak trees on the Heath. I think the owl's got a house in there. It's right by a rubbish bin and that was where I thought he got his food.' Fred is wide awake now, picking over the bits of reconstituted owl dinner. Laura glances at her watch.

'Come on. You'll have to leave it for now. Just hurry up and come down for breakfast.'

Fred scowls at her. 'All right, all right, there's no need to get in a psyche, is there?'

Laura doesn't answer. She bangs on Dolly's door as she passes and shouts, 'Breakfast Doll, come on,' with little hope of being heard above the whirr of the hairdryer and the thud of the radio. She runs downstairs and into the kitchen, imagining with savage pleasure the children's horror if she were to revert to a version of their behaviour and lie in bed refusing to get up or brush her hair or eat what is provided – Laura pours tea and places packets of cereal on the table, lost in her reverie, imagining herself lolling in the back of the car while her children drive, picking her nose, dangling her shoes from her toes and sighing at the choice of radio channel. It would be so enjoyable, such fun. Laura has forgotten how to have fun. Somewhere on the way to becoming a thirty-eight-year-old mother of adolescents, a wife manquée for fourteen years, she has left having fun behind.

Sighing, self-pity welling, Laura opens the fridge, reaching before she looks and thus dislodging a pyramid of eggs. One rolls out and breaks softly on her foot. 'Sod it,' she murmurs.

'If we had a dog your foot would be licked clean in a nano-second,' says Fred from the doorway where he has chosen to stand to eat his cereal. He prefers not to sit at the table, it makes the prospect of conversation with his sister more likely. He grins at Laura, and despite the small humiliations of the morning concerning owl spit and feet, Laura smiles back, love surging because he looks so scrubbed, his hair slicked back with a wet comb from his brow, freckles a splash across his nose, and the hollow at the back of his neck visible again now after a severe interlude at the barber's shop, reminding her of long-ago life when he and Dolly were babies and she lay with them in bed feeding them for so long it seemed for ever.

'Mum, why are you standing there with egg on your foot?' Dolly is at the table, her hair a sliding copper curtain as she leans over her bowl, shovelling spoonfuls of cereal into her mouth fast, flipping the pages of an exercise book between gulps. 'We've got a maths block test this morning. Do you know any algebra formulas?'

'You mean formulae,' Fred interrupts triumphantly.

'Oh, shut up, you swot,' growls Dolly, sticking out her foot to trip him up. Fred flounders but doesn't fall, and Laura is wrenched back from the misty memories of their babydom by them hurling abuse and shreds of breakfast at one another.

Having just read a manual on how to raise happy children, Laura suppresses her maternal instinct, which is to scream, 'Shut the hell up, you two, or I'll bang you heads together,' and opts for the psychologically correct response: 'I see that you are both angry – shall we all sit down and talk it through?'

Inigo walks in as Laura is saying this and looks at her incredulously. 'Get a grip, Laura. They're never going to take that hippy crap seriously,' he says to her, adding, 'What is that disgusting slime on your foot?' before clapping his hands like a tinpot dictator and yelling, 'Dolly! Fred! Enough.'

Irritatingly for Laura, they both shut up for an instant, but then explode into giggles.

'It's egg, Dad. Mum's covered in egg.' Fred sighs a last snigger and gulps milk from the carton. Inigo deliberately averts his face and props three spoons together to form a wigwam on the kitchen table. Fred looks at him, measuring up his mood. He decides to risk it. 'If we had a dog, it would have licked her foot clean by now,' he says, edging away towards the hall and his coat and bag as he speaks.

Inigo doesn't hear, he reaches into the fridge and emerges with three eggs. He rolls one out of his palm and on to the knuckles of his right hand while throwing another to Dolly. 'What did you say, Fred? Here, Doll, catch this. I liked your egg pyramid; shame Mum got to it.' He shakes his head sorrowfully in the direction of Laura's slime-smeared foot and reaches out to pull her towards him by her waist. 'I'm starving after eating that pile of organic horse shit last night. Who else wants scrambled egg?'

'We've got to go.' Laura glares at Fred over Inigo's shoulder, not wanting the dog row to break out this morning. 'We mustn't be late, they've got a maths test.'

Fred assumes an innocent and angelic expression and waves to his father. 'Bye, Dad, see you later.'

Inigo turns from the stove, a flowery apron tied neatly yet absurdly around his waist. 'See you tonight, Fred. Hope the test is OK.'

Dolly, twirling her school coat like a matador with his cloak, wraps her arms around her father, her bright hair sweeping his black-clad shoulder, ignoring the wooden spoon dripping butter onto the floor. Inigo kisses the top of her head, gesturing to Laura to take the wooden spoon. She does so, but drops it as Dolly begins her own personal dog attack on her father.

'Dad, come on, it's time we talked about this. We all really want a dog and—'

'Not now, Dolly, we've got to go,' Laura cuts in, grabbing her daughter's arm, trying to pull her out of the door.

Inigo narrows his eyes, crosses his arms and assumes an evil and inaccessible expression. 'Well, I don't want a sodding dog, so you can all go to hell.'

Dolly huffs and glares, tossing her hair crossly. 'You don't have to be quite so rude, Dad,' she says icily, and inwardly Laura applauds, although, with the childcare manual foremost in her mind, she knows better than to side with her daughter against her co-parent. Dolly flaps her coat insouciantly and turns on her heel, shouting back, 'Me and Fred think you only mind because you don't want to share Mum,' and Fred cannot resist calling from the doorway as he passes through it, adding his mite, 'You're daft to think you and a dog could compete, Dad. The dog would win hands down. I mean paws . . .'

Laura closes the front door behind them, hastily escaping the tirade she knows will follow, and herds the twins towards the car, pausing to check for forgotten bags and books, inspecting Dolly from a safe distance for signs of anti-father tantrum, smiling at Fred in case he is nervous about the maths test, chivvying and worrying like a veteran sheep dog.

In the car Laura turns the music up very loudly; it is the only way she can be sure that the children will not speak to her and that she will therefore have peace, if not quiet, in which to think for a moment.

The tape is a compilation of her favourite Country and Western songs. John Prine's inimitable croak cuts into her thoughts, soothing immediately. 'There's flies in the kitchen . . .'

'Oh no, it's slit your wrist time,' groans Dolly in the back. 'Mum, can we listen to our music instead?'

'Yes, in a minute, just be patient.'

Manoeuvring out of the quiet side street where they live and into the blaring, shunting London rush-hour traffic, Laura begins to relax. Time spent in the car is time off. Of course, it is better time off if the children are not in the car too, but even when they are, Laura is soothed by the fact that there is nothing they can do about forgotten homework, and even better, there is no need for her to nag them. She joins in with gusto, 'Make me an angel to fly from Montgomery, Make me a picture of an old Rodeo,' and flushed with pleasure at the music, and with her own faultless rendition, she glances in the rearview mirror to smile at her darling children, noticing as she does that there is a bus close behind, filling the back window of the car with its mud-stained redness.

The darlings loll vacantly, listless now the dog row has passed. Dolly is fiddling with her hair and gazing out of the window, Fred mouths the words of the song, not because he likes it, but because he knows it so well that he doesn't even know he's doing it. They are side by side, their school bags bundled between them, but each twin inhabits a separate world.

'You've got twins. How lovely, they must be so close,' people say to her when they meet her, avidly watching Dolly and Fred for signs of twinnishness. What these signs might be is not clear. They don't even look alike. Fred's freckles, his pale blue eyes, his determined chin and his hair the colour of wet sand come from Laura's mother's family, while Dolly has Inigo's narrow face and long elegant fingers, his curving mouth and dark grey eyes. Only her copper bright hair, and her skin as smooth and pale as cream are like Laura's. Or rather like they used to be, Laura thinks wryly.

Dolly catches her mother's eye in the mirror and scowls for no reason except she finds it quicker and easier than smiling. Laura sighs, trying to remember when life with Dolly was not like living with a temperamental opera diva. Fred has always been easy, but not Dolly. Dolly is difficult, and Laura finds Dolly especially hard work. With Inigo she is usually a more persuadable child, and has been since the moment she was placed in his arms, a crumpled infant bellowing her first breaths with flailing fists and a cross little face beneath a shock of hair. On that day, in the delivery room of the vast, dying West London Hospital, Inigo looked at his newborn daughter and began to laugh, wrapping her closer in her blanket, surprised by the rush of love this tiny creature prompted in him, amazed by her instant vigour and energy.

'She looks like a troll,' he said, and kissed her forehead. Fortunately, no one heard this pronouncement, as the twin about to be known as Fred was proving difficult to lure from the warmth of his mother's womb into this world, and every nurse in the room was occupied with watching the doctor as he snapped his forceps together and strode towards Laura on the bed. The sight of the masked doctor poised with his giant tongs was the catalyst needed, and Fred earned his mother's lifelong gratitude by appearing just in time, a calm baby with surprisingly elegant eyebrows.

Laura cranes round to see if Fred's eyebrows are still notable; he peers back at her crossly. 'What?'

'Oh, nothing. Just looking.' The thought of these thirteen-year-olds ever being tiny babies seems impossible; it was long ago, it feels almost as if it were in another life.

'Come on lady, get a move on.' Laura is brought abruptly back to the present by a jeering voice.

The bus has edged next to her so the driver can shout at Laura; with a hiss of air brakes and automatic doors it revs away into the traffic, leaving Laura dawdling at a green light. It takes her a few moments to realise where she is and what she should do next. The school run is something she executes automatically; any attempt at concentrating on it results in bewilderment. In fact the whole school operation is frequently bewildering, and because of the children being twins, Laura never has a chance to get it right next time. On the other hand, as Inigo is quick to point out when attending plays or singing competitions, at least they only have to go through all of this stuff once. There is more beeping behind her. She kangaroo hops forward in the wrong gear and Fred groans loudly.

'Mum, please don't drive like this when we get near school. And please can we turn your music off now and listen to something decent?'

'Mum can't help driving like this.' Dolly has taken one shoe off and is sitting in full lotus position examining the sole of her foot. 'Mum, can we stop and get some nail scissors? I think my toenail is growing into my foot, or maybe through it. It really hurts.'

'Not if you want to get there on time. Put your shoe on, Doll, please – you're taking up the whole seat sitting like that. Fred, find another tape, but please don't let's have Radio One, it makes me want to kill myself.'

School is reached with no further reference to dogs or pierced feet from Dolly, and just one hopeful request from Fred to stop for a gutting knife.

'You can't have a gutting knife. You're a child, not a mass murderer. What do you want it for anyway?' Laura parks on the zig zag of yellow lines outside his school gates, telling herself that it doesn't matter as they are too late for any other children to be still arriving. She climbs out, chauffeur-style, to open the door for her offspring.

'Oh, it doesn't matter. I'll tell you later.' Fred reaches up to kiss her then turns in through the gates and becomes the last of the seething horde of boys ebbing towards the school doors as the bell rings. Dolly is still in the car, scrabbling for her shoe.

'I'm afraid we're going to be late,' Laura says, edging out into the traffic to drive the short distance to Dolly's side of the school. They arrive, Dolly still half shoeless, searching beneath the back seat. Laura gets out of the car, bites her tongue hard to stop herself saying, 'Why didn't you keep your shoe on?' and bends to retrieve the spilled papers and books which cascade from her daughter's open school bag. A few girls run across the road and in through the gates. Dolly at last finds her shoe and shoves it on.

'Bye, Mummy, see you later. Will you get my swimming hat today? And I need a new pen, I think.'

Laura simply nods, watching as Dolly, suddenly alert and smiling, runs off, returns to kiss her mother, then lopes across the empty tarmac to the school entrance.

As Dolly vanishes Laura turns to her car. She loves the moment of getting back into it after the children have gone; there is a luxurious quality to the silence, and the day stretches before her, lit with possibilities. Contemplating these possibilities today, however, sinks her spirits; she could go to the studio she works in with Inigo, where she will arrive in time to take a self-satisfied call from Jack about his session with Manfred and the television crew. Maybe she could nip out at lunchtime to buy some dye. Laura is determined to have glamour in her underwear drawer, and has decided that the most satisfactory way to do this is to dye all her knickers. Peacock blue is the colour she has chosen to kick off with, and today will be a perfect day to start. Following the vital shopping, there will be an hour to tear up small pieces of paper, an ongoing project as Inigo plans to amass five tons of tiny torn scraps of paper and tip them out in Hyde

Park at dawn on the spring equinox. This installation is to be called *Fall Back* and was inspired by Laura's inability to remember which way the clocks go when they change in autumn and spring.

'It's easy, Mum,' Fred had told her patiently when the family were discussing it over supper. 'You have to remember "spring forward and fall back". I remember it because of leaves falling.'

This installation has caused consternation among the officers of the Royal Parks Committee, and Laura had to ask the Arts Council to use their influence in making sure the necessary permissions were granted in time. With less than a month to go until the equinox, she finally summoned the courage to ring them yesterday.

'Oh yes, Inigo Miller. I daresay we can persuade Royal Parks to relax restrictions for him – think of the publicity it will generate.' Laura was secretly irritated that it should be so easy for Inigo. He is on a roll at the moment, and is hotly tipped to win the Artist of the Year award next month. This accolade takes the form of a large purple sash and a small cheque, and is only given very occasionally. The last time was seven years ago, when it was awarded to Glynn Flynn, the artist famous for growing grass seed and mould over everyday items.

Inigo has been a favourite of not only the Arts Council, but more unusually, the public, ever since his signature Möbius strip was used as the central motif in the Regent Street Christmas lights two years ago. The lights that year were turned on by a beautiful, aging opera diva who, holding hands with Inigo, sang 'White Christmas' over microphones placed all the way up Regent Street. Inigo, who adores opera, and also soppy musicals, wept with the emotion of it all, and Laura had to bite her cheek very hard not to get overpowering giggles. Anyway, the exercise ensured that he became a household name, and the art establishment, fearful that he might defect to America, are still anxious to please him. Laura can afford to skive for a bit longer.

A beam of sunlight dazzles through the windscreen, and instead of following the hill down through South End Green towards the studio and its array of possibilities for her day, Laura parks the car on a street of redbrick terraced houses, curved so they seem articulated like a child's toy train, and walks between stout black bollards and on to Hampstead Heath. Another world. Here birds chirp as they flit from tree to shrub and the grass is vivid green and sparkling wet where the sun has transformed early morning frost crystals to winter dew. Laura closes her eyes and breathes in deeply. Increasingly and now without even trying to find an excuse, she is drawn to the Heath and the blast of outdoor life it offers. Today she strides towards the Men's pond where even though it is February, the sound of jocose bathing is brash above the birdsong. She pauses when the pond comes into view, enjoying the spectacle of a young man with a soft white body, poised on the jetty, one toe in the shallows like a classical statue.

'Come on in, Paul, you wimp,' yells his heartier friend, crossing the water with a few flashy strokes of front crawl then emerging, streaked mud grey across pink red flesh. Watching from a distance great enough, she hopes, to escape classification as a filthy pervert, Laura cranes to hear the conversation, as the Greek statue and the hearty swimmer argue cheerfully.

'I hate this,' moans the statue.

'It's character building,' urges the swimmer. 'Come on, it'll get rid of your hangover.' He splashes back into the water, and a boxer dog who has been sniffing around the edge of the pond leaps in with him. They cavort noisily, sending silver spray feathering across the pond. The Greek statue teeters, his calves flexing to hold his balance, his back alabaster pale in the sunlight above incongruous glamour trunks decorated with pictures of Marilyn Monroe. Laura walks on, grinning broadly to herself, Inigo forgotten.

A Labrador bounces towards her, beaming goodwill and enthusiasm, its breath a vapour cloud in the cold air. It is one of a trio she sees most days on the Heath, pursued by the day-dreaming figure of their fair and ethereal walker. Laura bends to pat the dog. Given that Inigo shows no sign of relenting on the subject of dog acquisition, she wonders whether she should take up professional dog walking. An outdoor career with canines is appealing, particularly today when the Heath is alive with image and incident. If Laura became a dog walker, her walks would have a purpose to them, instead of being no more than time borrowed from her working day. Her walks would in fact be her working day.

Having always prized the cerebral above the physical, Laura is surprised to find such a strong instinct for fresh air within herself. She thinks of the teetering Greek statue, and the hearty swimmer playing with his dog in the ice-cold winter water, and finds herself longing to go back to the pond and push the statue into the water. The glamour trunks would be ruined, of course. A snort of laughter wells up and out, and Laura stops in her tracks, leaning on a tree to laugh. Wiping her eyes she begins to walk back across towards South End Green and her car, smiling and nodding when she passes the ethereal blonde, now throwing a pink ball to her three Labradors. Dog walkers are friendly, they appear to have untrammelled lives, and this attracts Laura. To find pleasure in the gloss on a dog's coat, or to laugh as it rushes up to you with a stick to throw, are easy versions of happiness, and Laura responds gladly.

Back in the car, with five messages listed on her mobile phone, and all of them from Inigo, she stops smiling and punches in the studio number. Sometimes Inigo's search for truth and purity is too much like hard work.

CHAPTER 3

The promise of the morning has given way to spitting rain by the time Laura reaches Whitechapel, and clouds like bruises hang low across the street, vying with the watery February sun to create a vivid 1950s film-set light. Laura hums 'Singin' in the Rain' and parks outside the tombstone shop, noticing as she does so that they have changed their window display to include an arresting slab of skewbald marble and next to it a small, pig-shaped stone bearing the words:

With our deepest sympathies
the grandchildren

Wondering what, if any, phrase, might have sounded less incongruous with a pig-shaped headstone, Laura crosses the road to the building which houses the studio. The entrance is obscured by scaffolding and today by a large white van into which dusty-booted men are piling the contents of the studio above Inigo's.

Out comes a purple velvet sofa, a mannequin wearing nothing but a tutu, and a giant pink mule. Could any of the passers-by guess the nature of the business run from the studio by its office furnishing? Laura doubts it. None of the passers-by ever raise their heads from contemplation of the pavement, let alone look up high enough to see what is going on around them. As if to prove her point, two youths pass, both walking fast, one with his hands in his pockets, the other speaking into a mobile phone; both have their heads down and their eyes on the toes of their white trainers, blind to what lies ahead of them. Naturally, they walk straight into the purple velvet sofa.

Laura shrugs herself into the warm shell of her coat, hugely enjoying the street tableau this morning. The youths hardly miss a stride; they bounce off the sofa and walk on, with not a flicker of a glance up, no apology, no communication, not even a small, complicit laugh. The second one's phone rings as he passes Laura, so close that she can smell the musky waft of his aftershave mixed with tobacco. He answers it, and continues down the street beside his friend, both talking to people somewhere else, both unheeding of where they are, living internal lives.

Laura's own phone rings as she ascends the stairs. It is Inigo.

'Where are you? We've got trouble with the press in New York.'

'I'm on my way up the stairs.'

'Good. I'll see you in a minute.'

Wishing away the sinking sensation in her stomach,

Laura opens the door. She is in the studio in time to see Inigo utter these words and to hear him in stereo, although it is not easy to hear him at all as a lachrymose singer is wailing through a Bartok aria at full volume on the sound system.

'Here I am,' Laura mouths, hanging her coat behind the door and advancing towards him; he hardly pauses to greet her, but continues to pace up and down in the centre of the room. He is in a state, Laura notes apprehensively.

Inigo has a single bicycle wheel in one hand, and he is playing with it as he walks restlessly to and fro, bouncing the wheel down to the floor and up again, spinning it over and over so the spokes catch the light and glitter, blurring together to form a flat disc of liquid silver. Inigo collects the separate components of bicycles: wheels, saddles, frames, handle bars and gear mechanisms, and keeps them on permanent display leaning against the walls of his studio. Occasionally, in summertime, he picks out the necessary combination of these items and puts together a bike to ride between home and work, but a constant quest for perfectionism, spurred by the perusal of various bicycle magazines and websites, makes it difficult for him to stick with any single combination.

Laura knows better than to think he is making a bike to ride home on today. A wheel has always been a comfort to Inigo. He has one from a mountain bike suspended on wire from the ceiling at the back of the studio, next to a window, and he can spend hours there, looking out of the window, spinning the wheel.

A regression therapist once told him that in a past life he was a Flemish weaver sent to Norwich to make silk. While Inigo does not believe in reincarnation, something in him likes the idea of being haunted by ghost memories. However, today Flemish silk weaving is far from his mind, and the bicycle wheel is a tool through which he can express his frustration at the beeping answer machine and flashing computer.

He turns on Laura, bouncing the tyre in front of him as he speaks. Laura can hear nothing; she shakes her head helplessly. Displeased, Inigo pounces on the remote control and zaps Bartok down a few decibels. He grinds his teeth audibly and continues, 'I said, the gallery in New York left about ten messages last night, and now I can't get back to them because it's too early. D'you remember what time they open there?'

'I think it's eleven, which isn't for hours here. What's happened?'

Inigo grips the tyre like a steering wheel and moves it round and round in his hands. 'There's been a leak to the press about my show and I've had three major US newspapers and a magazine call me to talk about it and I'm not ready. I can't.'

Inigo also has celebrity status in America, where his work is venerated for being both obscure and eye-catching. He was artist in residence at NYU, when he and Laura were first together, in New York, and his exhibitions in America are always given a great deal of attention. Inigo enjoys this success, but likes to keep a strong front to hide behind. The leaking of information on a show he has not yet hung makes him feel vulnerable and paranoid. Now that someone knows what he is doing, his confidence could ebb until he decides to pull the whole show.

No one is more aware than Laura that while seeing is believing for Inigo's audience, believing is seeing for Inigo. This is where the whole thing starts to sag for Laura. It's the believing bit she's beginning to have trouble with, but it's her job to bolster him now, as it always has been. Laura and Inigo's business partnership grew out of their relationship. Supporting Inigo in whatever direction he chooses to take can be wildly frustrating. Too often, as now with the Park thing, Laura is left wading through swamping bureaucracy while Inigo skims ahead, evolving new ideas which she must make into reality.

The most extreme example of this was Inigo's first creation on returning from New York nine years ago. Driving to visit his mother in the comfortable Manchester suburb where he was brought up, he was caught for some time in a traffic jam in Birmingham around Spaghetti Junction. The result of four hours' contemplation of this concreted web of roads was daring and historic. Inigo suspended seven giant neon Möbius strips from the flyovers, embroiling Laura in more than five hundred hours of negotiations with insurance companies, crane contractors and the Highways and Byways department of the local council. It won Inigo international renown and brought Laura a very depressing crop of grey hairs. These are dealt with on a monthly basis at a discreet salon on Haverstock Hill and, she supposes, will continue to be treated until she is too senile to care.

Laura leans against the table, arms folded, trying to keep her voice level and reassuring, when really she wants to shout, 'Of course you can do the show. You always do, and we always have this conversation first. And I'm sick of it.'

Instead she says, 'The new work is looking great, Inigo. Why don't we talk it all through now and get something on paper to show them. Then they'll leave you alone.'

Inigo likes this notion. 'Good,' he says, bouncing the rim of the wheel on his palms. 'And we've got time before they open, haven't we?'

'Plenty,' soothes Laura, switching on her computer.

Inigo fiddles with his wheel and paces until twelve, winding himself into hysterics and being no help to Laura at all.

'I might forget what I'm doing, I might forget who I am. I think you should come too. Why don't we cancel the show and go on holiday? Maybe I should go to New York today. Shall I go to the airport now? Or not?'

'For God's sake, calm down!' Laura yells finally. 'None of this is necessary, everything will be fine. You know that.'

Inigo nods. 'You're right. God, I'm completely exhausted. I think I'll go and buy lunch. I need to get out.' Laura nods gratefully. She wants to print out the press release and have Inigo calm again more than she wants the dye for her peacock-blue knickers.

Death Threat by Inigo Miller

British artist Inigo Miller brings his latest work to New York next month with his extraordinary new show *Death Threat*.

The central image in the show is that of a tiny pastry-cutter in the shape of Miller's trademark the Möbius strip, beneath the shadow of a giant rolling pin. This is a simple installation with strong metaphorical qualities. Miller's work, increasingly, is concerned with mortality, with identity, with sexuality. Here his penetrating focus encompasses man's relationship to woman and throws a nod to the issue of domestic harmony in the professional workplace. With this powerful new work, Miller is distilling his thoughts to express the very essence of what it is to be contemporary man. As ever, he pushes the boundaries of expectation further out and he challenges fulfilment.

The show will include small biscuits made by Miller with the pastry-cutter. They should not be eaten. THEY TRANSCEND FOOD.

Born in 1960, Miller first discovered the Möbius strip when making paper chains with his grandfather. He was eight then, and it was not for another ten years that he met anyone who understood or even recognised the Möbius strip, originally conceived by the German August Ferdinand Möbius in 1876.

Miller has been showing with the CONCEPT gallery since he was twenty-one, when his extraordinary degree show at Goldsmiths Art School in London was bought in its entirety by CONCEPT and shipped to New York where an eager public bought every piece within the first hour of opening night.

Inigo Miller will be happy to answer any journalistic queries by email. You can reach him through his agent at jack@smackhard.com.

THIS INFORMATION CONCERNING INIGO MILLER'S NEW SHOW IS EMBARGOED UNTIL FURTHER NOTICE.

Most pleasing. Laura feels the press release has the necessary qualities of self-importance and absurd epic language to make it plausible to the Americans. The embargo, which Inigo suggested, is a brilliant idea, and a useful smokescreen, as so far nothing of *Death Threat* exists at all. She faxes a copy to Jack, sourly thinking that he should have been the one writing the press release. There is a mumbling beyond the door, and Laura opens it for Inigo, who enters backwards, balancing two Styrofoam cups of soup, a French loaf and a bunch of tulips in his hands, while dangling a paper bag of Turkish Delight from his teeth.

'Mmm, that looks wonderful,' says Laura.

'There wasn't much today.' Inigo puts down the Turkish Delight, rather crestfallen. 'I thought I could get bagels, but they were closed. The only escape from wet sandwiches was this girl with a soup wagon on the street opposite. It's Thai chicken. Is that OK for you?'

This unusual humility and concern for Laura is Inigo's way of saying thank you for her time and energy spent soothing him this morning. Generally, he is too lost in artistic contemplation to buy lunch, and Laura does it, relishing half an hour out on her own.

They arrange themselves at a small red table next to the window and sip their soup. The street below is shiny black from recent rain, the removals van has gone, and with it, all traces of the occupants of the upstairs studio.

'Did you see the fancy dressmakers before they left?' Laura asks Inigo. He nods, not looking up from the spiralling arrangement he is creating from tulip petals and dusty pink and amber squares of Turkish Delight.

'I couldn't believe it. They're leaving to move to Somerset.' From his tone of incredulity, Laura expected a destination a little more obscure, the moon perhaps, or Sao Paulo, but Somerset seems eminently sensible.

'What's wrong with Somerset?'

Inigo places a last block of Turkish Delight like a full stop at the end of his spiral; the yellow stamens and black centres of the tulips are as delicate as glass beside the soft dense blocks of muted colour of the sweets. Laura would like to wear the arrangement as a necklace. It is classic Inigo, and she feels a rush of frustrated affection for his childlike restlessness, his need to keep on making things. Even if she could pick it up and put it on, it would lose much by being removed from the red Formica table. Inigo stares at his creation for a long, silent moment, then, his artistic eye sated, he pops a bit of Turkish Delight in his mouth.

'It's so far away,' he explains, waving another piece in Laura's direction. 'You can't run a business or find your creative voice among fields. The countryside has too much of its own agenda with all the cows and nature and stuff. It gets in the way.'

Laura opens her mouth to disagree, but Inigo, his eyebrows drawn low and fiendish, pushes a powdered lump of stickiness onto her tongue.

'We all need the pulse of the pavement,' he says.

'You are ridiculous,' Laura laughs, but icing sugar hits the back of her throat, and she chokes instead. Her eyes water and she turns away. In the midst of her discomfort, a small voice in her head is saying: 'How long can you go on putting up with him?'

CHAPTER 4

'Hello. Whoisit?'

Dolly answers the phone. She has been sitting next to it all evening making arrangements with her friends, painting her toenails and occasionally glancing away from the television and towards the French vocabulary list teetering on the arm of her chair. The only reason she is in the room and using this phone is that her mobile has been confiscated at school. Laura was supposed to get it back, but she was too late to see Madame King the French teacher. Dolly has not yet decided to forgive her for this.

'Mum, it's for you. It's Hedley.' These are Dolly's first words to her mother since she came in. Laura smiles in recognition of the truce, and reluctantly Dolly allows her mouth to rise a millimetre at the corners. But a call from her mother's brother in Norfolk holds no interest for Dolly; she flops her wrist back and lets the telephone fall on the cushion beside her, shifting her long legs slightly to allow Laura room to perch on the edge of the seat to speak, while she continues to rake her fingers through her hair and chew gum. Fred zaps the television with the remote control to kill the sound, earning a grateful look from his mother.

'Hi, Hedley, how are you? I'm sorry I haven't rung you. I got your messages, but it's been so hectic. Inigo's off to New York soon to set up his new show, and someone's leaked the title, which is bad news.'

'What is the title of his show?' Hedley asks, glad that Laura cannot see that he has been reduced to making telephone calls from the airing cupboard in order to have privacy from the tyranny of Tamsin his teenage step-daughter.

Laura sighs. 'Hedley, honestly! What did I just say? I'm not supposed to tell you or anyone else anything about it.'

'Well, it doesn't matter now because it's already been leaked,' Hedley points out.

Laura laughs capitulation. 'All right, I'll tell you. It's called *Death Threat*, and the central image is the shadow of a giant rolling pin towering over a tiny pastry-cutter-sized Möbius strip. It was meant to have an embargo on it until the middle of March, as the show doesn't launch until April—' She breaks off, arrested by the muffled noises from Hedley's end. 'You sound very peculiar. Where are you?'

Her brother, trying to arrange himself for comfort as well as security on the second from bottom shelf, answers reluctantly, 'I'm in the airing cupboard.' He shifts a sprigged eiderdown from behind him and breathes, 'Aah, that's better. Isn't it time Inigo moved on from Möbius strips, or should the plural be Möbii? I shall look it up.' Hedley is always ready to be distracted by a bit of research. Laura cuts in, recognising the signs of her brother drifting away on a new tide of thought.

'You can't. It isn't Latin, remember? It's a German called August Ferdinand Möbius.' Laura's voice gathers exasperation. 'You know that, Hedley, you've always known that – and why are you in the airing cupboard anyway?'

Fred, bored by what he can see is going to be an extended interruption to his television viewing, hurls a cushion at Dolly to liven things up. His twin shrieks as the blue nail polish she has been applying in squiggles on a base coat of pink skids across her hand and gloops onto her French exercise book.

'Fred you stupid creep, don't bloody do that,' she howls.

Laura flails her hands, screwing up her eyes into menacing slits, hoping to mutely indicate terrible punishments if they don't start behaving at once. Fred and Dolly ignore her and hurl themselves into a full-scale cushion bashing session. Laura can hardly hear her brother, and isn't listening anyway, as her ears are straining to discover whether Inigo has heard the chaos from his cocoon of peace in the basement with the computer.

'. . . and I thought this would be the best place to come to talk to you,' her brother is saying. 'Actually, it's quite nice in here. Do you remember, we used to play Sardines here when we were young? I wish children now did that kind of thing. All Tamsin seems to want to do is stare at the television or talk on the telephone. I'd still rather play Sardines, wouldn't you?' Hedley sounds happier and more relaxed than he has done for weeks; hiding in the airing cupboard must be a good thing.

'How is Tamsin?' Laura asks, able to concentrate better now she has dragged the telephone, yanking the cord, out of the sitting room and into the hall away from the muffled thuds and squeals of the fight.

Hedley's voice wobbles with suppressed frustration. 'I cannot believe that parenting can ever be as difficult as my job of step-parenting,' he says.

Laura is silent, remembering the outraged agony of her brother when his wife Sarah told him she was leaving. She had met someone else. 'And it's not even a man, it's a female gym instructor,' Hedley had bellowed, adding in disbelief, 'And they've taken Tamsin.'

A year later though, Tamsin was back, with teenage hormones racing, a very different prospect from the child Hedley thought he knew. And Sarah has moved to a women-only commune in Turkey to find her inner self. That was eighteen months ago, and she still shows no sign of coming home.

'This is a classic instance of it; I've been trying to call you all evening but Tamsin wouldn't give me the telephone. She had it locked in the bathroom with her from six o'clock onwards.'

'Why don't you get her a mobile?' Laura asks, unable to stop herself being practical.

Hedley sighs. 'Oh, she's got one, but she's run out of money on it and I'm in trouble for refusing to take her to get another card at the garage. It's seven miles, for Christ's sake. I don't want to drive fourteen miles there and back at this time of night.'

Much goaded, he carries on, 'I don't seem to be able to get through to her at all – we don't speak, she won't look at me, we don't even eat together any more. She spends every moment that she isn't at school in the bathroom. She even eats in there – I found a plate of ancient peanut-butter sandwiches in the laundry basket this morning. I don't know what to do about her. I understand that this could go on for years.'

'Don't worry, I'm sure it will be better soon.' Hedley telephones Laura for advice three or four times a week, and it is clearly on the tip of his tongue to ask her if she will have Tamsin for a prolonged stay. A pink-faced giggling Dolly rushes past her up the stairs, waving the television remote control above her head. Fred follows, jaw set, furious. 'You loser, Doll,' he is shouting. 'If you put that in the bath, you've had it.'

The thump and hurtle of the twins' progress through the house is the same as it has always been, but there are other signs of impending teendom, and Laura is aware that life is becoming more dramatic every day – or certainly as far as Dolly is concerned. Taking her lead from Inigo, the biggest baby of all, Dolly hurls and slams her way through life. The tantrums over whether her jeans are clean or not are only eclipsed by mood swings over Dolly's rights. These vacillate between tragedy – which is anything to do with her mother, and comedy – which is anything to do with her teachers. Fred is easier to predict, more like a satisfying one-act play than the full-blown opera in a new language that is Dolly. Mystifying. Perhaps through Tamsin, Laura can find a way to talk to Dolly too?

Cheered by this optimistic thought, she suggests, 'Why don't we all come to stay with you in Norfolk this weekend? Inigo could do with the break, and frankly so could I. We haven't been to see you for ages. And I really mind that we don't come there enough. I'll talk to Tamsin a bit over the weekend and see if I can find out anything that might make her happier.'

Hedley appears to like this plan, but merely grunts, 'What about me being happier?' before adding more enthusiastically, 'Actually, it's a great weekend for you to come. I could do with some extra pairs of hands as we've got several hundred trees to plant.'

'Oh,' says Laura, not much liking the role of underling woodsman. 'I think I might steer clear of that.'

'What about Inigo?' asks Hedley hopefully. 'You could tell him it's like going to the gym, really good for muscle toning and all that.'

Laura is doubtful. 'You tell him,' she says, adding, 'Fred can help you too. Are you staying in the airing cupboard for the night?' She moves the phone away from her head to yell, 'THAT'S ENOUGH!' up the stairs following a shuddering crash from the top floor.

Fred's face appears at the top of the stairwell, rosy, his eyes cerulean, his expression worryingly angelic. 'Mum, quick, come up here. Where's Dad? There's bright turquoise water seeping out of the washing machine. We didn't do anything, honestly.'

Laura shouts, 'See you on Friday, Hedley,' and sprints up the stairs, or rather the first flight. By the second flight she is panting. Vowing to take up some form of exercise beyond not achieving yoga positions and watching other people walk their dogs, she hauls herself to the top of the house in time to witness the death throes of her washing machine. It has not enjoyed its role in her underwear dyeing project.

CHAPTER 5

When Inigo drives on the motorway, Laura sleeps. She knows she should be a support and talk to him, in fact she would enjoy this companionable way of conversing, side by side, the eye drawn ineluctably onward through the changing landscape, but she can never stay awake for more than five minutes. When the twins were younger, their needs occasionally roused her from slumber, and she would twist round in her seat to buy their silence with fruit or drinks, or lead them through the endlessly repeated chorus of 'Oh My Darling Clementine' and 'Sweet Molly Malone' (adapted, except for the death verse, to 'Sweet Dolly Malone'.)

However, the twins prepared for this journey with CDs and Dolly's new mobile phone. They have books and computer games, and Laura can see from the moment they leave home and Dolly and Fred both plug their ears with headphones and their mouths with gum, that they want no part in their parents' conversations. Inigo doesn't care whether he talks or not, because what he wants to do is drive, as fast as is humanly possible. He sees each notch he moves up on the speedometer as a personal victory against time, and he likes this crescendo of speed to build up through stirring highlights of epic opera – *Aïda* or *The Ring Cycle* are both a spur for Inigo's driving.

Laura dozes, floating in lovely time off. Today has been nerve-wracking. Inigo, having seen Dolly off to a disco the night before, decided to use strobe lighting to illustrate the story of Verdi's *Rigoletto*. Even an hour in the studio, with the blackout blinds drawn and light pulsing, not to mention the incessant repetition of the opening aria from the opera, left Laura with eye strain and a bad temper. Thankfully, at the end of that time, Inigo pinged up all the blinds and said, 'This doesn't work,' before removing himself to the computer for an afternoon stress-busting on Super Mario Karts.

Working with Inigo, in the same space all day, every day, talking, arguing, and endlessly listening can be suffocating. Sometimes at dusk, Laura leaves the twins glued to the television and goes out for a walk, gulping air, her ears singing with the peaceful joy of not being needed. This walk, through the winding down late-afternoon streets, past shops closing and restaurants opening, lit, at this time of year, by the friendly glow of amber streetlights, could become a necessity if only she had a dog. She must persuade Inigo.

Half-asleep in the car, she turns to look at him now. His profile is not encouraging. It is almost dark outside, but the glow of the instruments on the dashboard cast a green light up towards Inigo's jaw, highlighting the dark pits of new bristle growth on his chin and up towards his ears. Inigo's mouth is slightly open; it has been pursed to whistle disapproval at the low-slung sports car which ricocheted past a few moments ago, and soon it will be folded neatly shut, but right now Laura can see his teeth, and the set of his mouth, pulled back in a perpetual, slight grimace. Inigo's nose is beautiful, and in profile is the best way to see it. Face on, his eyes are too close to it, but in profile the nose sweeps out of his brow without indentation at the level of his arching eyebrows. It sweeps nobly on, but midway is interrupted by a bump, which should mar the perfection, but in fact serves only to enhance the fine length and proportion of the nose.

It is a boxer's nose, and it made Laura weak and breathless with longing when she first saw Inigo seventeen years ago, having bolted into his exhibition in Mercer Street in New York to escape a sudden summer downpour. Laura had been in New York for a year, studying film at NYU. She had another year to go, and she was missing home like crazy. She even missed her brother. Laura was on her way home from a class on creating the defining moment in a plot. She felt low and despondent; New York was breathless and humid, her apartment had no air conditioning, and her workload was greater than she could bear. She had no one to talk to about it, her fellow students were all so determined, so untrammelled by crises of confidence. Laura had a sneaking feeling this course was not for her. But what was? The humidity today was extreme; she held her hair up as she walked to let any small movement in the air play on her neck. She had a headache and was halfway home before she realised she'd left her coat in the seminar room. A clap of thunder and the hiss of summer rain invaded her thoughts, and she ran for shelter.

Inigo Miller was twenty-one that summer, and still wondering what on earth he was meant to say to justify his being here. He felt a fraud, but was in fact a success. His degree show had been lifted straight from art school and transported here, and it had opened with a queue around the block. Jack Smack, a creepy British agent, had offered to represent him, and since selling his soul to this whip-thin smooth talker, Inigo had hardly slept or stopped to draw breath, so constant was the round of interviews, meetings and exhibitions. Inigo made the most of every minute, convinced that he would be exposed as no big deal and shipped home at any moment.

Now he was talking to a smiling brace of Japanese art agents who smoothed their hair and nodded fervently when Inigo said he was thinking of taking his show to Tokyo.

'I want to have everything turned upside down. To re-examine it all from the perspective of another culture will be fascinating. I like to challenge my own perceptions,' he was saying, his tongue in his cheek. He didn't take it all so seriously then. Planning an escape as soon as possible, he glanced longingly at the door and saw Laura. In fact, he saw the back of Laura standing in the open doorway, smoothing the rain from her hair.

'Excuse me,' Inigo said to the Japanese. 'There's someone I—' He didn't finish his sentence because he had already gone. It was late June, and the hot streets streamed and steamed from this torrent of rain, and the smell of wet leaves hung in the air at the door of the gallery, making Laura shiver with nostalgia for her parents' garden and her childhood.

Inigo stood behind Laura, admiring her shoulders, her hair – everything about the back of her suggested the front would be wonderful. He couldn't think of anything to say to her, and he was afraid she might suddenly dart out into the rain again, and be gone without him seeing her face. The only thing to do was to go out and then come back towards the door and hope that if he smiled and said, 'Hello,' a conversation might develop.

Laura, glooming in the rain and relishing feeling sorry for herself, paid little attention when someone brushed past her to leave the gallery. But then he came back, presumably because he had forgotten something, and Laura looked up from her contemplation of the torrent swirling by the kerb to see Inigo, wet but smiling and suggesting hopefully: 'Hello, would you like to come and have tea with my Japanese agent?'

'What sort of Japanese agent?' Laura asked, smiling now, unconsciously reaching up to unknot her hair, shaking it onto her shoulders, unable to stop herself gazing at him.

'Successful, I hope,' said Inigo, grinning delightedly; it was easier than he had thought to speak, now he had started, and she was better, even better than he had dared hope from seeing only the back of her beautiful neck. Best of all, he hadn't missed his moment and watched her walk away without ever seeing her face. She was here, with him now. She was part of his success.

In the car Laura wonders if it's worth broaching the dog thing, and decides against it. Inigo is sulking anyway, partly because he had not wanted to spend the weekend at Hedley's house, and partly because Laura still hasn't got a new washing machine, despite the old one having broken five days ago. The fact that one is to be delivered in the middle of next week in no way placates him, nor do the neat piles of laundry in his drawers and cupboards. Inigo is a control freak, and no washing machine to him equals a worrying decline in standards at home and the eruption of chaos.

Laura is half-relieved that none of Inigo's clothes were caught in the turquoise flood which killed the washing machine – he would be unspeakably angry. It would almost be worth it though, for the entertainment value of seeing him in frivolous beach blue. Inigo does not like to wear bright colours. Indeed, he only really likes dark green, and the odd streak of grey. He hates patterns, and Laura has come to notice that there is an element of *Star Trek* in the close-cut way he wears his clothes. She suspects that this predilection for polo-necks is fostered by his view of the low standards at home. Inigo knows that if he had shirts, he would not be able to persuade anyone to iron them for him. He has no intention of ironing them himself, so it is not worth having shirts. With some effort, Laura withdraws from her musings about Inigo's laundry. It is time her mind became better occupied, but with what? For years now she has been looking after her family's interests and has forgotten how to have any of her own.

Inigo turns off the motorway and dark descends suddenly around them.

'When will we be there, Dad?' shouts Fred, his voice raised too loud because he cannot gauge it with his music blasting in his ears.

'Another hour,' Inigo answers, not hoping or expecting that Fred will hear him. He glances at Laura, but cannot see if she is awake in the soft dimness. He sighs and accelerates through the night towards Norfolk.

Laura had never expected that Norfolk, so much a part of her childhood, would become an important place to her again in her life. If she had thought about it at all, she would have imagined that her uncle's house, Crumbly Hall, would be sold when he died, and the place where she had spent her school summer holidays would become no more than a memory. She and Hedley both left for America before they were twenty, never thinking of looking back. Fifteen years later, Peter Sale died aged eighty-five and Hedley came back, leaving his university teaching in America, to live at Crumbly and run the small farm there. He thought he would just do it for a year or two. An outdoor life on the north Norfolk coast seemed a bleak prospect for a newly divorced academic, but the change of pace was what he needed, and life lived according to the seasons suited him, and even soothed him as he struggled through the aftermath of his marriage. After four years at Crumbly, Hedley recognised that he would stay, and that he loved it now in a way he could never have imagined loving a place. Only Inigo's lack of enthusiasm stops Laura visiting him there more often.

Hedley sees the headlights approaching along the drive, swooping up and down, raking spindly branches with their gleam then diving down into ruts and potholes. He hovers inside the front door, not wanting to appear overeager by going out to greet them, but unable to return to the sitting room where Tamsin is watching an unsuitable film.

'There's no such thing as unsuitable,' she snarled at him earlier, when he tried to suggest changing channels to the programme on the fruit flies and their habits. 'And anyway,' she added, having watched five stony minutes of the nature programme, 'your fruit flies are having sex and God knows what else. I don't think you've got a leg to stand on as far as suitable goes.'

Hopping from foot to foot in the hall, attended by Diver, the Labrador, Hedley empathises with the dog's single-note whining, and can almost believe that his own ears, like Diver's, are cocked towards the door. He wouldn't be surprised to find himself drooling. It is lonely here in Norfolk with only a taciturn teenager and a devoted dog for company. Hedley never envisaged himself as a single man, but since his failed affair with a neighbour, he has been on his own, and quite honestly, he can't imagine anything changing now. Reflecting that it is time he got out more and spent some time with adults instead of pandering to Tamsin and complaining to Diver, Hedley opens the door to his sister and her family.

'Inigo, Laura. Lovely to see you. Come in, come in.'

Laura hugs her brother, breathing deep as she steps away, loving the woodsmoke in the air, the hint of wet dog and the determined wafts of sweetness from a winter flowering jasmine scrambling up and over a plant stand in front of the fireplace in the hall.

'Hello, Hedley. It's lovely to be back. I'd forgotten how much I love the smell here, and it never changes.' Laura smiles, taking off her coat and walking through towards the kitchen.

Inigo, behind her with a bag of groceries, mutters, 'I hope you bought some wine, Laura. Hedley never has anything decent to drink here, and I could do with something now.'

Hedley stays to greet Fred and Dolly, jumping back as if scalded when he puts his hands out to hug Dolly and encounters a slice of midriff complete with a

56

diamanté tattoo below her belly button which reads STIFF.

God, she's becoming one too, he thinks despairingly. And last time I saw her she had plaits and still liked damming streams in the wood.

Dolly, chewing gum, her headphones dangling around her neck, dribbling a tune, gives him a long, expressionless look which makes Hedley want to shrivel to the size of a screwed-up pocket handkerchief.

'Hello, Uncle Hedley,' she says in the same lobotomised monotone with which Tamsin addresses him.

'Tamsin's in there.' Hedley points to the sitting room. Dolly spits her gum into the palm of her hand and throws it into the jasmine plant pot before vanishing into the sitting room. Hedley turns to Fred, braced for more of the same treatment, and is unnerved to find his nephew giving him a friendly smile as he crouches to stroke Diver.

'Hi, Uncle Hedley,' he says cheerily. 'Diver's looking well.'

'Yeeess,' says Hedley slowly, staring at him, fascinated by his civility, slowly warming beneath the uncritical expression on Fred's face. 'In fact, he's just become a father. I've been up at a friend's house looking at the puppies this evening,'

'NO!' bellows Inigo, who has removed his jacket to reveal a snug green polo-neck in very soft, lightweight fleece material which reveals every bulge of his biceps and chest and makes him look as if he has just been beamed into the dimly lit medieval hall at Crumbly from Planet Zog. 'On no account are you to take Fred to look at those puppies, Hedley. I will not have it.' Inigo paces about the room brushing invisible hairs off his sleeves and glancing venomously at Diver. 'They'll all shed hair like that one there. How can you stand it, Hedley?'

Hedley ignores this, recognising it as Inigo's usual combative arrival. He will settle down when he has had a drink, but until then will prowl and scowl and find fault. Rather like a dog arriving at another dog's house, Hedley thinks, amused.

Fred assumes a hurt expression. 'Dad, I hadn't even asked to see them, I hadn't even said one single word. I don't even know what kind of dog the mother is . . .'

In the kitchen, Laura leans against the Aga, enjoying the massaging effect its warmth has on her back. This Aga has been part of her life since she and Hedley first came here aged thirteen, dispatched from Cambridge by parents turned tight-lipped by the incessant volume of music and the ceaseless litany invoked by Laura and Hedley which scarcely varied from, 'I'm bored, when will you stop working and take us somewhere?'

Michael and Anne Sale, both immersed in academic research and uninterested in entertaining their children, sent them to Michael's half-brother in rural Norfolk. At the station they made a show of pretending to smile bravely, but in fact they were beaming in relief as they kissed their offspring and waved them off on the train, shouting down the platform, 'Make sure Peter notices that you've arrived, and always offer to help.' Then the pair of them returned to the library and their papers, the burden of the children a weight lifted now for ten weeks.

As their teenage status demanded, Laura and Hedley sulked as far as the first change on the train, but then they looked at each other and simultaneously grinned.

'We're having a new life now,' Laura whispered.

'We can do what we like,' agreed Hedley.

Laura cannot forget her first sighting of the house. And every time she comes back, no matter what the time of day or year, or the state of her mind, the first moment of seeing it gives the same lift to her spirits. It was a swooning July day, with flooding sunlight spilling across the fields and hedgerows as they drove from the station. Bumping down the drive, grey flint walls and mullioned windows reflecting wisps of cloud became visible through the dense foliage of the avenue of lime trees. And then the sea. Laura gasped as she saw its denim blue stretching beyond the house, seeming to be on top of it, but in fact separated from the gardens by a mile or more of marshland.

Uncle Peter must have been there with them, but Laura cannot recall him ever dispensing discipline or even food. Indeed, only vast effort and the assistance of a curling old photograph on the kitchen mantelpiece conjures his face for her at all, although she remembers his tall gaunt figure, leaning on a stick, his dog at his heels, gazing out across the early morning sea.

The mumbling kitchen radio bleeps the hour, and Laura pulls herself away from the Aga. Some raw potatoes have been left suggestively in a saucepan on the side. Laura pushes the pan across to the hot plate and reaches the photograph down. Peter was a mild man, an academic like Laura's father although he had chosen botany rather than history. Sixty-three when Laura and Hedley first went to stay with him, he had never married. His passion was reserved for bird and plant life, and for walking on the marshes beyond his garden, where he would spend all day weaving through the maze of silver-laced creeks with the certain step of one who has known every ditch and treacherous drain all his life.

From the beginning, Peter left the children to do as they pleased, and in doing so gave them his house to love. They explored every corner and cupboard, sneezing dust motes off old stacked books and clothes, bringing life and youth and new layers of chaos into the neglected rooms. Making it their own. Even now, Laura opens cupboards in the kitchen and knows what is in them with more certainty than she does in her parents' house. At Crumbly she and Hedley ran their own lives, ate what they wanted to when they wanted to, and acted out every adolescent whim they could there. Filling the kettle now, Laura remembers turning the kitchen sink scarlet with Crazy Colour hair dye when she re-fashioned Hedley's schoolboy quiff into a Mohican for a punk party in the village hall.

The windows glisten with steam as the potatoes boil and Laura doesn't notice them burn at the bottom.

She was so happy here in her teens, able to be herself, not pretending to be an academic like her parents and Hedley. It must be good for Tamsin growing up here; on behalf of her own children, Laura envies her.

'Come on, let's eat. I'm starving.' Inigo marches in, swinging a bottle of wine. He opens it, pours glasses for himself, Hedley and Laura, then stands fidgeting and ostentatiously looking at his watch to draw more attention to the lateness of supper. Despite his passion for cooking, Inigo never interferes in the kitchen at Crumbly. It's too medieval for him; doing anything culinary in the cavernous space makes him feel like a vassal, not a chef.

Laura feels like that all the time, but doesn't think it's worth mentioning. She drains the potatoes, ignoring the eager faces of Fred and Hedley hovering keenly like the Labrador Diver. She remembers her teenage culinary attempts at Crumbly. The meals were experimental and infrequent; at thirteen her cooking repertoire consisted largely of boiled eggs and cakes she liked to marble pink, purple and green with the small bottles of evil-looking food colouring the Crumbly village shop supplied. It has to be said, it hasn't increased much. The chicken pie she is placing on the table came out of Hedley's freezer ready cooked, and that's how Laura likes it. She calls Dolly and Tamsin through to supper, and everyone sits down at the long oak kitchen table.

'It's so nice to be back here,' Laura says, raising her glass to Hedley. He smiles, relaxing now the arrival is over.

'Cheers,' he says, slopping wine as he chinks his glass against Fred's water tumbler, and then Dolly's before reaching across the table to Inigo and Tamsin and his sister.

Home with their parents in Cambridge had seemed small, the rules petty and the city hard, grey and implacable after Laura and Hedley's summers in Norfolk, where the days were their own and the horizons stretched forever with no rules or boundaries to get in the way.

'Do you remember how awful it was going back to school after the summers here?' Laura asks Hedley, when everyone has got their food and is eating. 'And how we begged Mum and Dad until they let us come for Christmas, and it was the year there was that incredible snow.' Laura's eyes shine; she has her elbows on the table, leaning towards Hedley, who is looking puzzled. 'You must remember,' she urges. 'We went on a tractor to see the Sex Pistols play in Cromer.'

Dolly and Tamsin are drooped over their plates, shoulders hunched, hair flopping forwards to make two curtains, one rusty red, the other matt brown like stout. Dolly toys with a pea, but not keenly enough to put it into her mouth. Like Tamsin, her body language indicates torpor and boredom. However, when the girls hear the word 'sex', they both suddenly sit up, push their hair away from their faces and with pleased expressions begin to eat the chicken pie.

'Cool,' says Fred. 'Did they sing "God save the Queen"?'

'I saw them on *Rock Dinosaurs,*' says Dolly. 'Mum, did you get the dead one's autograph?' she asks, back to her usual animated self now.

Tamsin struggles to retain her sense of separation. 'The Sex Pistols are really rank,' she hisses. Hedley roars with laughter.

'That's exactly what they are, or rather were – you're so right,' he beams. 'And Uncle Peter thought so too. He had to wait through the whole evening inside the Town Hall where the gig was, because it would have taken too long to get home and then come back for us again.'

'I can't think why he didn't go to a pub,' muses Laura. 'But then—'

'I think we're all past caring now, aren't we?' says Inigo sulkily, and Tamsin, with her radar sense for discord, looks at him and then at Laura with interest. Laura sighs, and the sigh becomes a yawn and then another sigh as if she is meditating. She gets up to break the pattern and clears the plates away.

Inigo carefully removes his hand from the neck of the wine bottle he has been clasping. He has positioned the corkscrew so it is poised like a ballerina on the rim. But before anyone can exclaim at his brilliance, Laura reaches across past him for Fred's plate and knocks the corkscrew flying.

'Mum,' hisses Dolly. 'Dad had to think his way into that and you just knocked it down.'

Laura swallows her impatience ruefully, recognising that it is best to maintain an equilibrium even though every sense rails against it. She gives an apologetic half-smile, but Inigo just grins.

'Don't worry, I can do it again.'

Hedley has been preoccupied for the past few minutes; then his brow clears. 'Oh, I've got it!' he exclaims. 'The drilling starts tomorrow, there are trees to plant, and we've also got some men with ferrets coming. You'll like that, Fred, I think, won't you?'

'Ferrets, great,' says Fred, pushing back his chair and feeding most of his chicken pie to Diver.

'Not ferrets,' groans Inigo at the same moment. 'Honestly, Hedley, I don't know why you put yourself through all these charades. Drilling your fields, irrigating the crops, planting endless trees, worrying about rabbits. What is the point?' The twins and Tamsin, eyeing Hedley and Inigo scornfully, slide out from their places and troop back towards the television. Laura wishes they would stay and talk, but cannot see any reason why they should.

Hedley interrupts Inigo. 'You're a fine one to ask "What is the point?". Your work wouldn't stand up to much scrutiny with that as a criterion, would it? I mean, what a waste of bloody energy to go poncing around the world making bloody paper chains. I don't see the point of contemporary art. It doesn't make you think – in fact it's an excuse not to.'

Inigo ignores this unhelpful interruption and continues, 'You may as well accept that your role as a farmer is non-existent. What you are is a custodian of a small part of Norfolk. One day you will be bought by a rich Japanese businessman who will pay you a salary in order that he can come and take photographs of you going through the motions of farming. That's about as good as it will ever get, and that, I guarantee, is the future.'

Hedley pours wine into his and Inigo's glasses and looks at his brother-in-law with mild dislike, adjusting his look, when he remembers Inigo isn't technically his brother-in-law, to one of stronger disdain.

'I don't see why you can't accept that there is a valid existence to be had in rural England,' he says, determinedly keeping his tone well modulated and reasonable, as Laura has instructed him to do in his dealings with Tamsin, but is unable to resist a provocative little jibe at the end: 'And I haven't heard your defence for your way of life either,' he adds.

Inigo's eyes glitter and Laura isn't sure if it's the wine or the success of Hedley's baiting.

'I don't have to defend contemporary art,' he says loftily. 'Art has always been pilloried by philistines and it always will be. That doesn't ever stop the creative process. No artist will be put down by detractors.'

Hedley is astonished and quietly amused. 'I must say, Inigo, you are quite something. I don't know when I was last called a philistine – I'm a bloody Classics professor, in case you'd forgotten.'

'Oh, don't start this one you two,' Laura says wearily. 'You sound like Laurel and Hardy, you really do.'

'It beats your saunter down Memory Lane,' says Inigo defiantly, sounding so like a spoilt toddler that Laura wants to slap him. Inigo in giant baby mode is maddening, and unfortunately it is one of his most frequently adopted poses. Look at him now, bottom lip out, scowling as he pushes the debris of supper away from his place setting, where he has assembled a handful of candles, removed from the many candelabra placed around the hall. Lighting the first one he warms the base of the next until the wax is tacky and receptive, then presses the lit wick of the first into it, and so on until he has one long candle. Laura keeps her head turned towards her brother, ostensibly discussing Tamsin, but she can see Inigo out of the corner of her eye, and has to close her eyes and take several deep breaths, which she exhales in a ribbon, to stop exasperation spilling over within her. Thank God some of the yoga has sunk in.

Gathering her thoughts to the internal rhythm of 'I must focus on Tamsin, I must focus on Tamsin,' Laura makes her cupped hands into blinkers and leans towards Hedley. 'Tell me properly what's been happening,' she says.

Wrestling with the corkscrew and another bottle of wine, which Inigo, with a patronising smile, removes from him and opens, Hedley explains.

'Tamsin will be fifteen in April.' Laura nods. Hedley glances at her doubtfully, but her expression is sympathetic, and in direct contrast with Inigo's scowl, so to irritate him more than anything, Hedley launches in with detail. 'She's been telephoning her mother to discuss her birthday. It isn't for a few weeks, but Sarah's been so off-hand.'

Inigo leans back in his chair, balancing it on its two back legs and stretches, yawning. Hedley ignores him. 'The calls got off to a bad start when Sarah appeared to have forgotten who Tamsin was. By chance I came into the kitchen and found her sobbing by the telephone. I thought she must have had bad news, and I picked up the receiver. Sarah was on the other end saying, "Jasmine who?" and sounding lobotomised. I got rid of her and spent an hour convincing Tamsin that her mother was deaf and dim now she was nearly fifty, and should have an ear lift as well along with the soul cleansing she was enjoying in Turkey.' He gulps wine, rubbing his eyes. 'She has spoken to her now, but she resents her mother for having left her. Her form mistress at school says she needs someone to talk to about makeup and boyfriends and whatever else teenage girls obsess about.' Hedley coughs, to represent everything else in the teen repertoire. Laura tries to imagine him in the role of Agony Aunt and suppresses a smile.

Hedley rushes on, 'Anyway, Tamsin says her mother is a bitch from hell and won't let me mention her name or bring up the subject at all. And she says she wants to have a party here for her birthday, and I've no idea how to go about it.' He tips his chair forward and peers anxiously at his sister from beneath his lowered brow. He sighs. 'She seems to hold me responsible for Sarah's behaviour, and a lot of the time I feel that I am.'

Inigo pulls himself up from the table. 'I think you are,' he says. 'Sarah would never have left you if you'd stayed in America. You should have sold this place when you inherited it. You would have bought yourself freedom, and you'd still have a wife.'

Laura glares at him and looks pointedly towards the door. 'Inigo, just shut up, can't you? You don't know anything about Sarah, or about Hedley. If you did, you would remember that they were hopelessly unsuited, and splitting up was a huge relief for both of them. And to sell Crumbly would have been heartbreaking, as well as stupid. Think of the capital gains. Anyway, that was four years ago, and we've moved on.'

Inigo leans his giant candle against the Aga and prepares to leave the kitchen, but cannot resist a parting shot. 'Well, I think your problems start and end with this derelict heap of rubble, and the idea that its land pays for it is absurd. No one since Marie-Antoinette has got away with toy farming.'

'Your candle will melt if you leave it there,' warns Hedley.

Inigo grins wickedly. 'I know, that's the point,' he says. 'I'm off to bed so I can be up early to have a look at this ferret frenzy. I'll send the children up so you two can carry on bonding for as long as you want.'

Just to annoy him, Laura blows him a kiss. Hedley shoots him a suspicious glance, but Inigo is sweetness and light now, smiling benevolence at bedtime.

Laura looks after him wearily. 'He's good at making up,' she says into Hedley's silence, and then, feeling more is needed, 'I do love him, you know.'

She sighs. Hedley sighs too, then looking across at her says, 'It's a pity, I always wished you'd married Guy myself. Then you could have come back and lived here too.'

There is a silence. Laura laughs first. 'I think I'd better go to bed,' she says. 'Inigo won't like facing rural noises on his own at night – he's a real wimp about stuff like that.'

One of the things that Laura had found most attractive about Inigo when she met him was his passion for an urban existence. She didn't know he loathed the countryside though. He was in New York selling himself and he was loving it. Laura's small apartment on the Lower East Side was shared with a boy from Seattle training to be an opera singer and a Spanish hairdresser. Laura became a part-time waitress to subsidise her course. She knew no one save her fellow students but she could be who she wanted to be, and she thought she'd never go back to provincial life again. Meeting Inigo at the point where she wanted to give up and go home changed everything. The art world fascinated her, Inigo drew her into it, and gave her a role she enjoyed. Now though, leaning out of the bathroom window, watching the stars and breathing a shock of cold air, she realises that Hedley is drawing her back to Norfolk.

CHAPTER 6

Laura is woken at first light by Fred whispering, 'Come on, Mum, you don't want to miss the ferrets arriving, do you?'

The bed is warm, Laura's nose, exposed to the room, tells her that it is arctically cold – she must have forgotten to turn the heater on when she went to bed, out of practice with the primitive system at Crumbly Hall. There is nothing she would like more than to miss the ferrets arriving; she would love to wallow in this soft bed in the room that was hers when she was growing up, watching the light change through the roses scattered on the curtains, but Fred is tugging at her arm.

'Come on, Mum,' he is whispering loudly. 'If I can get up, I know you can. Dad said he was coming too, didn't you, Dad?'

Inigo groans and turns over.

'Mmm, later, just a bit later,' he agrees sleepily.

Fred pulls back the curtains with a clatter of rings, and Laura braces herself and throws off the covers.

The room is icy cold; she can't face taking her nightie off, so pulls her clothes on over the top. She follows Fred out into the sullen morning, inhaling damp air with each breath. Mud stretches in furrows towards a small copse where Hedley is part of a huddled group of men. They stamp their feet, and flap their arms, pacing around one another, their feet crunching through frosted leaves and crystalline grass. Feeling like King Wenceslas's slave, but with mud instead of snow, Laura trudges behind Fred to the spinney, half-listening to his torrent of information. '. . . the girl ones are called jills and Hedley says they are more difficult to train, but there's one I really like here called Precious. They like to eat dried food, but obviously dead things are better.'

This is truly ghastly, thinks Laura, waiting at the edge of the spinney for Fred to make himself known to the group. She wonders how soon she can mutter some excuse and go back to the warm oasis of peace that is the kitchen. Her fantasies about toast, and coffee-scented air, the newspaper waiting to be read, an egg to be boiled and eaten at leisure are broken by Fred. He ambles towards her, waving an animal.

'Here, Mum, hold this one while I put its harness on. It's a she and she's called Precious. I told you about her. She belongs to Jeff, over there.' A slither of ferret, pink-eyed and wriggling, is thrust into her hands. Intentions of being a ferret whisperer and a great help to her son suffer a setback.

'Urgh, it stinks.' Laura drops it at once, repulsed by the foxy aroma and the density of its blonde pelt.

There is something unnervingly smug about the ferret; even when dropped it retains self-possession, sniffing keenly at Laura's feet. Fred retrieves it, with a pained glare at his mother. Hedley nods a greeting to his sister and with Fred turns back to the group. Fred, showing all the ease with which Hedley greets everyone he meets, and none of his father's reserve, gets involved immediately in mending one of the electric ferret collars which beep when the animal is underground to help the owner find it.

Laura shivers in her coat, tucking her hands up the sleeves and stamping her feet to return some feeling to them. Now she has shown herself to be no use as an assistant, she can watch uninterrupted. This is much better, as she has no further enthusiasm for becoming a ferret groupie, and can think of nothing at all to say to Jeff or any other of the men bundled in balaclavas and muddy waxed coats now preening their ferrets as a prelude to stuffing them down into rabbit holes. A figure appears out of the white fog on the field, jogging towards them, his breath a pale cloud as big as his face in front of him. Laura is impressed to see that it is Inigo, up and dressed already and carrying a camera.

'Hi, Dad,' calls Fred in a stage whisper. 'Come and see.' He is in his element. Eyes shining, he darts between the three ferret men and Hedley, asking questions, watching each ferret manoeuvre intently. Inigo moves over to where Laura is standing.

'Some hellish chickens started screeching as if they were being murdered, so I had to get up,' he says, folding away the lens of his camera and shoving it deep into his pocket.

'I like your country casuals,' says Laura, grinning as she takes in his new camouflage trousers and jacket, and his black balaclava, pulled up like an ordinary hat at present. Inigo ignores her; he is fascinated by the group in front of them.

'I'm actually quite glad I got here so early,' he says. 'Tribal ritual like this is so important. Every country has a version of this, with men parading their killing machines in front of their women.'

A pheasant call cracks through the copse, otherwise the muffled conversation of the ferreters is all Laura can hear. Despite the gnawing cold, the unsavoury smell which now hangs on her clothes, and her own inclinations, she lingers. Inigo, still talking in his special, urgent wildlife programme voice, nudges her. 'Isn't it interesting? The women have got themselves dolled up, even though it's dawn in a muddy field. It's tribal paint, you see.'

Both entertained and exasperated by his commentary, Laura dutifully observes, and agrees that he does have a point – the two women in the group are made up with great care and peacock-bright glamour, and considering the time of day and the circumstances, they are giggling and flirting with unusual energy. Wishing that Hedley would introduce her, but at the same time thinking it silly to need introductions on a ferret hunt, Laura moves closer. The taller woman, Jen, is with the oldest man in the group. She has big fat curls of dark hair, and the red cheeks of a pantomime dame, and is wearing a large squashy coat like a duvet. She is paying scant attention to the ferrets, but with a lot of bobbing back and forth and winking, is making lewd jokes at her husband's expense as he pulls his ferrets. The jokes are much enjoyed by the trio of slightly aimless men standing about doing nothing because they don't have ferrets.

The younger woman, Marion, has pale pink lipstick, and a helmet of white-blonde hair which is in dazzling contrast with the flash of electric blue on her eyelids. She is quiet and pretty, her skin as soft and perfect as her pale sheepskin coat. Her boyfriend Jeff has two ferrets as well as Precious, and Marion stands attentively holding them like a pair of poodles on a short red leash.

Inigo moves closer, catching a little of the action on his camera. His somewhat sinister outfit gives the rustic scene an air of brutal depravity. Marion holds Precious up; her pudgy fingers with their blood-red painted nails sweep down the ferret's coat. Much to Laura's surprise, Inigo takes the ferret from her, holding it on his chest, stroking it for a moment. Inigo has always claimed to be useless with animals. Perhaps he needed to fondle a ferret to find his lurking animal instinct. Laura turns to Hedley to make sure he has noticed Inigo's heroic effort. As she moves, Inigo yells and starts backwards, his arms flailing. Astonishingly, Precious is clinging by her teeth to his chin, extended and dangling like a nicotine-stained Father Christmas beard.

'Bloody bastard rat. Get this hell fiend off me,' Inigo roars, staggering about with the ferret swaying, her jaw locked onto his chin. No one moves for several long seconds, then Hedley, as if suddenly defrosted, shakes himself and runs towards Inigo, shouting, 'Don't pull! Whatever you do, don't pull!'

It is too late. Inigo has recovered his balance, and with both hands clamped around Precious's plump waist he is trying to yank her away. 'My God, it's a fucking praying mantis,' he hisses, between clenched teeth. 'I'll have to go to hospital.'

The ferret fanciers huddle together, not liking this disaster in their midst, unconsciously forming a human shield around Marion in case anyone thinks it's her fault. Jen and her husband shake their heads and mutter to one another in disbelief, but no one steps forward to help Inigo.

'We'd better get on,' says Jeff. 'We won't catch these rabbits standing about all day.' He and his side-kicks move back into the wood with the other ferrets and become deliberately busy with beeping devices, terriers and nets.

Fred frowns after them. 'They should help Dad,' he says. 'They must know what to do.'

'They don't want to be responsible for it.' Hedley puts an arm around Fred, a rare gesture for him. 'Don't worry, we'll manage.'

'For Christ's sake get this thing off me!' Inigo yells. Laura rushes over, and not knowing what else to do, holds Inigo's hand, patting it absently. She is suspended between hysterical laughter and tears, and is fighting an almost overpowering urge to pass out. Inigo's chin with Precious dangling is a demonic sight. Blood begins to soak through and out of the ferret's mouth, seeping onto her nose, staining her head dark red. Behind Inigo, the hunched figures of Jeff and his friends burying things and crouching over holes in the ground, and the closing in of dank creeping fog, increases Laura's sense of nightmare. She clings tighter to Inigo's hand, suddenly letting go as she realises she isn't being helpful and her squeezing grip could in fact feel like another ferret to a man in shock. She glances up at his face, now deathly pale as though Precious has sucked all the colour out.

Hedley, his expression grim, attempts to prise Precious's jaws apart. 'They won't let go,' he says regretfully. 'Their instinct is to hold on, especially if someone has tried to remove them. My hand is too big, I can't get her to open her mouth.' He turns to Fred. 'You'll have to try, I'm afraid. Sorry.'

Fred steps forward, his face as white as the fog, eyes dark and wide with shock. He reaches up and inserts a finger into the ferret's jaw. Laura closes her eyes for a quick prayer to beg that Precious does not maim Fred as well. Immediately, though, Hedley's triumphant voice booms into the fog.

'Well done, Fred. She's let go. She's let go.' Laura opens her eyes to see Precious coiling down into Fred's arms, biddable and innocent save for the wine-dark mask which seeps past her eyes and trickles along her back. Inigo's legs fold and he crumples onto the earth.

'Christ. I've probably got bubonic plague,' he says, carefully running his fingers over the wound to feel the four toothmarks among the oozing blood.

Fred recovers from his shock the instant the drama is over, and is fascinated by the wounds. 'They're like vampire toothmarks. I didn't think you could get bitten like that in real life,' he marvels.

Inigo is not impressed. 'I'm delighted to be able to increase your knowledge of toothmarks,' he says sarcastically, 'but rather than leaving me here on the ground as a case study, I think you had better help me up and get me to a doctor before some filthy disease sets in.'

'Come on. I'll take you. What a vile thing to happen – it must be a rogue ferret.' Laura, still suppressing nausea and finding her face creasing into shocked laughter, helps Inigo up from the ground, holding her hankie over her mouth to hide her inane giggling.

'I don't have to come, do I?' asks Fred, with the natural callousness of youth. 'It's just that I want to stay and help do some proper ferret work with these guys.'

Hedley laughs, slapping him on the back. Laura leads Inigo, nursing flesh wounds and seething spirits, back to the house to be ministered to and fussed over by the girls.

Tamsin and Dolly are eating toast in the kitchen, both wearing pale green face packs as the final part of a lengthy morning bathroom session.

'OhmiGod, what happened?' screams Dolly, cracking the lower half of her mask in her concern for her father.

Tamsin drops her toast and runs to fetch the First Aid kit. 'I love cleaning wounds,' she purrs.

'Good,' says Laura, who doesn't. 'You clean him up then.'

Tamsin and Dolly happily settle down to mend Inigo. Their dabbing with cotton wool to the damaged chin and tender sympathy to the lacerated spirits perk him up a lot. This unexpected attention, followed by a telephone call to the doctor, has a tranquillising effect on Inigo. The doctor takes a suitably serious view of the event and agrees that tetanus is a danger, and that an injection will be necessary. As a committed hypochondriac, this is great news for Inigo. He puts the telephone down and announces triumphantly to Laura, 'You see, it is very primitive here. I shouldn't be surprised if you can get the plague too and a lot of other medieval illnesses that have been wiped out elsewhere.'

'Yes, you can,' says Hedley, who has just come in and is enjoying this train of thought. 'You can get ringworm, and cow pox.'

Inigo looks very alarmed; Tamsin rolls her eyes. 'No one gets cow pox! You're thinking of chicken pox.'

Inigo's visit to the local GP is enhanced by a discussion about primitive cultures including those in Norfolk, the doctor sensing a need in his patient to rant for a while after such an undignified accident. By mid-afternoon, Inigo is in recovery, and vocal in his desire never to set foot in the countryside again. Making the sitting room his salon, Inigo lounges on the sofa, his mobile phone in one hand, the television remote control in the other. Next to him, a laptop computer teeters drunkenly on a cushion while his new toy, the digital camera, records what it can see of his recovery from a tripod. The faded paper on the walls, the sagging scant curtains as much as the ash heap in the fireplace make an unlikely backdrop for this nerve centre of modernity. Inigo has made the most of his surroundings. He has readjusted the furniture, arranging a chair to put his feet up on, a table for a mug and a plate and the television all within easy reach of his sofa. Lying there he swigs whisky from Hedley's hip flask between telephone calls, and with Dolly's assistance is now working on the lighting.

His phone trills; he reaches for it. 'Hello, Jack? Inigo here. I'm in Norfolk, we should be back tonight . . . Yes, I know it's Saturday. I've been thinking about *Death Threat*—' He breaks off, waving his arm wildly. 'No, not there, Doll, now there's a lampshade frilling over the motor racing – anyway, Jack, are you there? ARE YOU THERE?' He hurls the phone into heaped cushions beside him. 'No proper signal here. Why is everything done so badly in the country? There's no need for it, it's just acceptance of incompetence.'

Laura, trying to read on the other side of the room, shuts her book. 'Inigo, we'd like to stay here until Sunday. There's so much for the children to do, and I've hardly seen Hedley, or got anything sorted out with Tamsin. And most of all, I really don't want to go back tonight.'

The phone cuts through her words and Inigo dives to answer it. Grinning, he sprawls, listening to Jack. 'That sounds good – well done . . . No, I haven't been running today. I thought I'd give myself a break because I've got sodding holes in my face . . . Yeah, some sort of feral beast called a ferret. I'm thinking of making an installation including a stuffed one and calling it *Death Threat II*, but I'm worried it would be a bit derivative.'

Laura returns to her book, jaw set, determined that she will not be coerced into going home a day early because Inigo is bored and wants to show off his war wounds. She turns the page, her hand trembling, angry blood rushing, burning her cheeks. Outside is the answer, and a walk, or else she won't be able to contain her annoyance and she'll start a row with Inigo.

Dusk is falling as she walks down through the garden and out onto the marshes, the Labrador Diver at her side, his nose down, vacuuming the evening scents as he goes. The fog has lifted, and the last gleam of afternoon sun is a primrose wash across the western sky. Above and below, sky and sea reflect a purple haze, deepening fast as the light fades. The cold air sears Laura's face, exhilarating and fresh, cooling her thoughts, mending her temper. She thinks back over the past months. These moments of despairing panic are becoming more frequent, more intense. She has a sense of suffocating, a need for air, for space to breathe. When did life become so stulti-fying, and why does she feel like this? It's not the children, they're difficult, but not yet impossible, Laura thinks, remembering Tamsin. They are in a lull before the hormone storm of teendom breaks. It isn't even really Inigo, although it is always tempting to blame her own lowness on him. But he's always been demanding and egocentric, and she has accepted it, lived with it and learned to use it as a shield to keep herself out of the limelight. Inigo's temperament makes it imperative that Laura should be the one who walks behind, picking up the pieces, but it's fine, she is good at it, and she has her own passions which can occasionally be indulged. Or she used to.

Wondering if she can remember what she really enjoys, Laura stops by the duck pond and chucks a stick into the grey water, its surface broken already by the evening breeze. A crashing splash indicates that Diver sees this as a game, then a beating rush of wings heralds three ducks flying up in perfect formation, quacking outrage as they vanish into the dusk. Laura can just make out the darker blob of Diver's head as he glides silently through the water, the stick borne high above the surface.

'Come on, boy, let's go back.' Laura turns towards home, frowning in concentration, trying to recall any pleasures that don't involve children, Inigo or work. What does she like? What makes her laugh? All she can come up with are dogs and country and western music – not that any of those songs make you laugh, but they offer incomparable solace. Laura has often felt her interests to be inadequate. With both parents historians and a classicist brother, her degree in film

81

studies always seems lightweight and not worth taking seriously, and with Inigo, it is essential for a bearable life to let his passions come first. Thus Laura knows a great deal she doesn't want to know about sport, and has been known to resort to reminiscing about her childhood to make it seem that she has hidden depths. Not that she needs them really, as Inigo has so much to say about himself and it's easier to think about him.

Ruefully she remembers a conversation with her friend Cally when Inigo gave up smoking. Enunciating slowly at first then speeding into a rant, Cally said, 'I can't believe this. When you gave up, you didn't think it was worth mentioning, and I didn't find out for months, but now you've actually rung me up to tell me Inigo's done it. Honestly, Laura, I keep telling you – get a bloody life.'

Cally's right; there should be something more to mark the passing years. If Laura were a man, she would label this her mid-life crisis, and perhaps buy a red sports car, or take up the gym. As a woman, social pressure suggests a face-lift or a toy boy, but she cannot imagine herself with either. But what can she have? Can anything physical staunch this sensation of loss and panic, or would it be better to have counselling? Back at college, twenty-year-old Laura would have known that all she needed was happiness. Her older self thinks what she needs is change.

Walking across the barnyard on her way back to the house, she peers through a doorway and into the big barn. Inside, the cavernous space is empty around one small, ancient tractor. Its tyres are almost flat, and dust and cobwebs have given the smudged blue panels a ghostly blur. Inigo would love it; it might distract him from going back to London. Laura hastens back to the house to fetch him to look at it.

The sitting room has traces of Inigo: his computer disks are stacked neatly in two piles, the cushions have been balanced along the sofa back, and a tennis player is thwacking a ball vigorously but silently across the television. Inigo, however, is not here. Nor is anyone else. Laura walks through to the hall to shout up the stairs, sensing more than hearing the pulsing beat of Tamsin's stereo system far away in the attic and wondering where Hedley and Fred have got to. The telephone rings. Laura picks it up.

'Hello?'

'Hello, this is Guy. I wonder if I could speak to Hedley?'

'Guy. Yes. Hello. How odd. I don't . . .' Laura tails off, obscurely embarrassed, suddenly tonguetied and desperate that he doesn't realise it is her, although she doesn't know why, and there is no reason why he should.

'Hello, hello, are you still there? Please could I speak to Hedley?' Guy speaks slowly, enunciating clearly as if to a long-distance, non-English-speaking operator. He must think she is a half-wit. In fact, he thinks she is Tamsin.

Laura doesn't speak but says, 'Mmmm.'

'Tamsin, would you take a message for me? He wanted to talk to me about organic weed warfare. Get him to call me back when he comes in, would you?'

Laura nods, then mumbles, 'All right,' and puts the telephone down. How fascinating that Guy, who has lain dormant in the outer recesses of her memory for years, should re-emerge both in person and on the telephone twice in one week. Cally, who lives on a houseboat in Little Venice with a cat called Hybrid, and has delusions of being a gypsy soothsayer, would insist it was portentous, but Laura knows better.

'Hi, Mum – look, I shot this pigeon. It was so cool, it just fell out of the tree when I hit it. I missed the other one that was flying – Hedley got that.'

Fred and Hedley clatter into the house. Fred is pink-cheeked and incandescent with excitement, waving his feathered trophy; Hedley, almost as delighted, is a long way from the tweedy academic he was for so long, bearing a gun, a stout stick and some sharp knives. Laura notices how attractive the trappings of outdoor life are, even on her brother. She must try and help him find a girlfriend. A motherly figure is what Tamsin needs in her life too.

Fred slaps the pigeon on the kitchen table. 'I'm going to pluck it and then we can cook it,' he says with relish.

'That's wonderful, well done.' Laura wonders what twisted element in her mothering makes her delighted when Fred spends an afternoon murdering helpless creatures but furious and frustrated if he should sit for three hours quietly occupied by the television. She helps them shed their weapons and waterproof coats, and makes tea for the three of them, as no one else is around, listening to their exchanged comments and observations about the marsh, astonished by the interest Fred shows and the knowledge he has picked up over a few weekend visits here.

'Mum, I think we should move in here and live with Hedley,' Fred announces, cramming a large piece of cake into his mouth to add, somewhat inaudibly, 'I don't ever want to go back to London, there's nothing to do.'

Laura laughs. 'That's exactly the opposite of Dolly's view. She wouldn't like it one bit; neither would your father.'

'No,' says Hedley emphatically. 'Inigo couldn't possibly live here. He'd be a nightmare – I mean he'd find it a nightmare.'

'Don't look so worried,' Laura whispers, leaning across the kitchen table as Fred moves out of earshot to graze in the fridge. 'It's never going to happen. Inigo can't even bear two nights here.'

Hedley's hairy eyebrows, which have been drifting down over his eyes, leap up to his hairline with surprise. 'Are you going then?'

Laura shakes her head. 'No, but I think he might.'

'He might what? I love it when you talk about me.' A warm hand runs over Laura's shoulders; she twists in her chair to look up at Inigo, all trace of his earlier truculence evaporated, now smiling at her, the four puncture wounds in his chin making him look as though he has just been sewn together.

Laura stands up, not ready yet to forgive him for trying to bully them all back to London. 'I thought you were going home.'

He kisses her forehead. 'I can't. I need to be with you. I'm staying for as long as you want to.' He is trying to be good. Laura decides to thaw.

She smiles at him. 'I found something you will love in the barn.'

'Take me and show me.' His eyes are dark; Laura's heart races looking into them.

'I will. After tea I'll show you.'

Hedley coughs, embarrassed by the intimacy of his sister and Inigo over crumpets and tea. Inigo has always been very un-English in his tendency to touch and stroke, and Hedley has never been able to relax and accept it, tending to look away, leave the room or change the subject while Inigo's hands move slowly across Laura's shoulders, or his hands tangle in the weight of her hair. Now is not too bad, they are simply standing still in the circle of one another's arms, so Hedley fixes his gaze a couple of inches above them and says, 'Good, so you're all staying. Marvellous. Let's tell Dolly and Tamsin.'

Laura breaks away from Inigo. 'Oh Hedley, I forgot to tell you. Guy rang – he wants to have a word with you about something organic.'

'How odd, he was talking about you the other day. Did you make a plan to meet up with him?'

'He thought I was Tamsin.'

Hedley sighs. 'Well, why didn't you say that you weren't Tamsin, you were you?'

'I don't know, the moment passed.'

Her brother claps his hand against his forehead in mock exasperation. 'Anyway,' he says, 'it doesn't matter. We don't want to go there – we'd have to see Celia and she's poisonous.'

'Who's Celia?'

'Guy's wife.'

'Oh, I see.'

'Is she poisonous to touch, or just if you bite her?' Fred has found a miniature axe and is chopping small pieces of kindling into matchsticks by the fire then lighting them one by one. Inigo crouches to help him, showing him how to split the wood so that each splinter comes away whole and springing from the block. Laura walks around the kitchen table in circles, picking up a cup, putting it down again, moving the cake plate from one end of the table to the other. It is disconcerting to think of Guy's life, and indeed his wife, existing here in Norfolk when, if she had thought about him at all in the past years, Laura had vaguely supposed him to inhabit a parallel universe.

It certainly seemed that he came from one when she first met him. Laura and Hedley were exploring a network of rutted tracks near Crumbly. Hedley had just passed his driving test, and the invisible Uncle Peter hadn't seemed to mind them borrowing the farm car and heading off all day. Driving in through an entrance surrounded by iron pig-stys, Hedley slewed the car in the mud, but persevered through thick fir trees, their evergreen shade creating a still, menacing light on this dark winter morning. They rounded a final bend in the track and Hedley slammed on the brakes with a jolt. 'What on earth is that?' he whispered.

Laura, who had been leaning back to reach for something from behind, turned and the breath stuck in her throat. Towering above them, so near their wheels were on the edge of the first rank of steps leading up to the front door, was a vast derelict building, so ruined it was hard to see whether it had once been a church or a house. A bell tower was tethered on one wall, and half a pediment straddled the front, but beyond the façade, windows without walls or floors behind them revealed the ghosts of rooms, now filled with falling beams and sprouting foliage.

Hedley had turned the engine off, but Laura tugged at him. 'Come on, let's go. It's creepy here.'

'No way. I want to look round.' Her brother got out of the car and climbed over one of the ground-floor windows. Laura waited, the radio turned on to keep her company. Hedley returned a few minutes later with another youth his own age.

'Laura, this is Guy Harvey. He lives here.'

The newcomer had dishevelled blond hair and laughing blue eyes, and when Laura said hello to him she had a flashing moment's thought that she had stepped into a lopsided fairy story and here was Prince Charming waiting to be rescued. In fact, Guy Harvey was the son of the local demolition man, and the two of them lived in a caravan next to the house. Guy and Hedley became inseparable friends and Laura tagged along with them more often than not, climbing in the ruin. They once had a picnic at night, the three of them lying, looking up at the stars, from a giant Edwardian bath teetering thirty feet up on a heap of rubble in the shattered east wing of the house. Laura was sixteen, and it was the first time Guy ever kissed her.

Alf Harvey, who had notably small feet and a round body which rolled from side to side when he walked, had bought the ruin when his wife died two years before Laura met Guy. His version of moving in was to arrive with a mobile home and a crane dangling a vast black iron ball, his plan to knock the ruin down and build a village of spanking new houses on the site. A man with a mission to flatten and renew, never to preserve or restore, Alf was astonished to find that his idea was met with disapproval in the neighbourhood, and before he could position his crane and ball for maximum effect, the local council's heritage officer arrived waving a preservation order. The building, or what was left of it, was preserved just as it was, beams exposed like bones on a rotting carcass, and even a shattered four-poster bed twisted in the remains of a doorway. Parking his mobile home in the stableyard, Alf set up residence with his son Guy, and spent the remaining years of his life trying to win over the planners. He had no interest in the fields and woodland, the streams and hedges which lay beyond the four walls of his giant white elephant.

Guy was an only child, fifteen and still missing his mother painfully. He began to mend the fences, lay hedges and unblock the choked stream so water could meander through the low-lying water meadows instead of flooding. Six months after his father and he moved in, Guy let his first field to a pig farmer; a year later he grew a patch of peas and another of strawberries. By the time he met Hedley and Laura, he had left school and was letting and farming the whole two hundred acres around his father's house and even making a small profit, driven by a barely recognised desire to create order.

Laura had never met anyone, save her Uncle Peter, whose livelihood came from the land. It was both quaint and impressive. She didn't know anyone of seventeen, either, who had left school. Guy, for his part, had never met a girl who found his life glamorous. They fell in love with the exoticism of one another.

CHAPTER 7

Back in London, it takes some days for the aroma of ferret to be eradicated from the car and every item of Fred's clothing. And as much as the smell clings to him, he clings to the memories of the weekend and the hope that Precious the ferret will have babies and he will be given one of his own.

'Anyway, Hedley said I could keep it there, so it's nothing to do with you AT ALL,' he roars defiantly at the end of a heated conversation with his father.

Inigo, stirring rusty sweet-smelling tomato sauce at the stove, is at his most implacable. For his weekly cook-athon he is wearing an apron Laura's mother Anne once gave him. It is made of yellow oilcloth with a red logo saying Camp Coffee, beneath which is a picture of a jaunty soldier marching about with a coffee cup. Inigo wears this apron every Thursday and for most of the weekend as he slices and chops vegetables, kneads and mixes dough and batter and cooks and cooks and cooks, laying waste to the kitchen and becoming more theatrical with each finished, and perfectly presented, dish. These are the meals for the week, and those that are to be frozen are carefully labelled and wrapped, and then placed in the freezer in chronological order of when they are to be eaten. All food preparation is taken out of Laura's hands.

There are people who are envious of Laura for having such a domesticated husband; indeed, her mother who telephones in the midst of the ferret discussion, reminds her, 'Of course it's marvellous he's such a cook, even if he does hate animals. It must be a price worth paying. After all, just imagine how awful it would be for everyone if you had to do it all.'

Laura appreciates the double edge of this thrust, and grins invisibly into the phone, thinking, 'Touché', but saying, 'I know, I realise it's extraordinary. It's one of his compulsions. He can't help it, it's the Jewish momma in him trying to get out. The maddening thing is that the children don't like the wild flavours he creates, and of course he won't listen or adapt. He's a megalomaniac in the kitchen. I have no role beyond skivvy. I'm a tweeny, in fact.'

Laura's mother is baffled. 'A tweeny? Are you? Do you mean the ones on television? How odd of you.'

She sounds displeased. Laura is not living up to expectation at all with nonsense about children's television characters and a husband who cooks better than she does. Not that Anne herself ever brought Laura up to cook. Oh dear me no. She was destined for the halls of academe where filthy food is served to intellectuals who use it merely as fuel for the engines of their minds, and have no sensory pleasure in it. Such a shame she decided not to pursue her studies further. Anne had always hoped Laura would stay in America and do a PhD after her master's degree, but of course she met Inigo. Maddening, but there we are. She wasn't doing anything proper like history after all, but a PhD in film – well, it would have been something for Anne to tell her colleagues at Trinity. She listens to Laura again.

'Oh come on, Mother, that's what they used to call the maids who worked between the kitchens and the rest of the household. You can't have forgotten.'

Laura hates herself as she utters the last sentence, but she cannot help it. In her family, a piece of knowledge imparted is a prize beyond gold. Throughout her childhood her mother, a history don specialising in The Age of Enlightenment, dispensed argument and raised questions, instead of cooking roast chicken and mashed potato. Of course Hedley and Laura, and their vague wispy father, were fed, but food was never meant to be enjoyed, not when there was reasoning or language to relish.

Clouds of steam billow above the stove as Inigo removes the lid from a pan of boiling water and begins to slide lengths of spaghetti beneath the surface. Dolly drifts into the room. Her hair is tousled, she has no shoes on, and is yawning mightily, as if she has just got out of bed. In fact she has been lying on the floor in the sitting room with her headphones on and her homework open in front of her, making a pyramid out of paperclips.

93

'Lay the table could you, Doll,' says Inigo, glancing up at her with a smile from his cooking. 'I doubt I'll get Fred to do it, he's too angry with me.'

From the tether of the telephone, Laura sees the troubled look on Fred's face as he glances between his father and his sister, and sensing his need of support, she says to her mother, 'I must go, I'll tell you about Hedley and his plans for Tamsin's birthday tomorrow.'

Inigo pours a trickle of oil into the bubbling pasta, laughing with Dolly over an incident at school. His glance flickers up to Fred and away again: he is punishing him with exclusion. Laura's temper rises fast, irritation spilling over so she has to bite her lip not to shout at Inigo. Maybe it would be better if she did shout at him, instead of shielding him from the frustration his behaviour causes. Fred scowls and sits down at the furthest seat from his father. Laura sits next to him, rumpling his hair and winking at him as Inigo serves them. It is Inigo's idea that they all sit down to eat together each evening. He likes to preside over his family, and he likes to be appreciated by them; without praise, Laura often thinks he would cease to function.

'Mmmm, this is delicious,' she says, half because it is true and half because she knows that Dolly and Fred will not be commenting on their food; instead, both are rolling it around their plates, Fred creating a mound of food in the middle, Dolly spreading hers into spaghetti waves like a nest around the rim of the plate. Fortunately, Inigo is discussing some final details for the torn-up paper event in Hyde Park, which is to be staged next week.

'We'll have to have a press release saying that spring is officially late this year,' he is telling Laura, 'and that the equinox in March didn't count because the weather was too bad. I don't think anyone will mind, do you?'

'No one you know will mind,' agrees Laura, 'but let's not make a big thing of it or we're going to look arrogant and stupid.'

Fred, who has given up toying with his food, tipping his chair back, humming a song and looking catatonically bored, perks up at this interchange.

'Could I come and help with the installation? I could miss school if Mum wrote me a note. They said any projects I did outside school were good anyway.'

This is just the sort of thing that cheers Inigo up, and he does not harbour grudges, particularly when he is receiving praise or attention. Grinning like the Cheshire Cat, licking his thumbs to remove the last traces of Parmesan cheese, he turns towards Fred. 'Do you think you'd like to help? I'd love to know how you think we can spread the stuff. There is literally tonnes of it coming on trucks.'

Suddenly Fred and Inigo are talking loudly across the table. Both of them have pushed their plates aside, and they are an advertisement for a perfect father and son act. Wondering if she will ever become used to the schizophrenic speed with which children – and of course Inigo – can mood swing, Laura leaves them discussing whether to use shovels or a wind machine to disperse the paper across the park. Drifting into the kitchen, she makes a mental list of her own more mundane activities, the most important of which has only just occurred to her. The press will have a field day on art as litter unless she can contain this whole, hugely energetic display somehow. Imagine twenty tonnes of torn-up paper swirling on the April breeze. The mess will be appalling.

Laura is at the sink, looking out at her small hemmed-in garden, soft green in the April dusk, every plant dripping from the recent shower. A chaffinch dives out of the cherry blossom on the wall and into her mind flashes the long-ago image of the summer kitchen garden at Alf Harvey's derelict house. The walls were tumbling on one side, but along the other three were planted huge, laden, espaliered cherry trees, and in her mind's eye, Laura can see Guy up on a ladder draping them in fruit nets to keep the birds out. That's what I need, she thinks suddenly, miles of fruit netting. I'll ring Guy tomorrow and ask where to get it.

Laura's heart thuds as if she is making a clandestine plan. Why is the thought of making a call about fruit nets clandestine? And what about Guy? How will she get hold of him? It would be odd to ask Hedley for his telephone number. Maybe he's in the book. She knows that Guy still farms the land around his father's house, and lived nearby until the old man died. Now he lives in a watermill he converted near Crumbly village, and has turned the pastures around it into his thriving organic vegetable business. Laura knows what it looks like because Hedley had a brochure from Guy's place in his study, complete with a small drawing of a pretty farmhouse set on the water. She tries to imagine life inside this picture-book house with Celia. But even imagining Celia herself presents difficulties. Laura cannot believe that Guy is married; she can't really believe he isn't still the boy next door whom she left behind when she went to America. Perhaps she should call Directory Enquiries now, so she can get the whole thing over with? No. She shouldn't be thinking so much about someone else's husband. What if Celia answers? She must remember to ask for the business number. And she's got her own family to consider, too. She must do it when they're all out, but there's no harm in getting the number now, is there?

Inigo and Fred have gone down to the computer to make a diagram for the *Paper in the Park* show; Laura can hear their voices rising and falling in bursts of animation as they draw it up on the screen. They will be hours. Laura goes in search of the telephone and finds it on the floor in the sitting room next to Dolly, who is lying flat on the carpet as usual, propped on her elbows, gazing glassily at the silent television. Suppressing an urge to kick the television screen or even Dolly to create some animation, Laura picks up the phone and dials, leaving the room. She bends forward and does a small and unchallenging yoga stretch, focusing on her breathing to try and eradicate the neck tension she is feeling due to her continued belief that what she is doing is illicit. It doesn't work.

'Hello, Directory Enquiries, this is Nicola speaking. What name is it?'

There is something about Directory Enquiries which maddens Laura. Provoked, she replies, '"What name is it" simply doesn't make sense. Do you mean "Whose number would I like?"'

A pause, signifying that Nicola is registering her as a nutter, before her flat nasal voice tries again. 'What name is it?'

Laura sighs. 'Harvey, Guy Harvey. Maybe Guy Harvey Organic actually.'

'How are you spelling that?'

'T.H.A.T.'

'Sorry?'

'I'm spelling "that" T.H.A.T. but if you want to know how to spell Harvey, it's H.A.R.V.E.Y.'

'OK,' says Nicola listlessly. 'What street name have you got?'

Laura speaks through tight lips. 'I haven't *got* a street name, I expect it's in the middle of fields. It's an organic vegetable farm. They supply lots of restaurants, you know. They're big news—'

Nicola cuts in, bored with this promotional aside. 'What town have you got then, madam?'

'I haven't got any town, it's in Norfolk. It's near the sea. I told you, it's an organic vegetable farm. You must have lots of them.'

'Sorry, I can only go by the name, and there's nothing listed unless you can give me a town.' Nicola is becoming more animated as the possibility of giving Laura the number recedes.

Laura thinks for a moment, remembering the different stations the local train stopped at, wondering which is Guy's station now. 'Sheringham,' she announces at last.

Nicola sighs with faux regret. 'Sorry, we've nothing listed for that name anywhere in the Sheringham area. Goodbye.'

Before Laura can suggest another name from the branch line Nicola's nasal voice has gone. Cursing, she slams the telephone down in its cradle, resolving to find out the number from Hedley tomorrow.

The doorbell rings. Dolly sweeps past her to open it, muttering, 'It's for me, Mum. Don't touch it – I said it's for me.' Her transformation is staggering. A few moments ago she was supine with dull, empty eyes, now she is prancing through the hall, swishing her hair, and opening the door to coo, 'Hi, Rebecca, I'm ready, let's go.' She leans back into the house to grab her jacket off the bottom bannister and is gone, rippling laughter following her and the equally animated friend. Dolly waves and shouts back to Laura on the doorstep, 'I'll be at Rebecca's, and I'll be home at eight-thirty. Byeeee.'

Laura waves back, hugging her arms around herself because there is no one else to hug now. They're leaving home, this is the first stage and then they will be gone. I've got to get a life, she thinks, eyes fixed on the swinging gate Dolly has not shut. Laura steps out to do it herself, and pauses at the gate, looking up at the mauve-rinsed evening sky, still watery and heavy with cloud but sparkling in the glimpse of evening sunshine. The flowering cherries in the street are all out now, and a foam of bridal blossom gives a festive air to the closed windows and gates of the neatly ranked houses. Laura and Inigo have lived here for ten years, ever since they came back from America, and although she knows who lives in the flats opposite, and in the divided houses next door on each side, Laura often feels that if she and her family vanished one day, none of their neighbours would notice they'd gone.

A raindrop splashes on the pavement in front of her, and another dollops onto her forehead, then there is a pause in which Laura hears before she feels the whisper of another veil of rain pattering up the street. A man turns the corner from the main road, his head bent, his hands in his pockets, legs scissoring fast towards her. Because his head is bowed, Laura sees the red scar like a fold on the top of his bald white scalp. She holds open the door.

'Hello Jack, what brings you up here after hours?'

Jack Smack makes sure he is well out of the wet before he removes his hands from his pockets and brushes his cheek against Laura's in greeting.

'I've come to see Inigo. We've got to sort out the New York show. We've already postponed it and they want him out there as soon as possible.'

'What a surprise, Jack.' Inigo and Fred have come up from the basement to stand like Jack with their hands in their pockets. Inigo slaps Jack jovially on the arm, but then returns his hand quickly to his pocket. Laura notices how simian the posture of males can be, toes out-turned, shoulders hunched, heads forwards. Feeling light and airy as thistledown among them, she ducks past and into the kitchen, suppressing an urge to thrust her own hands into the pockets of her jeans and lurch about in parody.

Fred comes through, his demeanour crestfallen. 'I don't think Dad will be doing the paper thing,' he says. 'Jack wants him to go to New York tomorrow to set up the show.'

'But he's not meant to be there for another two weeks – we've postponed!' Laura is aghast. 'And I've spent ages convincing the Parks Committee that we can do our paper installation . . .' She tails off, remembering it is nothing to do with Fred, and stalks back through to Inigo and Jack in the sitting room. Inigo is explaining the two elements of the New York show.

'First there is a cake.' He pulls a white paper model out from behind the bookshelf. 'Look, this is how I see it.'

'But it's a house,' says Jack, gazing perplexedly at the model which indeed is an architect's scale model of a modernist house.

'I know.' Inigo grins, twirling his pen on its nib like a pirouetting ballerina. 'Actually it's my parents' house, or rather it's the house they lived in before they split up. I made this at art school, but now I'm going to recreate the structure by making a cake tin to follow the floor plan and then filling it with cake-mix. The idea is that when it's been baked and turned out, the whole space inside will be full and impenetrable instead of empty and cavernous. It represents the conflicts of security and suffocation in a family home, and explores the nature of survival. It's called *Caked.*' He looks up at Jack measuringly. 'What do you think?'

Laura leans in the doorway. She is particularly keen on this project, and wants to persuade Inigo to do a whole show called *You Can Have Your Cake and Eat It* with all exhibits made of cake. It seems to Laura that this theme emphasises all that is absurd about conceptual art and delivers it with the supreme silliness of Marie Antoinette's famous cry, 'Let them eat cake.' Jack, however, is less keen.

'How can we sell this cake house?' he demands. 'Even your most avid collectors will balk at buying a cake.'

Fred, who has been sitting cross-legged on the floor, his chin resting on his hands, butts in, 'No, they won't. Everyone likes buying cakes.'

Jack casts him a look of mild dislike. 'Not at twenty thousand dollars a pop they don't,' he says. 'And I don't feel we can offer your work any lower than that, or we'll have people saying you're going out of fashion.'

'I don't think the cake should be for sale,' Laura offers. 'It's a statement of artistic integrity, it doesn't have a price on it.'

Jack's eyebrows whip up to where his hairline would be if he had one; he sees potential for publicity here.

'Yessss,' he drawls. 'I like that a lot, I really do.'

Laura beams; she is delighted, and surprised that Jack is so easy to convince. Pressing on while she is on the high ground, she adds quickly, 'But Inigo, if you go to New York tomorrow, what will we do about the *Paper in the Park* idea?'

Now Jack's look of dislike is directed at Laura. 'We haven't got time for that,' he interrupts, before Inigo can speak. 'And anyway, it was only an installation. We can't sell it. Now Inigo, what about the rest of the New York show. How is *Death Threat?*'

Inigo pulls a tiny silver figure of eight out of his pocket and holds it up. 'Just fine, thanks, Jack. Here's the baby, my smallest ever Möbius strip, and I've been working on rolling-pin projections for weeks. I'm ready to install this show now, but I wanted to finish *Paper in the Park* first. I think it will speak to the inner child in a lot of people, and spring is the moment to unleash that element.'

Jack's expression says very clearly that he thinks Inigo is talking nonsense, but that he can see a way to make mileage out of it.

'OK, we'll do it. We'll get you back from New York for it and you can arrive in the park in a helicopter. That way we'll get maximum publicity.'

'That way you'll wreck the whole thing before Inigo's even arrived,' says Laura tartly. 'The helicopter will send the paper everywhere.'

Fred interrupts, hopping from foot to foot with excitement. 'No, it would be totally cool,' he says. 'The helicopter can be the paper-spreader. Could I go in it too?'

Even Jack is impressed by this notion, his eyes flashing like cash registers as he imagines the storm of media excitement such a venture would create. Laura can hardly believe they are all being so stupid. Quite apart from the cost of hiring a helicopter, there is the small issue of permission. Royal Parks have taken a dim enough view of the whole project already. This would finish them off utterly. She opens her mouth to pour all this cold water on the project then closes it again. Why should she always be the voice of reason, the killjoy? Let them find out for themselves. The whole notion had always seemed pretty half-baked to Laura and now it has become truly preposterous.

She retreats upstairs to have a bath, armed with a weepalong novel and some bath essence Cally sent her, wrapped up in a large maple leaf and with a note saying 'Sugar is hot, xxx Cally.'

The bottle is long and narrow, like a test tube. Laura pours a few drops into the bathwater and, slightly horrified by the sickly smell, holds up the tube to read the ingredients.

This is Sugar Beet Intenscent, distilled to perfectly capture the organic, healthy scent of sugar; sweet and earthy as though the root has been freshly plucked from the soil, this is a polarising essence. You will love if you're hot, loathe if you're not.

Sugar beet? How is it possible that anyone has decided to make bath oil from sugar beet? It is a depressing and filthy feature of farm life, or it used to be. Now it has become a glamorous, sought-after beauty potion ingredient. Perched on the side of the bath, Laura giggles, rereading the label, much enjoying the preposterous tone. She turns it round, and on the back is a small picture of a millhouse. It is Guy's millhouse. Laura stares at the test tube in astonishment. Can Guy really be responsible for this drivel?

'What's going on, Mum?' Fred puts his head round the door. Laura waves the test tube.

'Come and smell this, and tell me what it reminds you of.' Suspicion in every shuffled step, her son sniffs the test tube and recoils. 'That's rank, Mum. It smells like rotting stuff. Why is it that weird green colour? You haven't put it in the bath, have you? It'll make you smell rotten. Don't come up to my room afterwards because I won't let you in.'

Laura promises not to pollute his bedroom with her presence, and reluctantly gets into her bath, not pleased by this new dimension of Guy. He must have changed more than Hedley has told her if he's writing pretentious nonsense like this on the side of bottles. And he's missed a great opportunity to gain more clients because he hasn't put his number on the bottle. Usually the bath is a good place to practise reaching a state of tranquillity, but Laura finds herself becoming more morose as each moment passes. How has it happened that she spends her days trying to get permission to chuck small pieces of paper around in a park, and her evenings soaking in liquid sugar beet? Where is the life she thought she was going to lead? The one where her intellect was going to burn brightly and she would have woken each morning with a sense of purpose? Is her whole generation as unexciting? Every horizon has shrunk to a point where Laura faces only domestic and practical questions. Even her interpretation of Inigo's work has become glib and cynical. Laura wonders whether there is anything left to salvage at this stage of her life, or whether the person she used to be has departed for good.

The luxury of introspection is fleeting, and Laura is unable to wallow properly in self-pity because she has too much to do. Inigo departs for New York with a bag containing one small metal pastry-cutter and a projector. Jack refuses to let him bring any clothes, saying, 'We only want hand luggage because we'll be pushed for time when we get there; I've arranged three interviews for you hot off the plane. We can buy what you need there.'

Pushing a laden trolley around the supermarket after driving them to the airport, Laura reflects that Inigo scarcely makes a move of any sort without someone – herself or Jack, or previously his mother – following him to make things easier for him. She pauses at the frozen food section and selects a bagful of spinach parcels, not because anyone at home will eat them, but because she is charmed by the small solidness of them. This sort of aimless shopping is not popular when Inigo is around, but Laura enjoys the tiny rush of triumph it brings. Mainly though, she is in the supermarket to procure crisps and drinks for Tamsin's birthday party. This event is planned for Saturday night, and Laura and the twins are driving up to get there in time to help set things up.

They arrive at Crumbly to find Hedley gloomily surveying the front hall. Tamsin is up a ladder, festooning a curtain of fairy lights across the fireplace.

The furniture has all gone, and lengths of rainbow-coloured fabric are draped on the bannisters while more are veiling the paintings.

'I don't see why it looks better with these rags everywhere,' says Hedley. 'What I wanted—'

'Well, it would have been better if we had loads of fake fur, but this is all we could find. I like it. Hello, Laura.' Tamsin smiles; Laura kisses her and gives her the present Dolly chose for her, muttering to Hedley, 'Well, she seems very cheerful. This is obviously just what was needed.'

'Cool, thank you.' Tamsin strips off her top and wriggles into the T-shirt in a flash.

Hedley sighs. 'Well, you should have seen her earlier,' he complains. 'I gave her an umbrella and a suitcase as her present and she said was I trying to say something.'

Tamsin is prancing about the hall in delight. 'Look, Hedley! Look what it says. I'm going to wear it tonight! It's totally brilliant' She turns round and poses. Please Can You Hold My Drink While I Snog Your Boyfriend is emblazoned on her chest.

'Oh no,' says Hedley faintly.

Laura and Hedley spend the evening in the kitchen, and as promised, do not go anywhere near the hall, no matter how loud the thuds and shrieks become. Hedley fidgets and coughs, paces up and down, and when Fred comes in, red-faced and panting for a glass of water, he pounces on him.

'What's happening? Is everything all right? What have they broken?'

Fred wrinkles his nose to express disbelief at his uncle's approach.

'Nothing's happening and nothing's broken,' he says in longsuffering tones. 'You should go to bed, or just chill out, Uncle Hedley.'

Laura laughs. 'Don't worry, Hedley, just think of the teenage parties we used to have.'

'I am,' replies Hedley in a doomladen voice.

To cheer him up and noticing an opportunity to bring Guy into the conversation, Laura remarks, 'I don't think we were so bad. You and Guy were always the drivers so you couldn't be.'

'You mean *I* was always the driver. You and Guy were usually holding hands in the back of the car,' says Hedley. This is not at all what Laura wanted to reminisce about in front of Fred, but Fred grins as he fills his glass with water again and looks at her enquiringly.

'Did you actually go out with someone?' he says, astonishment in every syllable.

'Yes, of course I did. It's not unusual, you know,' says Laura, embarrassment making her brusque.

'Was he a punk?'

'NO, he was perfectly normal. He's a farmer now – actually he was then too. Hedley knows him.' Laura is surprised to find herself flushing.

'You've gone pink, Mum,' says Fred. 'I can't wait to tell Dolly,' and with a sly grin he heads back to the party.

CHAPTER 8

Wednesday is the 'Free Ads' day. Laura remembers this with some pleasure on her way back from dropping Dolly and Fred at school. Good, she can go home and drink tea and read section 178, the 'Dogs Offered' column, and no one will know because Inigo is still in New York and the children won't be home until four o'clock. On the way to buy the 'Free Ads', Laura runs through the list of things she should feel guilty about. This is a daily ritual, sometimes she focuses on one subject and wrestles with it. It can be anything from Fred's cough to her own consumption of a slab of cake in the coffee shop on the way to the studio, or it can be an unanswered telephone call. These are mounting over the *Paper in the Park* show. Very shaming, something must be done. Laura lets herself into the house with her newspaper. Sometimes she simply reviews the list of things she feels guilty about, running through it with no hope of doing anything about any of it, but on other occasions she makes a plan of action and actually deals with the items one by one. Today, though, she has no room for feeling guilty about anything except having Guy's telephone number. Getting it from Hedley's desk at the weekend was simple, and made the horror of clearing up three piles of teenager sick just about bearable. She has not yet tried to use the number, however. To be honest, she is a little nervous that Celia might answer, and even though she only wants to know about fruit nets, Laura absolutely does not want to speak to Celia. How would she describe herself to Guy's wife? Would it be upsetting to Celia if she said she was an old friend or Hedley's sister or could she just be Laura Sale? None of it feels right to Laura. So she doesn't ring.

Hedley telephones as Laura is preparing to settle down for an hour of work avoidance with the 'Free Ads'. He is in high spirits because he has just diverted his telephone system to the dilapidated caravan in the farmyard.

'I'm going to make this my summer office,' he shouts. 'But listen, I need your advice. Tamsin's trying to persuade me to let her go to an all-night party with no parents this weekend. It's being given by that boy I saw her dancing with. I've already said no, but she thinks if she goes on at me enough I'll give in.'

'You weren't supposed to see that, so you've got to pretend you don't know about him,' Laura reminds him.

Hedley gives a cackle of pleasure at his own cunning. 'But now Tamsin doesn't know where I am so she can't get me. And even better, she can't get the telephone.'

'I don't think you should be treating her like the enemy,' Laura cautions him. 'She's quite alienated enough already, and things are supposed to have improved now you've given the party she wanted.'

'Too right she's an alien,' Hedley agrees, mishearing enthusiastically. 'Now I'm glad you rang, I've got an idea to put to you. It's—'

'I didn't ring, you did.' Laura eyes the 'Free Ads' and the almond croissant she is already doing penance for. 'I've got to go, will you call me later and tell me your idea?' And then, suddenly wondering if she can slip a question in without him noticing, she adds, 'Does Guy have an office number separate from his home number?'

'Guy? Oh, Guy Harvey. Of course. Umm. I don't know. Why do you ask?'

Absurdly, Laura finds this question alarming, and pretending there is a fault on the telephone line, starts shouting, 'Hello, Hedley? Hedley? I can't hear you? Sorry! Oh well, we'll talk later,' and she clicks the phone down in relief.

It is not until she has scanned every dog-related advertisement, including the 'Dogs at Stud' section, that Laura galvanises herself to go to the studio. Driving there, she is lost in a reverie of pleasure recalling the 'Dogs at Stud' section. There is only one entry, but it is fabulous. Cavolo Nero, a black pug of international calibre, is standing at stud. Hips, eyes and pedigree all first class.

Laura cannot get over this, and although she has never even contemplated pug life before, now finds herself longing more than anything to have a winsome female pug to take to meet Cavolo Nero. She recognises that her fantasies about Guy are getting out of hand when she can't help thinking it a sign of some sort that the pug is named after a fashionable vegetable which Guy probably grows on his organic farm.

Reaching the studio she is brought back to reality by six messages from the Royal Park offices about the restrictions on the *Paper in the Park* show. She no longer has any time to waste; fruit nets must be found. Striding in, she uses the momentum of arrival to propel herself over to the telephone, and without stopping to remove her coat, she calls Guy's number. It'll be the answerphone anyway, she tells herself as the number connects and rings.

'Hello?' It is Guy's voice on the other end, and not the answer machine. Oh God, what now?

'Hello,' says Laura, and stops. There is a long pause. Guy eventually speaks.

'Er, who is this, please?'

'Laura.'

Now the long pause is his. 'Laura?' He laughs. 'How wonderful. It was so surprising, so unexpected seeing you in that restaurant. I've been thinking about you since then.' He tails off, clearly feeling he has said too much.

Laura, her ear red hot with the handset pressed against it, does not answer. She wants to get off the topic of meeting and on to the safer ground of fruit nets, but she can't.

Guy coughs. 'But that was ages ago. It's much milder now, isn't it?'

'Yes, it is, but it's been dreadful for weeks,' Laura says automatically. She has always found talking about the weather soothing. Perhaps Guy has remembered this and is trying to make her relax. 'Guy?'

'Mmmm?' She can tell he is smiling by the tone of his voice. How can he smile like that when they haven't seen each other for all those years? And it's impossible not to smile back, so suddenly she is flirting on the telephone, which is exactly what she had been afraid of.

'I'm not ringing about anything except fruit nets,' she explains. 'I need to find some for Inigo's installation.'

'Inigo's what?' Guy sounds utterly blank. Laura suddenly realises she could have rung a farm supply shop and saved herself this pulse-raising conversation. It has all been a mistake. Guy's life is not hers to enter when she feels like it, and anyway he's married and she doesn't know him any more. You don't go around ringing strange men and flirting with them when you are nearly forty and have children and a partner and everything set up around you.

'Oh, it doesn't matter. I just need some fruit nets. But I think I know where I can find them. Goodbye, Guy, I—'

'No! Stop! I mean wait, don't go for a minute, Laura!' Guy is shouting.

'I'm still here.' She can only just whisper. She is making such a mountain out of this conversation, it's absurd. Her heart thuds in her throat.

'I'd like to see you. We've years of catching up to do. When will you next come to Norfolk? Why don't you bring your family over?'

'I don't know. I've got to go. Thanks, Guy.' Laura rushes the words out and puts the phone down. She is breathless and glowing, shaking even. It is absurd to be suffering this teenage agony over a man she no longer knows. She is shocked by her reaction to him, and by her sense of peeled-back years. It suddenly feels as if it was yesterday that they were last together.

The day before she left home to go to America and university, Laura caught the train to Norfolk to spend her last night with Guy. They had been together for a while now, all through Laura's A levels and her year working in the press office of a Cambridge-based theatre company. Her parents would have liked her to have done something more stimulating, but she was stubborn, and they knew she was leaving for NYU, so it didn't matter if she wanted to spend one last summer at Crumbly.

Laura and Guy both knew she would be going one day, but neither of them could really believe that the day would arrive. When it did, they were alone at the house. Uncle Peter was away birdwatching in Scotland, and no one knew they were there; not a soul telephoned and nobody came to invade their parting. Laura had made a picnic and they ate outside as the sun went down, flooding golden light up all the panes in the windows of the house behind them. Laura's bare feet felt the first dampness of night on the grass as a skein of ducks billowed overhead. Guy saw her shifting her feet on the ground and pulled her up.

'Come on, let's go for a walk.'

The soles of Laura's feet were hard from a summer of walking barefoot. She strolled easily beside Guy. Neither of them spoke. They reached the sea as the sun began to slip beneath the horizon, turning the flat surface of the water purple and pink. Guy pulled Laura closer to him, her ribs hard against his side, her hip bumping his when they walked. They followed the shoreline for a bit then paused again to listen to the sea.

Laura pulled away from Guy. 'Let's swim,' she said, and before she had finished speaking, she was unzipping her jeans, shaking them off and running straight into the sea in black lace knickers and her red T-shirt, twisting her hair high on her head as she jumped the breakers, laughing, and shouting back, 'Come on, Guy! It isn't cold, you know.'

Guy followed, kicking their clothes further up the beach, throwing his shirt up on to dry ground before diving under a swelling wave, his breath snatched by the shock as it broke. He caught up with her and they laughed, treading water, moving languorously now they had adjusted to the temperature.

Without taking her eyes from his face, Laura wriggled out of her knickers and her T-shirt, waving them above her head. 'Catch them if you can!' she cried, and threw them back towards the shore.

Guy laughed and wolf-whistled. 'I like the prim touch,' he teased. 'And I'm sure you're right to keep your kit on until you're underwater – you never know who, or what, might be watching.' And he lunged at her.

Laura squealed and splashed him back. 'Now yours,' she grinned, and dived down into the clear water, her hair spilling from its knot and smudging red-gold in the fading light, her arm and hands snaking out to yank at his shorts. Both naked, they stood on tiptoe in the water, floating, wrapped around one another, his body solid against hers, their skin hot where it touched and lapped with cold silk water.

'This is a good memory to take away,' whispered Laura, and Guy groaned suddenly, turning her face to his and kissing her gently at first, but harder, then harder still.

'I want more than a memory to keep,' he murmured, holding her head, stroking her wet hair, and pressing his mouth on her eyelids, her shoulders, her earlobe, licking the salt taste in the dip of her throat. He pulled Laura out of the water and lay down with her on the shirt on the sand, propping himself on his elbows to look at her. Laura laughed and hugged him, her arms around his ribs, fingers raking his back, drawing him closer all the time. A wave broke beyond them, lapping near their feet, as the last slice of the sun slipped below the horizon. Laura's breath was shallow, faster now, her eyes half-open, focusing on his face above hers. She bit her lip and shifted beneath him, gasping, tightening her arms around his neck.

Guy ran the tip of his tongue along her neck and rolled his hips, unable to stop anything now she was so close. Laura gasped and arched her back, locking her legs around him, shuddering and kissing him, pulling him to her as he held her close, his heart thumping, his arms around her in the sand.

The intercom buzzes and Laura starts, pulled back from the Norfolk beach with Guy to now and the Whitechapel Road. Guiltily, she picks up the intercom. 'Hello?'

'It's me – Cally. Let me in, can you? I haven't seen you for ages.'

Cally is in Whitechapel for her health; she has been attending a Chinese herbalist who is meant to be helping her give up smoking. It is not working. She bustles into the room and her vigour swamps Laura's guilty thoughts.

Laura slides her papers into a drawer and slams it, then bursting to confess, pulls it open again, waving the papers at her friend.

'Look, Cally, I've just hidden the number of the man I used to go out with. I've hidden it from you, because I shouldn't be telephoning him. It's absurd.' She presses her hands to her hot face.

'For God's sake, Laura,' says Cally, delving in her bag for her tobacco and papers, pushing to the depths of the cavernous holdall her newly prescribed and very expensive packet of sinister black-leafed Chinese herb. 'You're inventing a drama for yourself. What's the big deal? I can't believe you're getting so het up about it.' Cally drags keenly on her roll-up, her kind eyes narrowing with pleasure as nicotine thrums through her veins. 'Christ, that is such a relief. Do you know, I haven't smoked since Thursday because I was so worried that Mr Ming would notice tobacco in my aura or somewhere and refuse to treat me.'

Laura raises her eyebrows at Cally's roll-up. 'But what's the point of him treating you if this is what you do straight afterwards? You may as well save yourself the money and the journey and just get on with smoking at home.'

Cally, coughing now because she has smoked almost the whole cigarette in three greedy drags, shakes her head. 'No,' she gasps. 'No, I need to go because the fear stops me smoking until I've been, so if I go on Tuesdays, I only smoke until Friday at the latest then I stop for fear of Mr Ming.'

Laura stops herself saying she doesn't think that this is a very mature way to deal with addiction. Smoking is part of Cally; without it she is somehow diminished. The clanking bracelets as she delves into her bag, the hiss of the lighter, always a different one, embellished with feathers or cartoon stickers, glitter or tiny mosaics, and the trail of narrow half-smoked cigarettes which follow her through life are as much a part of her as her ready laughter and her flamboyant clothes. Today she is wearing a long fuchsia-pink velvet skirt and a lime-green and yellow striped jersey, between which a quantity of her midriff is visible. She grabs some of this exposed flesh, rolling it between her fingers.

'I'm on my way to the gym. Look at this, I've got to do something about all this. Will you come with me?'

Laura shakes her head. 'No. I've got too much work, and I hate the gym. I'd rather just go for a walk than be chained to a treadmill.'

Cally hadn't expected her to come anyway. 'Fine, fine,' she breezes, 'but I wondered if you and Inigo could come to supper next week. I want you to meet my cousin Gina. She's divorced and predatory, and I love her.'

'Yes, we'd like to,' says Laura. 'Inigo always loves a predatory female to flirt with.' She breaks off, distracted by a telephone ringing.

'I'm going, healthy living beckons.' Cally waves, stubbing her cigarette out and departing with a clatter of bangles and maximum door banging.

Laura swings around on her chair to the phone. It is Hedley.

'I thought I'd catch you at the office, Laura, to put this idea to you.'

'Oh, hi Hedley.' Half-listening, Laura turns on the computer to check her email; loud squawking sounds suggest that Hedley is in the hen run, and that he is upsetting the residents there. 'Ow, get off you sodding bird,' confirms this.

Laura is distracted from her screen.

'Hedley, why can't you ever ring me from anywhere normal?'

'I was going to, but Tamsin took the day off school saying she has an upset stomach and now she's on the Internet looking for porn, and she knows much more than me about it, so she can bar me from sites I know she shouldn't be looking at.'

'How do you know she's not doing her homework?'

'Well, she asked me how to spell vibrator, and I don't remember that being a word which came up very often in my O levels, do you?'

An email from Inigo flashes onto her screen, commandingly flagged, Read me. Idly Laura scrolls down to it.

'Oh well, she's fifteen now, she's bound to want to know all sorts of things like that,' she says vaguely. 'But what did you want to talk to me about?'

Hedley coughs, as is his habit when nervous. 'I wondered if you would like to have the Gate House. It's been empty since Mrs Jenkins went into sheltered housing, and I thought if you all had it you could come for . . .'

Laura's head is about to explode. She has opened Inigo's email and has been reading it while Hedley talks:

Darling, I'm pulling *Fall Back*, I'm afraid, as *Death Threat* is mushrooming here and I've been offered a post on the board of the Met. It's a position they're creating for me of Artist In Residence. I don't know if I can say no. What the hell – I don't want to say no. It's a year from September or October. Isn't it great news? Email me back. XI.

Laura moans low and angrily, more or less growling in fact, as a prelude to swearing.

Hedley stops his sales pitch to shout at the hen behind him, 'Oh, for God's sake you stupid creature, what now? It's not as though I'm sitting on you, is it? Oh! It's not you making that noise? Christ, it must be Laura. How weird of you. Laura, is that you? What's happened?'

There are so many things in Inigo's message that Laura cannot believe, her mind swims, and tears of rage prick her eyes. She blinks them away, and focuses on the first and least complicated point. The sodding Royal Parks people must be told. Thank God she hasn't wasted any time over fruit nets. There is so much to do, including speaking to Inigo immediately.

Laura stops moaning and says to Hedley, 'I'll have to get back to you. I can't think right now, I've got to speak to the Royal Park keepers.'

A cockerel crows next to Hedley's ear, partly obscuring his cross words. 'You've gone completely barking, Laura. Ring me tonight or the offer closes.'

Oh God, now Hedley is behaving like Attila the Hun as well. What is it with all these men? 'I will,' she promises.

'Good, because if you don't want it, I'm going to put an advertisement in *The Lady*,' he says, adding as an afterthought, 'Do you think I'll get a lady? Because I was thinking it might be the secret to finding someone to share my life.'

'Well, if I take the house, I'll help you look for a life partner,' Laura promises, with half her attention on the computer screen. Hedley says goodbye and Laura returns to the email to give it her full attention. She begins to shake, and wants to cry, pressing her fingers hard against her eyes then looking again at the screen.

The selfish creep-faced bastard,' she mutters to herself. 'Who does he think is going to pick up the pieces of all that negotiation over the park? And what about the children if he goes off to live in New York for a whole bloody year? And what about me? How come Inigo thinks he can make decisions that affect all of us without consulting any of us. Actually, I think I'll do the same. I like the idea of a country retreat and Crumbly is the perfect place.' She grins to herself, relishing the thought that Inigo will loathe it.

The telephone rings again. It is Manfred the German art collector she and Inigo met with Jack in March.

'Laura, I have been planning a new home for my collection and I want a piece by Inigo Miller to be the focal point,' he says, delighted to have got her when he thought he would have to speak to that smarmy agent Jack Smack. 'I'd like something three-dimensional. I expect Inigo would come and install it himself, *nein?*'

'Yes, of course he will.' Laura's mind is whirring, wondering if she could persuade Manfred to buy *Paper in the Park* – or at least the paper bit of it.

'Could we arrange a meeting to talk about it, please?' Manfred rustles his diary expectantly.

Laura looks out into fitful April sunshine over the blossom-strewn streets and offers a date next week. Manfred agrees, and Laura has a rush of adrenaline, reminding her how much she used to enjoy working. However, now she has a new list of priorities, and the first is to do what she wants to do instead of what Inigo wants her to do. Her big plans for getting everything in perspective should surely begin with a call to the stud pug, Cavolo Nero. The children will like that, and it will be good for them to have to take care of something themselves. And then on to Inigo to listen to his excuses and check a few details like when he's bloody coming back to sort his mess out, and then . . . and then. Laura isn't sure what then, but doubtless something will come to her. Perhaps she could take a short scriptwriting course? After all, she is a film school major, and she can't have forgotten everything they taught at NYU.

But all a short trawl into her memory reveals are flashes back to hot nights hanging out in the Italian bars below Washington Square, smoking and arguing about Tarkovsky. Personally, Laura never really saw the point of Tarkovsky and managed to fall asleep on three different occasions when taken to the Film Forum by a languidly handsome final year student called Bradley who smoked grass throughout the films while Laura stuffed popcorn and wished she hadn't. She put her uncool behaviour down to being English and unused to the twenty-four-hour existence of New Yorkers, but she always found that she was a little removed from the lives her fellow students lived. It was as if she were breathing on glass that would never splinter to allow her through into their world of getting high, going clubbing and falling in love. New York in the early 1980s was as wild and outrageous as you wanted it to be, but Laura remained slightly aloof. No matter how unzipped the parties, how swinging the weekends, she remembered to eat at least once a day and she wrote to Guy, long letters once a week.

Guy, who still lives in Norfolk near Hedley. Guy who really loved her once. Until she met Inigo. Refusing to allow herself to think slowly and rationally, Laura dials Hedley's number and, ignoring the background sounds of chugging engines and falling masonry (Hedley is demolishing a wall by backing his tractor into it), says, 'Yes please, dearest brother, we'd love the Gate House. Thank you so much for offering it. Let's talk about it properly later.'

The thought of speaking to Inigo is creating a sick space in Laura's stomach, so she deals with the Royal Parks first instead. They were clearly very worried by the project, as they accept the last-minute cancellation without a murmur. However, Laura does not wish to let Inigo know this yet; she would like to think that he will suffer a little over his appalling behaviour. She looks around the studio for other distractions and is delighted to notice the unopened post on her desk, and also a very satisfying amount of dust on top of the computer. Gladly she bustles to the sink to find dusters and polish, and while she is at it, what about mopping the floor? It hasn't been done for months, and still has a faintly purple tinge at the point where Laura had bumped into a trestle table upon which Inigo had created a multi-coloured mountain range using nothing more solid than heaps of powdered pigment.

Mopping now, Laura can afford to hum. It is such an easy job compared with the task then, when the air and the whole studio had filled with rainbow motes, and anything damp burst into a smear of Technicolor as pigment settled on the kettle, in the sink and all over Inigo's newly washed rubber boots and hood which he had been wearing while welding a steel plate to support the larger, lunar pigment landscape he planned to execute next. To be fair to Inigo, he hadn't been very angry then, but he had also done nothing to help clear up the mess. Laura was forced to forgo the Private View party they had been invited to, and spent until eleven at night trying to get the place clean again. Inigo went to the party, and then on out to dinner.

It is three o'clock by the time Laura surfaces from her domestic frenzy, and time to leave the studio to fetch the children. No time for traumatic telephone conversations. She locks up and departs, her chin set in defiance, if only Inigo could see it. The weather, not usually a prominent feature of London life, matches her mood as she waits outside Fred's school gates. The troubled sky has formed a low wedge of cloud from which bad temper in the form of hailstones is suddenly released, pinging down onto cars, bouncing off the pavement and tapping vociferously on Laura's windscreen. This is good, as it means none of the other mothers will come to talk to her. In her present frame of mind, to have to make sleepover arrangements, or hear how well someone else's children are doing at violin, would be the last straw. Laura has reached a point where she only wants to hear bad news.

Fred gets into the car scowling. 'I hate school. Just because I made a small joke, a really small one and was showing Shane how to walk like Mr Stevenson.'

This is just up Laura's street today. 'How does Mr Stevenson walk?' She kisses Fred, a gesture he accepts without any acknowledgement at all.

'As if his pants were wet,' he rushes on, bursting with injustice. 'I got detention at lunchtime and I couldn't go to the drumming seminar. They had someone really famous and really old like The Beatles but not them and I wanted to get his autograph for Dolly.'

Laura manoeuvres the car round to the girls' school gates, where Dolly is waiting, head bowed. Her school coat is much too short, shorter indeed than it was this morning. Laura decides it is best not to notice this. Dolly has it draped around her rather than worn, so she looks like a bedraggled painting of a saint with smooth long plaits and her face pale, indeed mauve in the cold.

'Guess what,' says Laura, when Dolly has arranged herself in the back and they are heading through more hail for home.

'What?' says Fred, not looking up from the *Nintendo* magazine he is reading. Dolly doesn't even pretend to be listening; she hunts in her bag for her mobile phone and begins punching in text messages to her friends.

'We're going to live at Crumbly,' says Laura, mustering all the enthusiasm she can get into her voice and feeling like a children's television presenter as she does so.

'Cool, can I get a ferret? When are we moving? We'll need our own dog, won't we, Mum?' Fred bounces up in the passenger seat, lit with excitement.

Dolly wraps her coat more closely around her and announces in trembling tones, 'You may be moving to Crumbly, but I am staying here to complete my education.' She sniffs and turns her nose up, suddenly an ambitious student under siege.

Laura laughs. 'Oh, come on, Doll. It's only the weekends, you know. You'll both be going to school just as usual.'

'I don't want to go to school as usual. I want to leave London and go to a school in the country,' says Fred. 'Why can't we just leave Dolly here with Daddy and move in with Uncle Hedley full time?'

'Oh, we're not living with him, we're going to have our own house there. It's the Gate House – it's that cottage down towards the village.'

Dolly unwraps herself and leans over towards her mother, astonishment causing uncharacteristic animation. 'You mean that ruined hovel?' she hisses scornfully. 'You're crazy, Mum. What does Dad think anyway? I bet he doesn't want to go there.'

It is pleasing to Laura that Dolly's early flair for language is still discernible, and she enjoys her pithy use of 'hovel', but otherwise she doesn't much want to be drawn.

'You'll be in the dog house when Dad gets back,' Dolly goes on scathingly. Then, more cheerfully, 'Speaking of dogs, can we get one now Dad's away and you've decided to do exactly as you please?'

'Maybe,' says Laura, not particularly meaning it but wanting to hear what it sounds like to almost agree to becoming a dog-owner. It sounds great, so she follows it up confidently and positively by saying, 'Yes, why don't we?'

There is a stunned silence before Dolly and Fred begin their favourite debate over what kind of dog and what it should be called.

Laura interrupts, 'I'd like a pug. A black pug. There's a stallion pug, or whatever you call them, called Cavolo Nero. Let's see if we can get one of his, shall we?'

'You can't have a pug, it's so embarrassing, and when we go to Crumbly, Diver will eat it,' moans Fred, but Dolly claps her hands and says, 'Mum, what a brilliant idea, and Dad can't complain because they hardly look like dogs, they're more like a bad joke, or a weird guinea pig. I know what, let's say it's a guinea pig. He'll never know.'

Telephoning Inigo that evening, Laura can scarcely focus on his iniquities, so many and various are the secrets she is keeping from him. She has spoken to Cavolo Nero's headquarters and discovered a batch, no sorry, a litter of baby pugs in Suffolk, ready to go to homes in a few weeks. Due to a marriage bust-up, the breeder has two of the tiny darlings, presently known as Bruschetta and Aïoli, suddenly homeless.

'It was the same old story,' the breeder sighs, her voice neatly clipped to reveal maximum world-weariness. 'The wife ordered them as a final revenge on the husband, and when he saw the bill, he stopped the cheque. Of course, she couldn't afford to pay for them. Can you?'

Horrified, convinced that this pug breeder has Mystic Meg qualities and can see into her head, much more clearly than she herself can, Laura gasps then recovers. 'Oh yes,' she says carefully, adding nonchalantly, 'But remind me how much they are again, could you?'

'Seven for the dog, seven-fifty for the bitch – you can take your pick. I must go, someone's come about the ferrets. We'll expect you on Friday evening. G'dbye.'

Panting, Laura puts the phone down. Dolly is next to her, hovering anxiously. 'What did she say? Has she got any? Can we have one?'

Laura sits down, sinking her face into her hands. 'Dolly, they cost seven hundred pounds,' she says in awed tones. 'Can you imagine paying seven hundred pounds for a dog?'

'Yes, easily,' says her daughter, with all the insouciance of someone with exactly thirteen pence in her purse. 'We can all contribute. He can be a quarter each of ours. No, maybe a third and leave Dad out. A third each is . . . is . . .' The girl goes slightly cross-eyed with concentration, and Laura, noticing this and remembering it is not the first time she's seen Dolly squinting, is stabbed with guilt that she has not made her an appointment with the optician.

'A third each is two hundred and thirty-three pounds,' says Fred, who has deliberately not been taking an interest because he wanted a manly Labrador. 'Or if it's a quarter each, it's one hundred and seventy-five pounds.'

'See?' says Dolly, who doesn't herself. 'Not too bad really, is it?'

'No,' says Laura dryly. 'Not when you consider that Dad is actually paying all the quarters.'

The call to Inigo is briefer than planned because he has Jack with him and is downtown, walking along Mercer Street towards the gallery where they are meeting New York's most revered and feared art critic, Gerry Lavender. Inigo is bullish, lapping up the attention and accolade, and enjoying being a star in New York. It is like speaking to a stranger. Laura does not try for long.

'I've sorted out the Royal Parks about *Fall Back* and it's all fine. What do you want me to do with all that torn-up paper though? It's in the fancy dressmaker's studio in bales, but someone might want to rent that before you're back. I think I could get Manfred, that German collector, interested in it.'

'Yeah, whatever you want,' says Inigo with so little interest Laura would like to throttle him with the telephone wire. If he notices this lateral thrust at his absence, Inigo ignores it. 'That's great, babe, do what you like with the paper. I'm glad you've called now because I want to know what you think of the Met's offer?' Inigo only ever calls her 'babe' when he is showing off, and doubly when he is in another country showing off by telephone.

'I don't know, Inigo. I don't know what to think about it. It's all quite removed, you know—'

'Yeah, well, I'm glad we've talked, babe. I'm gonna give the story to Gerry Lavender to break. I'd better fly babe, I'm almost in the gallery and Lavender is here ... Hey, Gerry, good to see you, man. Listen, babe, we'll talk later, OK?'

The telephone clicks and he is gone. It takes Laura a moment to realise that tears of rage and frustration are pouring down her face. Dolly and Fred glance up from the television and see her crying. At once they rush over, spreading their arms, engulfing her.

'Don't cry, Mum, he'll be back soon.' Dolly strokes her mother's hair, then her cheek.

Fred wraps both arms round her waist and squeezes; she laughs, breathless.

'Mum, you'll feel so much better when we've got a dog, you just won't believe it. You'll probably never cry again,' he says.

Laura wipes her eyes, and blows her nose on Dolly's handkerchief. 'I think you're right,' she says, and smiles.

CHAPTER 9

Inigo always makes an unpleasant fuss about having supper at Cally's house. On the way there this evening he is bolshy: jet-lagged because he arrived back in London this morning, cross because his reception here was not rapturous as it had been in New York.

'You could have told me you were going to be at home not the studio,' he grumbles, flinching exaggeratedly as Laura, who is driving, swerves the car while attempting to put her seat belt on.

'I didn't know. I had to be at home because Dolly had a sore throat and needed to go to the doctor. I didn't know she was going to be ill until this morning.' Laura is patient only because she is preoccupied, negotiating across slow traffic, weaving through side streets across north London to Maida Vale and the canal.

'Why can't she live in a normal house?' Inigo is too big in his bulky coat for Cally's narrow gateway covered by a collapsing arch of roses, not out yet but showing sharp leaves. He squeezes through, dislodging a shower of water droplets which scatter behind him. Cally opens the door to greet them and a hot smell of spices and cooking bursts out, hitting the chilly spring air.

'Inigo, I'm glad you're back safely.' She kisses him, winks at Laura and follows them onto the houseboat. At the far end of the long narrow room, a table is laid and beyond it, curled up on the sofa with Hybrid, Cally's large ginger cat, is a woman wearing a black lace dress which clings like a stocking to her body. Inigo, poised to make an unpleasant remark about lentils, Cally's most frequently offered dish, changes his mind and his expression.

'This is Gina, my cousin,' says Cally, wiping her hands on her skirt before pouring drinks.

Gina is a big hit with Inigo, and by the time they are all sitting at the table eating Cally's curry, Inigo has discovered some of the more intimate details of her divorce (she never really loved him, so when he turned out to be gay, although it destroyed her ego, her heart remained intact), and also that she lives very near them in Hampstead.

'It's great, Laura,' he enthuses, forking tarka dal to his mouth with no hidden agenda at all. 'Gina lives in that house with the silver front door.'

'We drive past it every day to school,' says Laura. 'The children will be fascinated that we've met you – they are always fantasising about who lives there.'

Gina looks alarmed. 'I'm very sorry, I don't think they'll be at all pleased that it's only me and not a famous pop star.'

133

'But at least you're on television,' says Cally encouragingly, and tells Inigo: 'Gina is the presenter of a talk show called *In the Daytime.*' Inigo is a little crestfallen to hear this, and Laura deliberately drops her fork to hide the choke of laughter that bubbles up in her as he chews his rice and re-assesses Gina.

Gina swallows half her glass of wine in one gulp. 'Yes, I'm on telly, and I was married to a performer, so I suppose I've earned the right to paint my house a silly colour.'

Into the general laughter, Inigo starts talking about music, and then he says, with a self-deprecating cough, 'But of course my only claim to fame is through Leonard Cohen.'

Laura rolls her eyes. If she had a pound for every time she's heard this story, she'd definitely have enough to buy a pug outright by now.

Gina's eyes are big; she tucks her hair behind her ears and blinks. 'How come?' she asks obligingly.

'He slept with Suzanne from that song,' says Cally, who has heard it too, getting up for another bottle of wine.

'Ooh,' says Gina, eyeing him respectfully. 'Did she feed you tea and oranges?'

'That come all the way from China?' Laura adds, swinging her legs under the table, wondering why everyone always asks exactly the same questions about bloody Suzanne.

'What did she look like?' Even Cally, who's heard about it at least three times before, is interested.

Inigo hugely enjoys this anecdote. If truth be known, it is much more enjoyable now as a story than when it was happening. Suzanne was fifteen years older than him, and although the sex was great from his point of view, he couldn't help worrying at the time that if you've had Leonard Cohen, a twenty-year-old from Manchester might not cut much ice.

'She looked great,' he says. 'I met her at a roller disco in the San Fernando Valley when I was visiting UCLA. She had long shaggy curly, dark hair and she wore tight jeans, like those ones Laura's wearing now.'

Laura obligingly gets up and does a pirouette, making a hideous face at Cally as she twirls. Both Cally and she dissolve giggling and pour each other more wine.

Gina is still in the song. 'And you spent the night for ever, but did you know she was half-crazy?'

'She wasn't crazy, she was chilled out; she had a great figure, and dark skin, and a bit of a beaky nose. She was thirty-five then, I suppose, and she was looking for some fun.'

'Blimey,' says Gina. 'It sounds just like another Leonard Cohen song to me.'

'Is she dead yet, do you think?' Laura muses.

Inigo, slightly annoyed, protests, 'No, of course she isn't, she'd only be about sixty. I haven't read anything in the papers anyway, have you?'

There is a silence while they all think of Suzanne drawing her pension. Gina breaks it, getting up with a smile, pulling the clinging fabric of her dress away from her stomach.

'I'm going to be the party pooper,' she says. 'All that talk about rock legends has left me feeling exhausted and ancient.' She blows a kiss across the room towards Laura and Inigo. 'It was nice to meet you,' she says.

CHAPTER 10

All the windows of the car are open to the bottom as Laura, Dolly and Fred head north-east out of London on Friday afternoon. Inigo is not with them. His displeasure about the Gate House has not had a chance to ignite, as Manfred turned up with a large cheque for a piece of artwork that doesn't exist.

'How could you not have told me he was coming?' Inigo had yelled the day before, in the studio loo, where he marched Laura when Manfred arrived.

'I forgot.' Laura crossed her arms and tapped her toes and said, 'Anyway, you'd better get out there and start talking fast. You can do something with all that paper.' An arrested expression crossed Inigo's face. He pinched her cheek.

'Yes, I can,' he said slowly. 'It's papier mâché. I want to create the cramped space around a man in a commuter train reading a newspaper. Yes, I know how to do it, I've been thinking about it for ages. Clever girl, Laura, clever girl.' Stifling an urge to kick him, Laura smoothed her skirt and preceded Inigo back into the studio to make a fuss of Manfred.

'It's called *Infill* . . .' Inigo, suave and confident, talked Manfred through the piece, and agreed to install it this weekend in Manfred's new private gallery in Berlin.

'Laura will come too?' asked Manfred hopefully.

'Maybe next time. She's needed here at the moment,' Inigo said, shaking his head regretfully.

Laura is fed up with Inigo; he simply pleases himself and rides roughshod over her plans. He should be coming with them to help them move in this weekend, but when she told him she'd taken Hedley's Gate House, he glared at her in disbelief, then said, 'Well, if you've decided that without me, then you can sort it out without me.' Laura's crossness is fuelled by the sneaking knowledge that she has not behaved particularly well herself. She orders a taxi to take him to the airport without mentioning the pug.

An unexpected few days of balmy sunshine have brought spring onto the streets in a bustle of full-blown blossom and people in T-shirts and bare legs. In the car, Laura swigs water and succumbs to blandishments from her offspring to stop for ice cream. The traffic is intense and slow, overheating in the lazy warmth of the afternoon. A black car with brown tinted windows screeches up next to Laura, thumping with reggae music, the driver leaning into the windscreen, wraparound dark glasses obscuring his face.

'How can he see out at all?' Laura marvels. 'It must be pitch dark in there with the windows that colour. Why on earth doesn't he take his sunglasses off?'

Fred clamps his hand to his brow and rolls his head against the seat to look at his mother. He is grinning fondly. 'They're not sunglasses, Mum, they're shades, and he can see fine because tinted windows only look tinted from the outside. Inside they're normal.'

The traffic surges forward and Laura indicates to cross the final roundabout before the motorway and freedom. 'How do you know?'

Fred shuts his window and slides down in his seat as the car gathers speed. 'I just know. Do you like this music, Mum, or shall we put some of yours on to help you stay calm?'

Laura is white-knuckling the steering wheel, her jaw clenched in a rictus already and they've only just hit the motorway. She attempts a laugh, but it comes out all pitiful, and more of a bleat. 'Don't worry, darling, I'm much better now than I was. I'm used to going fast.'

Dolly and Fred look at one another, but say nothing. All are remembering the last long-distance journey Laura and the children attempted without Inigo. In January Laura had decided to take them to Cambridge to visit her parents. It was a chilly, ill-lit day, with fog creeping along the edge of the motorway, billowing from time to time across all three lanes. For no reason she could think of, Laura had become hopelessly alarmed at the wheel, terrified by the proximity of vast lorries thundering past her, hypnotised by their spinning wheels and gasping pressure brakes, as she tried to hurry in the slow lane. Dolly had been forced to lean daringly forward between the seats to reach the radio and change it to soothing classical music, as the pulse of Fred's favourite station had Laura yelling, 'Quick, quick, I can't cope, it's all too fast, even the music. Put something soothing on, or I might crash the car.' Feeling rather than seeing their horrified expressions, she attempted to gloss over this possibility. 'I'm sure I won't, don't worry. But I might, I just might.'

Fortunately, because she was craning to see the next service station, Laura failed to hear Fred's background muttering of, 'But we're only doing sixty, for God's sake. What's your problem, Mum?' She managed to retain a semblance of control until the car was parked by the air-fill pump of a petrol station and she was sobbing into her phone at Inigo, 'You'll have to come and get us, I can't drive any further, it's too scary.'

'Laura, Laura, come on, you can do it, you know you can.' The familiar sound of Inigo's voice as much as his words was reassuring, and Laura felt steadier. Then a very young blond boy, driving a brand new silver Land Rover, had approached.

'Are you lost? I can help you, I work on the Formula Three track over there. I know my way around here like the back of my hand.'

Dolly rolled her eyes. 'I don't believe it. We're getting sympathy from racing drivers now. This is so uncool. What is Mum like?'

'It's getting worse,' hissed Fred. 'She's asking him to let us follow him.'

Dolly shook her head. 'No. She can't. She wouldn't.'

But she could and she would. Laura, beaming relief, drove smoothly and calmly the last thirty miles through the fog to Cambridge escorted by a twenty-year-old racing driver and two cringing children. Inigo had laughed and pulled her into his arms when he heard.

'I love the way you have no shame,' he cried, kissing her forehead. Laura couldn't see what there was to have shame about; she was just glad to be alive.

Since that occasion, when she can be bothered, Laura has been practising breathing exercises and Pilates, and she is sure they will both help immeasurably. She has also taken the precaution of purchasing a tape version of *White Fang*, the only choice, among various hip and thigh diets and Engelbert Humperdinck collections, in the petrol station that could appeal to all three of them. She, Dolly and Fred thus arrive at Pug Paradise, the beguilingly named home of Cavolo Nero's offspring, emotionally shattered and a little afraid of canine capabilities.

It immediately becomes clear that Pug Paradise, a small pink house surrounded by fields of sheep outside a sleepy town in Suffolk, is a very wonderful place. Laura peers through the wicket gate and up a path between white narcissus, red tulips and little blue grape hyacinths to the kitchen door. Without having met her, Laura longs to have the life that Marjorie the pug owner leads almost more than she wants the pug itself.

Marjorie greets her, a dead pigeon swinging in one hand as she comes through the gate, the other positioned ready to shake with Laura.

'Hello there. I'll just feed this to the ferrets and then we can start. You two could do with a bit of fresh air, couldn't you,' she says, nodding at Dolly and Fred as they climb out of the car stretching and yawning, rubbing tired eyes before they can compose themselves and grunt a greeting. Marjorie clearly has little truck with teenagers, and folds her lips in disapproval, looking at them measuringly. 'Why don't you come and help me give this bird to the ferrets. Can either of you pluck?'

'I can,' says Fred, rushing to catch up with Marjorie who is climbing steps up to a thatched barn and a line of dog kennels. 'How many ferrets do you have?'

Dolly holds back, scowling at her mother. 'Why are we looking at ferrets? We're here for the pugs and I want to get to Hedley's in time for *Top of the Pops*.'

Laura has got out her camera and is photographing the flower beds, and a trio of enchanting lavender-coloured hens who are pecking about next to a tub of primroses. The scene is exquisite and desirable. She has to breathe deeply to prevent herself from panting with longing.

'This is so lovely. I think we should try and do something like this at the Gate House. It's got a garden, I think.' Then, as Dolly's remark sinks in, she lowers the camera, saying anxiously, 'But you know we aren't staying with Hedley, don't you? We've got our own place now. Hedley has lent us some old beds and we're moving in tonight. And I'm afraid we haven't got a television.' Laura braces herself for the wrath of Dolly to engulf her like a tidal wave, but nothing happens. She realises she has instinctively closed her eyes and hunched her shoulders for impact. With no little effort she shakes off the fear of teen rage and quickly stands tall, wiping her hands over her face and assuming an alert, *Blue Peter*-ish expression, very glad that Marjorie is off doing something gruesome with ferrets and hasn't seen her being idiotic.

Dolly's fury has been curbed by the appearance of five teeny pug puppies on the lawn. 'Look, Mum, have you ever seen anything so sweet? Please, please can we have one? You can have all my lunch money for next term and the one after to pay for it.'

Laura can't help thinking that at two pounds a day, the lunch money isn't going to make a lot of headway into the gigantic pug debt they will have if she succumbs. Dolly is on her knees beside the puppies and they are climbing over her, wriggling and snuffling, yapping their delight. Two are jet black, and in the evening sunlight they gleam exotic and irresistible, while the three brown ones (known as fawn, Laura remembers reading) are a blur of soft cuteness. Tears start at Laura's eyes. She wipes them away as Marjorie and Fred approach, Fred carrying a chocolate-coloured ferret.

'Mum, this is Vice. Marjorie's husband rescued her from Budgen's car park and they've taught her all sorts of tricks and she doesn't bite like Precious and if you get a pug, couldn't I have this dear little ferret – please, Mum, please.'

Laura puts both hands behind her back, determined not to be bitten by this creature. Her thoughts stray to Inigo, and how much he is annoying her at the moment. Marjorie looms, a brisk, kindly presence, with a good, no-nonsense approach to life, illustrated by the one short conversation Laura has had with her. Marjorie would never stoop to using animals as a tool to defy her husband; Marjorie would never allow herself to be blackmailed by her children.

Laura coughs, and gingerly reaches to stroke the ferret. 'Slow down, Fred, we need to think about all this very carefully.'

Marjorie rests a hand on her arm and whispers importantly, 'I must tell you, your son is very gifted with vermin. Very.' She blinks, and her watery gaze slides back to Fred. 'I don't often like to recommend ferrets to children, but he is exceptional.'

Reflecting on what a simple and effective ploy it is to praise a child to its mother, Laura nods and almost agrees to the ferret. With an effort she manages instead to say, 'Yes. Well, let's see when we've talked about the pugs. Which are the ones needing homes?'

Marjorie suddenly squats on the grass, then rolls down until she is lying full length, an arresting spectacle with her laced-up shoes and pleated skirt. She calls out, 'Bruschee-etta, Aaa-ïoooli, here, pups, here now!' And from the tumbling mass on Dolly's knee, the smallest black, and one fawn puppy pounce up to Marjorie and hurl themselves on her chest.

'Bruschetta is the bitch. Aïoli is the black dog. Both perfect pugs. Faultless.' Marjorie sits up and taking each puppy in turn, fondles them, turning them over, pinching their ears gently, splaying the pads of their paws. 'And you know all the pug protocol, of course, so I won't go into that with you, but do look, they're responding to training awfully well, and they're only seven weeks old.'

Marjorie topples them onto their backs and they loll, tongues protruding pinkly, looking absurd and like Chinese lions on the springy grass. Laura finds that her mouth is hanging slack and open with longing. Fred prods her; even he has been beguiled by the snub-nosed enquiring faces of the baby pugs.

'Come on, Mum, you know you want one – that's why we came. It's just what we need to catch the rabbits in Norfolk. Just choose.' Laura realises he must be smitten to imagine that a pug could catch a rabbit.

Dolly rushes up to her mother, yanking her arm, begging with tears in her eyes, 'Oh Mum, I think it would be such fun,' she whispers.

Laura imagines herself in the garden she believes to exist at the Gate House. In her mind's eye, she is sitting at a small table under a lilac tree in full bloom. A few hens, just like Marjorie's in fact, scratch about nearby, and a manly figure, perhaps even Inigo, can be seen doing something useful and not balancing things, over to the right, while to the left Dolly is picking a perfect bunch of fragrant flowers in happy animation instead of sulky torpor and Fred is leading a chocolate ferret through a tiny box hedging maze and teaching it to remember its way, as a true ferret whisperer does. The tea tray is there, and so is the pug, smug and black on a cushion at her feet. The picture is perfect. Highly camp perhaps, but perfect.

Laura, with the sensation of walking off a cliff, shuts her eyes and says firmly, 'Marjorie, we'll have Aïoli, the boy, if we may. Oh, and the ferret too. We'll collect them next weekend.'

Laura and the twins depart, very much poorer and none the wiser as to what 'pug protocol' might be.

'Oh, we can look it up on the Internet,' says Dolly, embracing as much of her mother as she can without garrotting her from the back seat. 'Let's get going to Crumbly now, we've got to make a dog room immediately.'

'And a ferret house,' adds Fred.

Laura, accelerating northwards, is so touched and delighted by her children's excitement that she has no remorse at spending Inigo's money on something he will detest. Adolescent enthusiasm is a quality beyond price.

Enthusiasm fuels Dolly, Fred and Laura all the way from Suffolk and right up to the front door of the Gate House, where it runs out abruptly.

'We can't get in, there's no key,' moans Dolly from beneath a pile of pillows and clothes. 'I can't carry all this and there's nowhere to put it down.'

This is true. Looking around, Laura is surprised by how her memory had pruned and weeded the garden, which in reality is a seething mass of early sprouting nettles and brambles with a few bright yellow daffodils dropping their petals into a small dank pond. It is dusk, and the air is damp and cold; a low white mist, which Laura remembers is the sea har, creeps into the further reaches of the garden. Shivering, she dumps her box of food on a rickety old chair by the weed-strewn path and kneels by the front door, feeling with her hands for a stone under which a key might lie.

'Mum, quick, there's a goat here, and its udder is massive. Shouldn't we milk it?' Fred rushes from the back of the cottage where he has been exploring, his trousers dark up to the knees with wet from the tangled grasses.

'I didn't know we were having a goat,' says Laura faintly. 'I just want the key.' She looks up at the darkening sky and, astonishingly, sees a key dangling from a piece of string tied to the old apple tree. 'What a weird place for a key,' she marvels.

Dolly snatches it. 'Oh thank God, let's get inside and then we'll think about the sodding goat.'

From the state of the garden, Laura had been dreading what might be in the house, but to her relief the electricity is on, and Hedley has clearly been making an effort. A small and ancient Rayburn stove is lit and giving off delicious heat. Dolly and Fred rush as one to lean against it, both wrapped in duvets, their lips tinged blue because the warmth of today has left them bare-legged and unprepared for a chilly evening. In front of the Rayburn is a chipped red gloss painted table and four multi-coloured chairs that Laura remembers decorating one teenage summer. On the table is a jam jar of tulips and a note.

Welcome Laura and family.
   I've sorted the house out a bit. Sorry about the goat, I had her at home, but she kept getting out and coming back here. I think she's missing Mrs Jenkins. Could you just keep an eye on her and I'll make plans for her next week? Her name is Grass. I'll drop by to see you all at breakfast-time, with Tamsin if I can get her up. Love, Hedley.

Laura presses her hands over her eyes. 'We're acquiring animals as if it's Christmas,' she says bleakly. 'A pug, a ferret – and now a goat. She's called Grass and I think we'd better try and milk her before she explodes. It doesn't sound as though Hedley has even thought of it.'

'How, how, how?' clamours Fred, hopping with excitement at the prospect of an interactive animal. He and Dolly rummage for boots in one of their dustbin bags of clothes. Laura, frustrated by trying to choose what anyone might wear, finally packed everything by pouring all the contents of the children's drawers into black bin liners. Surely it will be a perk of having her own house that she will leave country clothes here? Inigo will love that degree of domestic organisation, it might make up for the dog. Or the goat. But definitely not for the ferret. Nothing will make up for the ferret.

Dolly and Fred vanish out into the dark wielding a cup and a saucepan, Fred's torch dancing a beam before them. Laura looks helplessly at the tide of clothing chaos spreading across the bumpy tiled floor of her new kitchen. She needs to get all this stuff put away, but there is nowhere to put it. In the end she drags it in a heap to the bottom of the stairs and dumps it. They can sort it, she decides, hearing their voices as they pass the window.

'Here we come, Grass. Don't worry, we're highly qualified milkmen,' yells Dolly.

'I'm going to aim the milk so it goes into the cup first and then flows over and into the pan,' boasts Fred.

'Fat chance,' laughs Dolly, and Laura grins, as they move away towards the shed busy answering the call of nature instead of indulging in their usual evening activities which include zapping life away on a computer game. It is, she muses, a proud moment for a parent when offspring choose to milk a goat over watching *Top of the Pops*. Not that choice had much to do with it, of course, as there is no television, but Laura takes great pride in the fact that they haven't even mentioned *Top of the Pops* since they arrived here.

Twenty minutes later, when the twins still haven't come in and she has cooked three rather rubbery omelettes and made lovely unhealthy Angel Delight for pudding, Laura heads outside to find them. She has a candle in a jam jar, but still she stumbles through the now inky night, regretting the lack of a street lamp glow in the countryside for the first time in her life.

'Ow, bastard,' she curses as a bramble spirals around her ankle.

'Mum, are you there?' Dolly's face, ghostly pale in Laura's candlelight, appears over the half-door of the shed. 'Grass kicked Fred and it's bleeding into the milk and Fred knocked the pan over so we've only got a tiny amount.'

'Oh well, I don't think we were planning to make ice cream with it.' Thankful to be able to see where to go, Laura steps over the last few brambles and enters.

'No, but I thought we could make goat's cheese and we could sell it at the school fair next week.' Dolly's arms, and even loose strands of her jaunty

150

pony tail, droop with disappointment. Laura hugs her.

'What a good idea. I hadn't thought of goat's cheese.' She is beginning to see the point of Grass.

Dolly and Fred have hung the torch on a hook in the roof, creating a well of light at the centre of the shed. Madly illuminated, with vast threatening shadows, Fred, nursing his bleeding hand, is squatting on the straw next to the goat. He and Grass look to Laura like extras in a voodoo horror film. Grass chews a mouthful of leaves placidly, her long yellow eyes unblinking and expressionless until Fred leans forward to touch her udder; she then aquires a look of evil cunning and a back leg springs like a piston towards Fred's face. He dodges and tries again, this time successfully grabbing her. There is a satisfying hiss and Laura imagines a foaming stream of milk hitting the pan, swirling creamy and full.

'Mmm, wonderful,' she says, not noticing that she has stepped onto a pile of goat shit, black pellets round and coarse like peppercorns.

'It's not going very well, Mum,' says Fred, passing the tin saucepan to show her. Laura is surprised and disappointed to see that the milk hardly covers the bottom of the pan and what they have is gruesomely tinged with pink. 'It takes forever and she hates it. I'm starving and I've had enough. I wish I hadn't spilt some.'

Laura rubs his shoulders sympathetically. 'I would have spilt it too,' she says. 'Let's give up now. You've done so well, and I should think that getting any out is a bonus for her. We'll try again in the morning. She'll be better then because it's when you're meant to do milking.' Laura is pleased with this notion, it makes sense. She is doing well so far as a country-woman, and with the prospect of goat's cheese in the morning, is pretty convinced that soon they will be self-sufficient. Congratulating herself and her children silently, she unties Grass who promptly steps back onto her foot, squishing it deeply and painfully into another pile of droppings. So great is the pain that even a combination of fluent swearing and karmic deep breathing takes several moments to soothe Laura.

'Shit. Oww. Bugger. Literally shit,' she groans. 'I wonder if this bodes ill for all our animal husbandry? We'd better buy a goat manual tomorrow.'

'Let's call Dad and tell him what we're doing,' says Dolly, holding her mother's arm and guiding her back towards the cottage as if she is a very ancient person. Laura rather enjoys this.

'Mmm. Yes, we must,' she agrees, while thinking, He'll go spare. He thinks this is a decent centrally heated holiday cottage with double glazing; and he hates all animals, so he's not going to like hearing that we've already got a goat.

She sits down for supper with the children and lights a festive candle in a jam jar. 'But let's not talk to him right now,' she adds. The omelettes are a small triumph; they taste much better than they look. This is an improvement on the last time Laura made omelettes, when no one could eat them because they were so full of eggshell and grease from the cooking oil she used in place of butter. She is bullish now, fuelled by two glasses of wine and feeling not unlike Elizabeth David. Defiance grows as she washes up in the ancient green-stained stone sink and thinks, What the hell, it's time I did what I want to do for a bit. He always does, let's ring him and tell him.

She calls Dolly away from her self-imposed chore of decorating the loo door with the family photographs Laura has brought with her. These photographs span the whole of the twins' lives and are kept permanently in the back of the car in an old box. Laura likes to have them with her wherever she goes, as she has a longstanding fantasy that she is going to stick them into an album, thus editing her family life to an existence of magazine glamour and happy smiling picnics.

Dolly has begun her collage with a picture of Inigo baking, his arms a blur of flour, his expression relaxed, almost beatific, and nothing like it will be when Dolly tells him what they are doing. Next to it is one of Laura bathing the two-year-old twins, dishevelled with drops of water, pushing back her hair from her face and laughing. The tiny twins are laughing too. Laura stares at the snapshot, and feels nostalgia for that moment and a hundred like it. They were still in New York then, and life was simple. Inigo was a struggling young artist and Laura looked after the babies, none of this working together nonsense which now engulfs her life.

Dolly, waving a phone in search of a signal, climbs onto a chair. 'Hello? Hello, Dad. It's me, Dolly . . . What? Oh bugger, the signal's gone.'

The chair wasn't good enough, and now Dolly is standing on the kitchen table, towering over Fred who is carving a handle for a stick he found in the garden. The light from the one dusty lamp is dim, and Fred has his torch precariously balanced between the bread and a mug to illuminate his work. Dolly, redialling, crouches suddenly and makes a platform for the torch, securing it so no matter how she moves on the table, it remains stationary.

Fred grins, she stands up again, shouting, 'Dad, can you hear me? We're at the Gate House. It's like really medieval, there's green stuff dripping in the bathroom – it's so cool like a dungeon to look at but I so don't want to ever have a bath in there, and we've got a goat, it's like really adorable—'

'I think that's enough for him to get used to for this evening,' Laura interrupts hastily, reaching up for the telephone. 'Hello, Inigo? Inigo?' She can hear nothing.

Dolly shakes her head. 'It doesn't work, Mum. All he said was "Fuck" and then he got cut off. We'll have to ring him from a land line tomorrow. Where do you think there is one?'

Relieved, and virtuous because she has tried, Laura heads for bed, earlier than the children who are listening to a band called Wet Biscuit or similar on the radio. They are listening to the radio together. Laura allows herself a small smug moment. It's like *Cider with Rosie*. Well, all right not exactly, because that was set in the West Country; maybe *The Go Between*, which was definitely set in Norfolk. Actually, not *The Go Between* – that repressed-love thing isn't quite right. Anyway, this moment is very good and it's definitely like a rite of passage novel set in the twentieth century in Britain but not *Trainspotting*. Laura loves it all, especially the fact that she is suddenly remembering snatches from so many books. Wishing to keep the cosy mood alive, she finds herself a Fair Isle jersey in her own dustbin bag, to wear on top of her nightie.

Laura's bedroom is small and in the eaves above the Rayburn. Despite the warm chimney breast, the temperature in the room is bracing, and it looks as if it will remain so, as the low casement window is jammed open and obscured now by thrusting clematis stems and a tangle of rose thorns. Hedley has added some homely touches in here, Laura notices. Two balding skin rugs from the attics at Crumbly have been hurled onto her floorboards, and another smaller skin inadequately covers the large mattress. The window is at floor level, and Laura drags her mattress into the middle of the room, positioning it so that she will be able to see out in the morning. A large beetle bursts through the foliage at the window and scrambles across the ceiling towards the light bulb, buzzing crossly. It misses and bounces off to swerve at Laura. She shrieks and hides her head in her hands, turning off the light and jumping onto the bed, hating the late-night business of lowlife creatures. In the dark she fumbles for socks and a scarf to add to her night attire, and would complete the outfit with a woolly hat if she could be bothered to go downstairs to get one. Making a mental note to buy hot-water bottles tomorrow, Laura falls asleep.

She awakes with a start. There is no thump of music from downstairs, so Dolly and Fred must have gone to bed, but there are loud trundling noises near her head. Outside an owl hoots mellifluously, adding to the eeriness of the moment. Laura's heart beats violently, she is stiff with fear; it takes an effort to relax her shoulders enough to move her arm. Holding her breath, she slowly reaches out to turn on the light. Two mice look at her for a moment, then whisk out of sight, scampering beyond her bed and under the skirting board. Laura presses her hand against her mouth and manages not to utter a sound. She leaps off the mattress and runs down to find a woolly hat, the horror of the notion that the mice might build a nest in her hair pumping through her veins so she feels wide awake. It is almost light by the time she can relax enough to fall asleep again, and in the darkest moments, Laura admits to herself that Norfolk has a long way to go before it can compete properly with London. She drifts off amid happy thoughts of restaurants, shoe shops, florists and cinemas with not a mouse to be seen anywhere in the light, mud-free streets of the West End.

Sleep is short-lived. Laura is woken by raucous birdsong. She tries stuffing a pillow in the window casement, but the dawn chorus continues unabated. By seven o'clock she is dressed; she stands on the doorstep with a cup of tea, watching the sun begin to sweep between the trees beyond her garden. It is impossible not to smile. Laura is suffused with a sense of peace, and holds onto this moment while her tea cools, before wandering out to have a proper look at the garden. Surrounded by a small wooden fence, and facing a clearing on the edge of the beechwood, Laura's Gate House is like a child's drawing, squat with a pointed gable above the front door and castellations like steps meeting at the top above her bedroom window. The garden at the front is neat, with a central path from the gate to the front door, and another path leading round the back, past a small orchard and an overgrown vegetable patch, to the shed where Grass lives. Beyond that is an area of rocketing nettles and long grass, a small silted-up pond, and then the path reappears by a dilapidated greenhouse, bringing Laura back to the front garden again.

I can walk around my house, she thinks, when she has done it. What an amazing feeling. Laura and Inigo's house in London is terraced, her parents' house in Cambridge was a semi-detached villa, and Crumbly, although it isn't joined to any other house, is impossible to walk round because of the hedges and barns which abut the building. Laura does it again a few times, reminding herself of Pooh and Piglet's search for the Woozles as she follows her own footsteps through the long grass and back to the front door. On her third perambulation she notices that the drain under the kitchen window is blocked and she stoops to prod it with a stick. A frog, glistening bright green, scrambles for cover. Laura crouches to see where he has gone, and is startled to find a community of them leaping and darting away from her.

'Aah, I see. You are migrating to water. You need the pond to be cleared so it can fill up.' Laura sets to this task with vigour. It is much more satisfying than unpacking clothes, and more necessary. Another frog leaps from a tussock as Laura heaves sedge and old netting from the pond. She hopes he will spread the word.

She is in the kitchen, making a bacon sandwich – the most effective sensory alarm clock for rousing her children – when Hedley arrives.

'You look the part,' he says, taking in Laura's mud-covered jeans, her boots flung across the doorstep. She turns to him, wreathed in smiles.

'Oh Hedley, it's so wonderful, thank you for this. It's going to be so great.'

'It is a repairing lease,' says Hedley, feeling that this euphoric moment is the right one to slip in the small print. 'I've got the papers here for you and Inigo to sign.'

'He's not here – he had to go to Germany. Anyway, this is my thing, and I want to be the leaseholder.'

Hedley raises his eyebrows. 'Well, I suppose you can sort that out between you,' he says. 'But let's get it done now.' He moves to clear a space for his papers. 'Eugh, there's a toad on the table. Is it Inigo, here after all, in his country attire?' Hedley enjoys his own joke hugely, nudging Fred who has appeared, rubbing his eyes.

'Oh very funny,' says Laura. 'Actually it's one of my frogs. It's waiting for me to finish cleaning out its pond.'

Hedley groans. 'It is so typical of you to start managing pondlife, isn't it?' he remarks. 'But you know these aren't frogs, they're toads and they don't need a pond, the drain is fine.'

Laura remains defiant. 'Well, I want to make them a pond. Anyway, I'm not making it, I'm restoring the one that's there. How high do you think the water table is here?'

'Not very high, the soil is too sandy. Now this is what you sign, Laura.' Hedley flourishes his pen; his sister takes it and is about to sign when a thought occurs to her.

'Actually, I don't want to seem untrusting, but can we sort out the goat first?'

Hedley reaches across to the plate of bacon, as does Fred.

'We're keeping the goat, Mum,' says Fred. 'She's part of the Gate House furniture.'

Laura senses that she is in a losing position with this argument. 'Oh all right, we'll keep her until Inigo comes.'

Dolly appears, tousled in the doorway, clutching her phone.

'God, do you sleep with that thing glued to your ear?' Fred asks, pouring cereal into a cup and filling it to the brim with milk before sliding several heaped spoonfuls of sugar in for good measure.

Dolly ignores him. 'Mum, Dad just called. He's coming back tomorrow and he's coming here.'

Hedley groans. 'I wonder if he'll want to come too?' he says half to himself. 'Laura, I was going to ask you all to come with me to a christening tomorrow, but I don't think Inigo would like it.'

Laura is quite sure he is right. 'No, Inigo doesn't believe in what he calls the bourgeois patina of religion that you get in the Church of England. It's one of his pet subjects, like farming.'

Hedley gets up to leave. 'A patina is usually thought to be green,' he muses, a faraway look in his eyes that Laura recognises as his scholar's expression.

'Mmm?' she says helpfully.

Hedley recalls himself. 'Anyway. Yes. Well. I'll keep well out of Inigo's way tomorrow then, but if you want to come, Laura, or you two –' he glances towards Fred and Dolly, '– Tamsin and I will be here to escort you at eleven-thirty.'

Fred watches him down the path, and turns to Laura. 'Mum, he may be your brother, but he's weird.'

'Yeah, I'm glad I'm not Tamsin,' agrees Dolly. 'He's like from another planet or something.'

Laura isn't listening. She looks around the kitchen at the debris of breakfast and decides not to do anything about it.

'I'm going to do gardening until lunchtime, and this afternoon we'll go and buy some junk to fill this house with. And if either of you can find the nobility of soul to clear up the kitchen I will be grateful for ever,' she announces, already half out of the door, the toad balanced on a tea cosy on her hand because she remembers reading that human skin burns them.

'But will you pay us?' Fred shouts after her with a grin.

Laura decides that to try and turn the house into a palace of civilisation suitable for Inigo in twenty-four hours is not feasible. Beyond purchasing some lamps, bedspreads and a lot of cracked but beautiful pearl pink china, and plonking vases of grape hyacinths and wallflowers on every windowsill, she does nothing. The mould-green walls in the bathroom remain unbrushed, the Rayburn is not scrubbed, but outside, the garden begins to take shape. Laura's back burns where her muscles have stretched and pulled as she digs and heaves, weeds and chops. Fred finds a rusty lawnmower in the shed next to the goat and, Laura assumes, by making some pact with God or the Devil, manages to make it work. His first circuit around the lawn is witnessed and applauded by Dolly and Laura; then they lean against the fence, eyes closed, drinking in the warm afternoon sun and the smell of cut grass. As she climbs into bed, Laura realises she hasn't thought about Inigo almost all day and it has been bliss.

CHAPTER 12

As promised, Hedley is back the next morning, unusually smart in a suit, a red shirt and a tie with sunflowers all over it. Tamsin is with him, also very dolled up, although seemingly for a different, more retro occasion as her outfit consists of a crocheted silver mini-skirt, a purple fluffy coat, and knee-high pink suede boots.

'Is Inigo back yet?' Hedley asks nervously.

'No, he said he wouldn't be here till this afternoon, so I'll come to the christening first. Whose is it anyway?'

'Hedley's old girlfriend Venetia,' says Tamsin. Hedley looks at Laura, agonised.

'Oh yes, of course.' Laura smiles brightly at him, remembering rumours of a romance when Hedley first came to Crumbly.

'I'm the godfather,' he says, wielding a small wrapped package. 'It's a Swiss Army knife – what do you think?'

Tamsin, finding this conversation achingly boring, slouches up the narrow stairs to find Dolly. Moments later, music thumps through the ceiling, and Fred, forced out by the sound, appears, rumpled and sleepy but friendly.

'Mum, can you ask Dolly to play something decent. Her music is so sad, I even prefer yours,' he mumbles.

'Your children are always asleep,' marvels Hedley. 'And they're nice to you,' he adds, as Fred drapes himself over his mother's shoulders and kisses her cheek as she sits eating toast at the kitchen table. 'I wish Tamsin was nice to me like that,' Hedley sighs.

Laura opens her mouth to answer, but leaves it dangling as the doorframe is filled, the sunlight blocked by Inigo. Unshaven, eyes pink-rimmed and bloodshot, skin pallid, he walks straight up to Laura and puts his arms around her, dropping a bunch of lilies onto the table behind her.

'You're very early,' she says, blinking amazement.

'I was missing you too much,' he says, bending his head to kiss her.

I hope he isn't going to spoil things, Laura thinks. Shocked by her own ungenerosity, she pulls herself together and smiles back into Inigo's ardent gaze, wondering why he always has to be so full on about everything, but amazed that he still makes her heart pound. She is off-balance seeing him here, annoyed in fact; it was such a relief not being affected by him, and now he's the biggest thing in her new kitchen, and he's brought the exotic, incongruous waft of hothouse flowers to the country.

Dolly, as excessive as Inigo, bounces into the room, clad in a small strappy top and tiny skirt, waving a selection of fleeces and cardigans, and hurls herself on her father, wrapping her arms around him, nuzzling his coat.

'Dad, do you like our house? We've got a goat – come and see me milk it, quick.'

'Won't you be frozen, Dolly? That's not much of a skirt for April.' Laura is ignored.

'Its name is Grass and it's a nanny goat,' adds Fred. 'It's got these really gross toggles dangling off its neck and a beard, it's so cool.'

Correctly interpreting the grossness as the best bit, Inigo follows Fred and Dolly straight outside again without even speaking to Hedley, and round to the shed, accompanied by Tamsin, a little wobbly on her stiletto heels, but uncomplaining, much to Hedley's surprise.

'We've got a ferret and a pug to confess next,' Laura whispers to Hedley.

'Your children have such a good effect on Tamsin, why can't it stretch to Inigo as well?' Hedley complains, rising to leave. 'You can't come with me to church if he's only just arrived, but don't forget the christening lunch at one. It's in the house at the end of the village on the right.'

Laura, conscious of an almost irresistible urge to escape Inigo and go with her brother now, follows him out and, keen to look busy, begins half-heartedly slashing at some nettles with the bread-knife. Inigo, armed with a small shark-skin sketchpad, and still wearing his long black coat, emerges from the goat shed with a cheerful spring in his step. He stands, pencil poised, watching Laura for a moment, making her feel like a work in progress instead of a person.

'You can't do it like that – you need a proper scythe, like the Grim Reaper. I'll take a shower and then we'll go into town to get one, shall we?'

Laura puts the bread-knife into his outstretched hand and follows him into the house. 'There isn't a shower, I'm afraid, just an ancient cast-iron bath in that room there.' She points to a room beyond the kitchen. 'It's probably the most gruesome room in the house,' she warns him.

'Downstairs, how novel,' says Inigo, fussily shaking the towel he finds on the floor before heading into the dank pit that is the bathroom. Laura's heart sinks further. She hates it when Inigo decides to make the best of everything; it is so wearing because it is all a front.

The sound of sluicing water in the bathroom reminds her that she hasn't washed up from breakfast. Filling the sink, she marvels that Inigo is still cheerful. The odds are stacked against it: he loathes the countryside, he hates animals, he finds disorder maddening and dirt repellent. She has rented a cottage, or rather a hovel, without consulting him and moved into it in his absence. It must be a huge blow to his control freakery. Suddenly Laura feels entirely unable to deal with him when he comes out of the bathroom. It will be better if he gets used to the Gate House without her there; that way she can avoid being defensive.

Leaving the washing up to soak, and grabbing Dolly's pink sequinned cowboy hat and a very unsuitable pair of metallic purple high heels she bought yesterday in a junk shop, she shouts through the bathroom door, 'I've just got to go and help Hedley with something. You go to town for the scythe – Woolworth's will be open, and I'll see you later on.' Then she runs out of the house, putting the shoes on halfway down the path, and hoping that the very old skirt embroidered with mirrors and the faded sage-coloured T-shirt she put on this morning after frog work will be smart enough for a christening lunch.

Hastening through the village, Laura is glad that the early morning sun has been replaced by glowering light and a slicing wind, so no one is out to watch her hobbling in her ridiculous shoes as she passes. She slows down, partly through discomfort as a blister is forming, and partly curiosity.

Little has changed in Crumbly village at first glance; indeed, it is reassuringly identical to her memories. Even the chickens at the pub are the same over-sized and over-friendly breed that used to hop up onto the bench next to you if you chose an outside table for a drink. Laura pauses and stoops, putting out a hand, hoping to entice one of these creatures away from its business scratching up primulas from a tub by the pub door. The hen pauses, and looks at her severely. It groans horribly, perhaps indicating that it doesn't much like what it sees and struts off to continue with its work in the flower bed by the pub wall. Walking past the creaking sign, Laura realises with irritation how Hampstead life has changed her when she is shocked for a second by the name. The picture is of two chocolate box black kittens, but even so the words 'The Black Boys' are startling now. There must have been a politically correct uprising in the village since she was last here: Laura vividly remembers the old sign, admittedly faded and in need of renovation, depicted two small African boys in white shirts and little skullcaps standing in front of a boat.

The first time Guy took her out for a drink on their own they came to The Black Boys. When he summoned the courage to ask her out, they agreed that the village pub was acceptable on the grounds that it was summer and they could sit in the garden, away from the curious eyes of Hedley and the rest of the cricket team, who spent most evenings, no matter how gentle and warm, in the smallest, darkest bar. Laura had hardly ever been to a pub before, and not wishing to let him know this, copied Guy and ordered draught beer. She shudders, remembering the sweet earthy taste, so revolting she almost gagged in front of him. Eyes watering, she asked him to get her something else, and Guy laughed and went back to the bar for wine. Feeding peanuts to the hens, Guy convinced her that they were Chinese Lap Chickens, originally reared alongside Pekineses for the royal household. She had believed him and, fascinated, had taken the story home to Hedley and Uncle Peter. Peter blinked and nodded vague corroboration, but Hedley grinned knowingly and said, 'Come on, sis, you should never believe anything a man on a date tells you.'

Laura had flushed, felt foolish and protested, 'But we weren't on a date, I just went for a drink with him. Is it not true then?'

The next time they saw one another, Laura challenged Guy. 'They said never believe anything a man on a date tells you, Guy, so what have you got to say to that?' she teased.

He looked alarmed. 'Am I accused of lying about chickens or taking you on a date?' he asked, pulling her towards him so close she could feel his heart beating against her own. 'Because I'm guilty of both.' And he bent over her and kissed her on the bridge in the village, where anyone could see them.

She is on the bridge again now, pausing to look down out of almost forgotten habit to see if she can catch a glimpse of a lazy brown trout. It takes a moment to see anything more than her face and the sky reflected in the slow dark water, but then her eyes become accustomed and her focus shifts below the surface to undulating weed and there, beside a flat stone, is a trout, doing the fishy equivalent of treading water as it remains in the shadows, swaying but never moving and facing upstream.

'Why do they always face upstream?' she wonders aloud and nearly jumps out of her skin when a voice behind her answers, 'That's how they get oxygen into their gills.'

It is Guy. Different from when she saw him in the restaurant, and more as he was long ago, tousled and crumpled in dishevelled jeans and a worn shirt the same faded blue grey as his eyes. He is sitting in a sputtering low-slung car, and is looking more or less up Laura's skirt as she hangs over the bridge. Red heat creeps up her face; she feels he knows she was thinking about kissing him. Guy rolls a cigarette with one hand. Laura wonders if he always does that or if he is trying to impress her. She finds herself staring at his teeth which are white and even, and his skin, already tanned even though it is April – no, Laura suddenly remembers that it is May the first today,

'Are you going to the christening?' Guy asks her. 'If so, may I drive you the remaining few yards?' Laura nods and fumbles with the door, glad to be able to sit down as her knees have gone weak.

'Where's your wife?' she asks, now almost horizontal in the sagging passenger seat of Guy's car.

'She's gone to a hunter trial – where's your husband?'

Guy changes gear and Laura is flung back even further. 'He's gone to buy a scythe in Woolworth's.'

'A scythe? What for?' Guy's voice is full of amusement, and hearing this from an idiotic dentist-chair position enrages Laura. Inigo has as much right to a scythe as anyone. There is no time to put Guy straight on this one though, or to mention that she has become a neighbour, because they have arrived. Laura is hurled forwards against her seat belt as Guy pulls up.

'You don't seem to have much idea how to drive, this car,' she mutters.

Guy pauses as he is about to get out, looks straight at her and says, 'I'm sorry, I was nervous.' He yanks a skateboard out from between the seats, and noticing the astonishment on her face, explains, 'It's my christening present. But I think the big boys will have to look after it for a few years until Harry's old enough.'

'Oh no,' Laura gasps. 'I wasn't thinking about the skateboard – I mean, I haven't got a present. I didn't even know the baby was a boy.'

'Don't worry, you can share mine,' says Guy.

Laura follows him through a gate and into a garden. It is hard to get to the house because a small girl clad in a wetsuit and snorkel is dragging a paddling pool out of the front door, attended by a parrot.

'Put it over there, put it over there,' scolds the parrot.'

'I AM TRYING TO!' roars the child. 'And shud-dup Gertie or I'll christen you.'

'That's Venetia's daughter,' says Guy. 'She's obvi-ously taken the wet bit of the christening to heart.'

Relieved that her own clothing cannot possibly seem out of place when the junior hostess is clad in neoprene, Laura enters the cottage, stepping over strewn dolls and cricket bats in the hallway to see into a crowded sitting room. There, behind a huge jugful of white narcissus and moulting pink cherry blossom, Hedley is talking to a majestic woman in purple, hold-ing her glass for her as she lights one cigarette from another.

'The thing is, they should always have a toast of some sort in the church,' says the woman, waving her cigarette and casting a trail of ash onto her skirt and the white bull terrier nestling close to her. 'Champagne is good, but if you want a change there's nothing wrong with a nice bracing vodka and tonic in the morning, is there?'

Tamsin has taken off the shaggy coat she was wearing this morning to reveal an outfit made up of the sleeves of a navy blue jersey without any middle bit. Instead of the middle bit she has on a tiny camisole. Impressed, Laura wonders if these are the modern equivalent to leg warmers. Tamsin beckons her over, waving the pink drink she is sipping from a Teletubbies plastic beaker. She is perched on the back of a sofa near the music, with a boy about her age and another a bit younger with an ice-cream moustache.

'Hi Laura, these are my friends,' says Tamsin, simpering sweetly, her voice a soft coo, and a million miles from the grunts she usually favours her family with.

'These are Venetia's sons Giles and Felix,' adds Guy, introducing Laura, and she grins at them and wishes she had brought Fred and Dolly.

'Hello,' says Felix, the younger one, not looking at her but staring at her shoes. 'Mum's got some shoes like that,' he says, dreamily extracting a piece of chewing gum from his mouth and clamping it to the side of his cup. 'She says they're bloody agony.'

'They are,' laughs Laura.

Giles pokes his brother. 'Felix,' he hisses, 'you're not supposed to swear at christenings.'

'Well, we've had the christening, and Harry made such a racket in my ear I think I'm a bit deaf now. I don't know why Mum bothered having another baby.

There were enough of us already.' Felix's chin sinks forward almost onto his chest, and he stares more fixedly at Laura's shoes.

Giles tries to jolly him out of this gloomy train of thought. 'Oh come on, Felix, Harry's all right, he's only a baby and he can't help it. They did give us a trampoline when he came.'

'Yeah, but I wanted a PlayStation much more.'

Giles rolls his eyes at Tamsin and gives Laura an embarrassed grin. She touches Felix on the shoulder and says, 'Do you think my son Fred could come and play on your trampoline some time? He would love to meet you, he wants a PlayStation too.'

Felix brightens. 'Does he? Mint! Maybe we can save up together. I've got seventeen pounds and I've asked Mum to pay me all the pocket money she owes me for the whole of my life which is twelve years of one pound a week because she never gives me *any*, which is . . .'

'Don't get in a psyche about pocket money,' warns Giles.

Guy brings Venetia over to meet Laura.

'Mum, look, she's got the same shoes as you and her son wants a PlayStation,' says Felix.

'I got them in a junk shop yesterday,' Laura says, looking doubtfully at the shoes.

Venetia giggles. 'The one just beyond the village? In the barn?'

Laura nods. Venetia carries on, 'Then I bet they are mine – I sold him a chest last week and all my shoes have disappeared and Giles has just told me that The Beauty – that's my four-year-old, the one outside with the parrot – was making it into a shoe shop. It's my own fault, I was so stupid not to look inside it.'

Laura laughs. 'Well, you must have them back now, as long as you don't mind a barefoot gate-crasher, or perhaps I could borrow some wellies.'

'Don't be ridiculous,' answers Venetia, sloshing wine into two glasses and passing one to Laura. 'It's such a good sign, I wouldn't dream of taking them back. They're yours now.'

She moves off to speak to the vicar. Laura looks around the colourful room, full of laughter and friendly-faced people, and compares it to the Private Views and parties she usually attends. At these, everyone is one age – forty – and pretending not to be. Invariably they are clad in black, no one smokes, only a few defiant people drink, and hardly anyone laughs. Sipping her drink, she admits that in London Inigo is the best person to talk to at parties, the only irreverent voice. His favourite trick, last employed at a dinner given by the National Art Fund with the Home Secretary present, is to draw naked cartoons of other guests and pass them to Laura while she is talking to someone.

'Here, I need you to hold onto my inspiration,' he whispered on that occasion, and tucked a drawing of the Home Secretary in all his glory folded like a paper aeroplane into her belt.

Laura gazes around the christening party. Without knowing Venetia at all, she is sure that this is how she would like her life to be, conveniently forgetting that yesterday she wanted it to be like Marjorie the pug lady's. But no matter how idyllic Marjorie's garden and animal life is, this house has all the vibrancy and chaos that a family home should have. From where she is standing, Laura can see through to a kitchen painted vivid yellow, pictures by the children stuck haphazardly over the walls, and a fat white dog asleep on a black feather boa in front of the red Aga. Laura thinks of her own white and steel London kitchen, and of her new mould-speckled one at the Gate House. Could she create a vivid world like this one? And it would have to be her own creation. It would be perfect and easy to get Dolly and Fred over here now, but there's Inigo. She tries to imagine him here, perhaps talking to the vicar about fund-raising for the new bell, as Hedley is doing, but it is impossible. Inigo would be uncomfortable here, where a toddler has just stuck a finger into the chocolate christening cake, to the huge amusement of Venetia and her mother standing together toasting baby Harry. He would not appreciate a life where every situation is beyond control, and every surface is covered; he would create an atmosphere. He is too different a species.

Laura moves across and makes a space for herself on the window seat, squeezing in next to a large cat and a pile of what look like more of Tamsin's sweater sleeves with no middles. Outside, the wetsuit wearer and the parrot have dragooned Guy into helping them, and the paddling pool is filling fast. The little girl flourishes a bottle of bath essence and pours a long gloop of blue into the water. Bubbles rise; she and the parrot caper about shouting, 'Hubble Bubble, Hubble Bubble.' The clouds, threatening all morning, are now lower and menacing. A wind whisks up, and Guy persuades the two bathers to come inside with him just as rain bursts from the darkest cloud onto the road and the garden. Laura thinks of Inigo and the scythe, Dolly and Fred and the goat, and decides it is time to go; the only trouble is that she will be drenched. There is an embarrassing Pac-a-Mac in her handbag, but no weather could be foul enough to persuade her to put it on anywhere near this house full of flowers and colour. Indeed, she is determined from today onwards to become the kind of person who doesn't even know what a Pac-a-Mac looks like. At least she didn't choose it, it was Inigo who bought the mac; always on the lookout for ways to waste money, he was delighted to find something so mundane at such a price in Bond Street one day when they were looking at Cork Street shows together. He tucked it into her bag, joking, 'Here's something for a rainy day.'

As she hovers by the front door, watching the sky, waiting for a moment to dash, Guy appears.

'Can I give you a lift back to Hedley's?' he asks, chivalrously flourishing a Barbie umbrella he has pinched from an overcrowded chimney pot in the hall. He holds it over her head and they set off into slapping cold rain. Laura bumps against him as they negotiate the gate, and her heart beats in her throat.

Guy's neck and chest are wet where rain has crept down his open shirt.

'I'm not staying with Hedley, we've just moved into the Gate House.'

They have reached the car now. Guy unlocks the door for her and bundles her in. Laura scrambles to stuff the Pac-a-Mac to the bottom of her bag in case he sees it. His shirt is wet through across the shoulders. Laura rubs the raindrops off her bare arms and legs and shivers.

Guy turns the heating up and starts the car, murmuring almost to himself, 'So you've moved into the village have you? Now I'll believe anything. You said you'd never be back, do you remember?'

'Well, I'm not back.' Laura shifts crossly, yanking her seat belt over her. 'Not full time anyway, but we love the Gate House. And I'm very excited to be here again. At last.'

Nearly twenty years ago, Guy had driven her to the tiny local station and said goodbye. She was dreading the possibility that they might be the only people waiting there for the train, and they were. Guy stood on the platform next to her, and the glass windows of the railway house on the opposite side of the track reflected him back, his hair shaggy over his eyes, face obscured because he was looking down at a stone he scuffed with his shoe on the platform. Laura saw herself next to him, her hands deep into the pockets of her jeans, biting her lip, not speaking but restless. She pulled her hands out of her pockets, accidentally brushing against Guy's bare arm. They both jumped as if electrified and stood a little further apart, not looking at one another. Laura rolled back on her heels and prayed the train would appear right now out of a hole in the earth.

She swayed and tried to whistle, wrapping her arms around herself, making herself narrower and less visibly there on the platform with Guy and the flooding sadness of the September light. Her throat was dry and she couldn't whistle, nor could she speak; no words came into her mind to fill the loud silence.

'Saying goodbye is a mistake, you know,' she said quietly. 'You should go now.'

'Will you come back?' Guy knew that whatever he said would be wrong, but surely this was the worst? How needy, bleating and desperate he sounded. He watched Laura's reflection, her hair whipped across her face by the sun-baked breeze, edged now with the chill of autumn. He saw her glance up at him, angry and upset.

'I can't. I don't belong here. I need the city. This is your place. I can't come back.' Her words were cruel, harsher than she ever meant them to be, and her eyes were bright with tears.

'You don't know what you're saying,' said Guy and the reflection of him and Laura standing side by side on the platform blurred and smeared in his hot eyes as the train arrived, grinding and hissing as if it were steam. Laura's hands were cold and stiff when he held them to kiss her goodbye.

CHAPTER 13

The conversation Laura has been dreading since Inigo walked into the Gate House on Sunday morning does not occur until they are back in London and ensconced in weekday ritual and routine. Cally calls to find out if Laura has got a life yet.

'Yes, I think I have, but Inigo hates it.' Laura should be at the studio when Cally rings, but she is avoiding Inigo, and pretended to have a dentist appointment this morning.

'How do you know?' Cally's bracelets jangle against the phone and Laura imagines her lighting her cigarette.

'He's avoiding me as much as I am him. He doesn't like the fact that I'm doing my own thing.'

'Well, whose fault is that?' demands Cally. 'You've spent years pandering to him and giving in, so this will be a horrible shock.' She laughs. 'Even I feel a bit sorry for him,' she says.

'I heard him telling his mother he had to come home

early from doing the installation for Manfred because he was so freaked out about the goat,' Laura confesses. 'He went straight to the airport without bothering to check on the flights out and he'd missed every single one. He had to spend the night in the departure lounge and catch the first flight in the morning.'

'Serves him right,' says Cally stoutly, hearing guilt in Laura's voice. 'Look, you must need a change if you're making these big decisions without him now. You're angry with him, and you're right to be. Tell him he shouldn't have tried to railroad you about that Met offer in New York. Stand up to him, Laura – it'll be better for both of you in the long run.'

Laura nods slowly. 'You're right, but it's not easy.'

In her mind is Inigo at the Gate House, or as he phrased it, 'The godforsaken pit you are so keen to call home.' Laura could see what he was thinking as clearly as if he had said it: she, Laura, seemed to have regressed to the nursery, surrounding herself with unsuitable animals – well, a goat at any rate – and wandering off with strange men in sports cars without explanation whenever she felt like it. Confounded, he struggled to be helpful and supportive, but without much idea how, as the place seemed good for nothing but demolition. His instinct when the balance of his family is rocked like this must always be to try to realign it. But how? And he doesn't like squalor. He sees Laura enjoying squalor and it makes him uneasy. Even returning to London from the Gate House has not dispelled his unease. Inigo is biding his time, Laura is sure.

So when Laura reaches for the telephone in the middle of their discussion about whether a cottage in the country is sustainable, with Inigo about to go and work in New York for a year and Laura unable to decide whether she and the children should go too; when she reaches for the phone and calls the blacksmith in Norfolk to ask him to make a tether for the sodding goat, Inigo does not shout, stamp or whirl himself into a frenzy of rage, he sits calmly in the white kid chair across from Laura, spreading his hands over the soft arms and waiting. He wonders if Laura knows that the chairs they are sitting on are made from the hides of tiny goats like Grass. The thought gives him savage pleasure, but he is pretty sure she will hate to be told. Laura puts the phone down with a sigh, and crosses something off in the big green notebook she has with her all the time now.

'Sorry, I had to do it now. I'd totally forgotten and Grass must have a tether by this weekend so we can start getting the garden under control.' She smiles apologetically at Inigo, very much as if they are mild acquaintances at a parish council meeting, and clasps her hands, blinking encouragement. Clearly Laura has not been trying to imagine herself in Inigo's shoes, as he has just been urging her. Inigo is crestfallen and at a loss.

Making the most of his morose and abjectly confused air, Laura announces, 'I think you should know that we have a ferret and a pug on order. I'm picking them up on Friday.'

Inigo is gob-smacked. He opens and closes his mouth several times, but that's all. Laura is hugely relieved. Really it has gone rather well. She lies back in her chair relaxing her hands; she's been twisting her handkerchief since she and Inigo got home from work; she hardly stopped to eat supper, and even then it was spaghetti so she twisted that instead. It has been a burden, concealing the truth from Inigo, and she'd hoped he would be back in Germany for at least another week. It's not that she doesn't miss him, it's just his absences create such a welcome break in routine, as well as unlocking spare hours Laura never thought she'd see again. These spare hours are more precious than ever now she is embarking on a new and rapturous love affair with Norfolk.

She leaves the room under the pretence of making tea, but forgets what she's doing when she gets to the kitchen. Her thoughts are running away with her, and she couldn't bear for him to know that she is thinking like this. It feels like treachery to acknowledge that if Inigo had been in England when Hedley offered her the Gate House, she would never have dared to take it. She is longing for him to go back to New York and get on with making his biscuits for the *Death Threat* show. In fact, despite the outrageous way he broke it to her, Laura cannot now think of one good reason why Inigo shouldn't take the fellowship at the Met. Of course he should. It would be marvellous. But there's no way she's going with him.

It's odd that he hasn't seemed keen to discuss it; instead he harps on about the Gate House and whether it needs damp proofing and how to get gas there. She never thought it could happen, but a bit of Inigo is turning into his mother, the home and hearth bit, already quite pronounced enough in Laura's view. Look at him now, flicking through a magazine to find a new cooker for the Gate House. It's madness. It's got a perfectly good Rayburn. OK, so it needs to be filled with coal three times a day, but that's fine. Hedley lights it the afternoon before they come, to give it a few hours to get up to speed, and if the house is a little smoky, there are windows which can be opened. Honestly, Laura can't see what Inigo is fussing about.

She can, however, see the spirit of his mother Betty, her fat short hands raised in alarm at the prospect of putting up with something old when you could have a new one, nail polish dripping blood red as she stabs her fingers through her hair and shakes her head, fussing and worrying about every breath the twins took until they were five and she began to find them a bit much. A widow, she remains unceasingly anxious about Inigo, her youngest child, her only son. Inigo's two sisters fled the suffocation of their mother's love in their late teens and both emigrated to Canada, but Inigo couldn't leave her, he knew it would break her heart. When he had his first show in New York and was away for months setting it up and travelling, Betty lost two stone, mainly from her upper arms, as she willingly showed anyone who would look. She would have pined away entirely, had Inigo's gallery not taken pity on her from her daily phone calls, and sent her a ticket to come over for the opening night. Inigo was not pleased. Laura met him the day Betty left again, and Inigo was ripe for freedom and for fun.

That was a long time ago, however, and while Inigo hasn't started to look like his mother, he has already inherited her old-ladyish fussing skills. On balance it is better he fusses like her than looks like her, given that Betty has black-rooted platinum hair and immaculate make-up, incorporating shimmering blue on the eyelid and a slick of rhubarb pink on the mouth. Inigo has not inherited her gait either – although the scampering trot with which she approaches life is, Laura is convinced, caused by the effort it costs her small feet, never encased in shoes without heels, to support her colossal bust on an otherwise sparrow-like frame.

Inigo is bashing the page of a magazine now with one finger, reading out the copy for the cooker of his choice. 'Yes, you see it says here that it has an electric oven and gas hobs, and if we could just get gas there – or wait – what if we get an industrial cooker . . .' He is off, flipping through the magazine again.

Laura takes off her shoes and curls her legs under her, wondering how far from the point Inigo will go this evening. It doesn't matter. She too wants to avoid talking about what is happening to the small safe unit of their family. And what about the new animals? Can he possibly have accepted them?

'I'll look it up tomorrow, or later tonight on the internet.' Inigo has finished with that topic. He stands up, and moves towards Laura and puts his hands on her shoulders. 'Let's go to bed now,' he says, his eyes darkening as they do when he gets passionate. He leans down and lifts her hair from the nape of her neck, breathing in the scent of her, his breath on her skin making her shiver with irritation more than pleasure. He is trying to control her again. Inigo kisses her forehead, then her eyes, obliging her to close them. 'Just give me the dog woman's telephone number first, will you?' he murmurs. 'I'll send them a donation and thanks in the morning, but you can't have the dog, it won't work. The house I can deal with, even the goat, but not a bloody dog, or one of those foul feral beasts. I won't have it.'

Laura leaps up as if he has poured scalding water on her back. She twists round to face him, scooping her shoes back on because subconsciously she wants to be taller for this. 'It doesn't matter what you won't have because you won't be here,' she says quietly, and she can't look at him because there is pain and panic all over his face and it makes her hurt too.

'I might not take the fellowship.' Inigo moves to stand leaning on the fireplace, looking down into the empty grate, his back hunching and knotting as he flexes his fists in his pockets and clenches his jaw to stop himself turning around to reach out for Laura.

Oddly detached, as though this is all happening on television and not to her, Laura steps forward to lean on the fireplace next to him.

'Look, why don't we just let things run for a bit,' she says. 'You're busy with *Death Threat*, whether or not you take the fellowship, and I want to try a bit of rural life while the children are still at an age where I can get them to come with me. I think it will be good for them.' She puts both hands around his arm, hoping he will turn to face her. 'I think it will be good for all of us.'

The silence is enormous. Laura isn't sure what she has just said, but she has stood her ground. When Inigo moves round to look at her, she meets his gaze steadily, her face grave. Unexpectedly, she sees a slow smile at the corner of his mouth. Honestly, he is impossible; now she's grinning back and it should be awful right now, not funny. He hasn't taken her seriously. As if he can hear her thoughts, Inigo whispers, 'You're just so irresistible when you're serious.'

Laura gives up. She links her hands behind his neck and kisses him slowly. Later, in bed, fitted against him in a coil of sheets, she remembers the pug is still on order. Most pleasing.

CHAPTER 14

Laura has owned a dog for three weeks now, and while she would say without hesitation that her own life has improved one thousandfold, Inigo has told his analyst that their life as a couple has become unspeakable. Laura is never at home, or indeed at work. She is either on the Heath with Zeus, as Aïoli has been rechristened, or she's at puppy training or at dog psychology sessions. Indeed, Inigo has decided to see an analyst mainly out of jealousy because Zeus was seeing one. Inigo's counsellor finds this most interesting, and is using Inigo as a case study for his book on regression. Laura pays scant attention because she is house training Zeus, and can't think of much else.

In protest, and because he needs to be there, Inigo has gone to New York. There, everyone is making a huge fuss of him, most particularly those who want to appear both international and intellectual. He is the toast of the town, but Laura has no issue with his absence and certainly has no idea when he may be back. Her domestic life has vanished with Inigo, and she very much enjoys not having to cook proper meals or having to keep the house rigorously tidy. She finds it a huge relief that the eggs are just in their box now, not balanced precariously, and that no magnets are suspended between doorways, nor are candles teetering askew on the mantelpiece. The space left by the absence of his glittering, restless energy is comfortable and easy. Laura, folding clothes she doesn't bother to iron with Inigo away, imagines how cross he would be to think of her settling comfortably into his being away as if it were a pair of slippers, huge padded slippers in the shape of Garfield. How Inigo would loathe the idea. She almost feels guilty for enjoying it.

Laura sorts the clothes into piles and takes a small heap of rainbow-bright garments into Dolly's room. Swinging open the door she is too vigorous and the handle bumps the shelf behind, dislodging a pile of books which thud down onto a rack of CDs. The discs spin out across the floor, slicing silver blue as they skate beneath the bed, under the chair, everywhere. Cursing her clumsiness for catching her out here where it matters, rather than in Fred's room where it wouldn't, Laura drops the clothes and kneels down. A throb of exhaustion, familiar accompaniment to all her clearing up, pulls at Laura's shoulders, and she sighs. Dolly is missing Inigo horribly. Laura alone is not enough parent for her, and not the right one for her baleful, leg-swinging insolence. Impotence wells daily as Laura tries to get Dolly to do her homework, or run down the street for a pint of milk.

Later that afternoon, Dolly plonks herself and her school bag on the kitchen table and drinks milk out of the bottle, her eyes on Laura even as her head is tilted back, and in them a wordless challenge. Laura takes a deep breath and turns away towards the window, hugging Zeus with ridiculous tears hot behind her eyes, ashamed that she has no idea what to do, or what to say to her daughter. The idea that she can help Hedley with Tamsin is a joke now. Her own daughter has become a hormonal teenager almost overnight, and none of the preaching works in practice. Dolly's answer to the smallest request is to flick her hair and reach for the telephone to call Inigo. As she does this at any hour of the day or night with no regard for the time lag, her relationship with Inigo is volatile. A curt ten seconds during a breakfast fracas over whether or not Dolly would eat anything other than crisps before school had her in tears.

'He said, "It's three in the morning so this had better be bloody important,"' she sobbed to her mother, wilting and pulling her jersey down over her pulled-up knees.

This moment is the catalyst for Laura suggesting she brings a friend with her to Norfolk, a breakthrough moment so satisfying in its effect on Dolly's deportment and her mood that Laura decides Fred must have someone too.

Locking the car on the Heath road high above Hampstead village, Laura gulps the summer air hungrily. The tantrums Dolly indulges in at the moment are suffocating; it is a relief to get her to school and take Zeus out for his daily stroll. Everything Laura imagined about having a dog is true; and that it should be true about an almost toy dog is doubly pleasing. Walking Zeus is a vital release from life at home, and she is fascinated and entertained by the dog-walking fraternity she has befriended. Conversations with them involve no questions or observations relating to anything but the dogs, and are thus very soothing.

This morning, Laura is pleased to see Lola, a woman who walks a pack of eight dogs most days. Lola is on the slope below the Plague Pit, giving her gang a good run off their leads. Laura greets her, noticing that Lola's plum-coloured wig is a little lopsided today.

'Hello there, Zeus,' says Lola, stooping to pet him. It is usual on the Heath to greet the dog, not the owner. She nods at Laura and then down at her own clothes. 'I'm all muddy because at ten to seven this morning, I saw Sue Whippet coming towards me – she's a loose cannon now, that woman – she used to walk with me sometimes but I changed my times.' Lola nods vehemently, and the tangle of dog leads round her neck jangles. 'I did. I can't stand her, I'm just not up to it at that time of day. You know what she's like?'

Gripped, Laura shakes her head, keeping her eyes on Zeus as he pings between Lola's dogs, rolling over and jumping with them in the springy grass.

'She's one of those types who say, "If you can't afford a Bosch fridge, you shouldn't have an Italian greyhound because they can open all the cheaper models." Her whippets are like hell hounds—' Lola breaks off as she and Laura approach the Men's pond and lets rip an earsplitting cry; all her dogs come racing up from their distant points of play. Without breaking the stride of her conversation, she attaches each one to the correct lead and gives them a chocolate drop.

'How do you audition the dogs you walk?' Laura asks.

Lola sucks in both cheeks, and assumes a haughty expression. 'All the dogs I take on have to work together, and I don't like collecting them from apartment blocks.'

'What do you mean?' Laura asks blankly.

Lola clucks. 'You know, all those big marble entrance halls and closed-circuit cameras – you can imagine what it's like going up in the lift to fetch the dog with this lot in tow. Mayhem. Specially on the way home. I like a dog with his own front door.'

Laura can't stop herself saying proudly, 'Zeus has his own front door.'

CHAPTER 15

There is no electricity and an ominous dripping sound echoes wetly from the bathroom in the Gate House, accompanied by a bad smell. Zeus has been sick three times in the car, and Vice the ferret is loose and has gone to ground somewhere under the back seat. This is Laura's first attempt at going to the country alone since moving there. What she imagined would be a lovely bonding adventure for herself and the children is turning into the usual mutiny, with herself as chauffeur, slave and pack animal. Airily planning to buy food for supper on the way at a wholesome farm shop, Laura forgets that such outlets shut at five, and has to resort to a petrol station. There, fantasies about home-baked bread and organic lamb cutlets are subsumed by a reality of three half baked rolls and a sweaty hunk of cheese. Laura hurls her bags onto the kitchen table and turns to welcome the guests with a big fake smile.

'So this is it,' she beams. 'Rural bliss,' she adds unconvincingly. Dolly's friend Rebecca and Fred's friend Shane back nervously out of the door, trying not to let her see that they are holding their breath to ward off the awful smell. Dolly comes in to get a jug to milk Grass and scowls at Laura.

'Mum, this place stinks. How could you do this when I've got Becca staying? And I've sprayed my deodorant and your scent in the car but I can't get the smell of sick out, or the smell of that disgusting ferret.' Dolly points her chin accusingly at her mother and swirls out of the door, slamming it as she goes.

Laura and her one adult guest, Gina, look at one another but say nothing for a moment. Gina reaches into the carrier bags of shopping and pulls out two cans of ready mixed gin and tonic. She passes one to Laura. 'I'm bloody glad I had the sense to get a six-pack of these at that God-awful garage. I had a funny feeling we were going to need an instant hit. Does she always treat you like that?'

Laura swigs her drink. 'Yup. Well, more and more of the time anyway. I wonder where the fuse box is?' She gazed around hopelessly.

Gina, unpacking the ten Pot Noodles Dolly insisted on buying at the garage, discovers the fuse box in the larder and restores electricity with one flick of the trip switch. 'Right, that was easy, let's find the smell now,' she says, and marches into the bathroom wielding a bottle of bleach. Laura watches her go, obscurely irritated by Gina's swamping practicality. She hadn't intended to ask her, in fact she hadn't asked her. Gina, cousin of Cally and new occasional friend, walked past as Laura was packing the car.

'You shouldn't be doing that,' she observed after several moments of watching Laura attempt to heap suitcases into the tiny space left around Dolly and Fred and their friends, all sitting like waxworks in the car, their four pairs of headphones separating them from the world.

Gina poked at a pair of boots disparagingly. 'No girl should be doing that. What's the point of feminism if it doesn't get rid of things like car packing? Where's your delicious husband?' Laura turned to face her and missed catching her own open suitcase which fell, spilling books, her alarm clock and underwear across the road.

'In New York,' Laura sighed. Gina's eyes narrowed. She knew Inigo had left for the States weeks ago; she'd been with Laura to the cinema directly after he left. They'd seen a truly awful art film about a family in Taiwan in a high-rise block. It went on for four hours – long enough, as Laura had pointed out, to get to Paris and have supper much more enjoyably.

'Still?' Gina drawls, draining the word of every last drop of inference.

'Yes, still,' agreed Laura, beginning to retrieve her belongings from the pavement.

'Your poor thing,' said Gina, in a pitying tone which suggested that she, as a divorcée, knew just what 'Still' meant. Hovering, unwilling to leave Laura, Gina tiptoed forwards and picked up a very tired-looking bra, her perfect midriff on show above low-slung jeans, so toned it didn't even crease as she bent.

'Here you are. Mmm, this does look like an old favourite, so don't leave it, will you.' She draped the bra carefully over the roof of the car, and caught sight of the car's occupants. She peered in at them for a moment before turning to Laura, her face crumpled with concern.

'Oh darling, you're all on your own with THEM.' She shuddered. 'I tell you what, why don't I come with you to the country? I've been longing to see your place and I'm free this weekend. You'll need back-up with THEM or you'll never survive, you look exhausted already. Poor love.' She leaned forwards to hug Laura across the spilled suitcase, her bracelets jangling, her arms thin and cold but strong as wire. 'Just wait a moment and I'll get a few things. What fun we'll have being girls together. I love the country.'

Laura began to mumble, 'There isn't room,' but Gina, moving surprisingly fast on her slingback heels, was already out of earshot. Laura could have jumped into the car and driven off without her, but there was no other way of avoiding Gina's company. Gina came.

'Mum, can we shoot some pigeons?' Fred appears, Shane hovering behind, shrouded like a spectre in his hooded sweatshirt. Both boys are armed with giant catapults. The catapults look like advanced and kinky torture instruments with black rubber grips and dolloping lengths of nude-coloured rubber tubing, but Fred has assured his mother that 'all they do is kill birds and stuff – nothing worse, I promise, Mum.'

The boys rush off, tailed by the snuffling, bouncing pug, the ferret leering from Fred's pocket like a glove puppet.

'Don't forget you've got Zeus,' Laura calls after them. 'He's got no sense of direction so you'll need his lead if you go far.'

Alone for a moment, she half-guiltily leaves the unpacking, preferring to head for the garden, where the last of the evening sun spills its warmth onto her back. Soaking up the peace she turns and tilts her face, closing her eyes, and leaning back on the wall. At first the only sound is her own breath slowing then, as if she has reached the point of trance in a textbook meditation session, Laura's head fills with the gentle coo of doves, the rustle of leaves and the distant honky tonk of an ice-cream van. All tensions dissolve and she opens her eyes, blinking at the bright paradise of her garden. And the weeds.

Gina, having dealt with whatever it was in the bathroom, and earning Laura's undying gratitude for not telling her about it, wanders out to the garden to join Laura crouched in her newly dug vegetable patch, planting salad leaves beneath a swinging row of old CDs Fred has set up to scare the pigeons away. Laura is immersed, singing to herself, all monstrous details of the journey erased by the long June evening, her children's voices happy and, even better, not too close, a can of gin and tonic finished beside her and the promise of more as Gina approaches, shedding her shirt to reveal a pink and purple bra which hardly covers her voluptuous bosom.

'Gosh, how wonderful not to be overlooked, and the sun really is warm, isn't it?' she cries, tripping through the daisies and settling herself on a small stool Laura likes to think she will sit on to view her garden but never does. Laura sprinkles water over the last of her seeds and stands back to view the Beatrix Potter loveliness of her vegetable plot. This area, an eight-foot square of freshly turned earth with neat edges and hospital corners, is in marked contrast to the rest of the garden. Laura is about to launch into a poetic explanation of happiness and its link for her with the soil, when there is a scream from the shed and Grass bounds out bleating and trots straight across the middle of the vegetables. Becca, waving a rope like a lasso, follows, breathless.

'She bit Dolly and stamped on her foot,' she pants, 'but we've got loads of milk.'

'She'd be better as goat curry,' Laura mutters, as Gina, almost topless, sets off in pursuit of Grass who has swerved out of the gate and is heading down the track towards Crumbly, still bleating balefully. Dolly hobbles towards her mother, pink-faced and swearing fluently. Laura decides it's best to pretend she can't hear Dolly's language and begins a soothing litany. 'Don't worry, darling, let me see. Ooh, how painful. Shall I kiss it better?'

Dolly pushes her away impatiently, reaching into her pocket for her mobile phone, today fetchingly clad in a fluffy pink cover, and begins stabbing the keys. 'Oh shut up Mum, I'm not a baby. I hate that fucking goat. Why can't Hedley take it away? It isn't even ours and I'm never milking it or going near it again. I'm texting Tamsin, and Becca and I are going to see her right now, and I don't know when we'll be back.'

Dolly rushes into the house to complete her tantrum with the required hefty door slam. Becca skulks behind, feebly prodding her own more conservative pale blue plastic mobile. She sends her message then looks up at Laura whispering, 'Umm, sorry Laura,' before she too whisks into the house. God, the opera of Dolly's life is becoming more gothic every day, Laura thinks, but before she can decide whether to follow her, there is a shout from the gate and Hedley, grinning hugely, enters with a swagger, dragging the still bleating Grass.

'Found your house guest in distress,' he smirks, turning to help Gina over the tiny step up to the path, clearly much too difficult for her to manage alone, and taking some time to remove his appreciative gaze from her cleavage.

'Darling Laura, I just couldn't manage to catch her until these charming men appeared.' She bats her eyelashes at Hedley and murmurs to Laura, 'Honestly, everyone in the country is so ruggedly handsome, especially your delicious brother. Why didn't you tell me about him?' Laura stares, incredulous, but there is no guile in Gina's expression, just good old-fashioned come-hitherance, and it is directed at Hedley. Amazing. Laura has no time to think more because the garden is suddenly full of people as Guy and then Tamsin follow Gina in through the gate, and Fred and

Shane, liberally covered in bits of twig and leaf, abseil on a frayed rope down from the big oak tree.

Laura has a sense of her whole being unravelling from the top of her head downwards as everybody begins shouting their business at once:

'Mum, Mum, Zeus got his head stuck down a rabbit hole in that field and I didn't dare pull him by his legs in case—'

'Laura, that goat is impossible! It tried to eat my bra, thank God your brother came to my rescue—'

'Laura, d'you know where Dolly is? I wondered if she'd like to come to the disco in the village hall—'

Guy grins across the wall of sound at her, apologetically shifting a basket of vegetables from one hand to the other, and handing her a bunch of fragrant sweet peas. 'Hedley said you would be here this weekend, so I came to check on the goat, and I thought you might need some veg, but I can see you're already growing your own—'

Laura thanks him, wishing that she, like Gina, was wearing a lovely girlie bra instead of baggy jeans with mud caked on the knees and a shapeless old T-shirt of Dolly's with Elvis wrinkling with age on the front. Gina and Hedley are standing so close together it's surprising they can see one another to speak, but from the shouts of laughter, they are clearly managing fine. A piercing scream from Dolly's bedroom window penetrates the clamour, and Laura's heart misses a beat then pounds in terror. Everyone stands as if petrified for a millisecond. The screaming continues, on a crescendo, and there is a stampede towards the house. Hedley, made omnipotent by the vision of Gina in her small amount of clothing, is first in, choosing to climb onto the roof via the water butt and enter through the window of his niece's room. Laura, huffing up the stairs, is convinced she is about to die of a heart attack and makes a mental note to sacrifice all pleasures starting with tinned gin and tonic, and to become super-fit and virtuous if only Dolly is still alive when she gets to her. At the bedroom door she takes a deep breath, but Hedley is there first and opens it from the inside to greet her.

'She won't stop screaming, but I think this is the cause.' He waves Vice, the ferret, above his head, and Fred leaps to reclaim her.

'Oh, I wondered where she'd got to.'

'She was in Dolly's knicker drawer,' whispers Becca, herself on the verge of tears. 'And I think she bit Dolly. After the goat I think it was the final straw. Dolly says she's going back to London and never coming here again.'

Fred rolls his eyes, tucks his ferret into his pocket and says without rancour, 'Dolly's mental. She's always in a psyche nowadays – she thinks it makes her seem older, but I think it's sad.' This pithy summary of his sister's character does not help, and he is bundled out of the room by Laura.

Everyone looks with interest at Dolly, including Grass, whose unwelcome presence upstairs in the house Laura notices with a rising sense of panic. Grass, masticating busily, coughs, and spits out a pink thong. Recognising Dolly's favourite underwear,

Laura whisks it behind her back and stuffs it in her pocket.

Becca translates the next scream, staring at the floor, discomfort scarlet on her face. 'And she says she hopes Inigo leaves Laura and that she can go and live with him in New York and never see another animal as long as she lives.'

'Oh, for heaven's sake!' Laura has really had enough of this absurd scene and is beginning to think that Dolly is doing it on purpose to punish her for Inigo's absence. He's been away for two weeks now, and even Laura, still fed up with him, is beginning to long for his return.

Guy edges into the room and walks up to Dolly, standing rigid and hysterical next to a drawer full of tangled underwear, both Tamsin and Becca draped protectively around her. He takes both her hands in his and rubs them. 'Come on Dolly,' he says gently. 'You need to snap out of this.'

Laura has to clench both fists and press her arms to her sides to stop herself rushing forward and slapping her daughter, but to her immense relief, Guy is getting through to the three girls and Dolly's screams begin to subside until she is sitting sniffing on the edge of her bed with her arms around her attendant nymphs, both of whom are murmuring gently and stroking her hair. Drained, Laura creeps away towards the stairs, keen to get Grass out before Dolly notices her. Grass has other ideas, and digs her hooves in, snaking her neck to snatch at the white muslin curtains Laura hung in a fit of domestic enthusiasm last time she was here.

Laura tugs as the ribboned edging quivers in the goat's mouth, but too late, Grass chews and swallows violently, the twin toggles at her throat dancing hairily as the ribbon slides down. Laura wants to cry, but is damned if a bloody goat and a curtain will reduce her to tears. She grits her teeth and yanks at the rope. Grass resists.

'You are evil,' Laura says between gritted teeth. 'I want to kill you.'

'Come on now, don't let's get this out of proportion. It's only a curtain,' soothes Gina, who has emerged from Dolly's bedroom with Hedley in bossy big sister mode. She slaps the goat's bony bottom, and Grass gallops down the stairs, with Laura running at her side, determined to maintain this small measure of control. Dusk has fallen before any normality is regained. Guy and Hedley secure Grass in her shed, and with ostentatious hammering, then announce that it is fixed. Dolly still won't speak to her mother and Laura is exhausted by trying to penetrate her stone wall daughter and longs for her to simply vanish.

Suddenly, Laura's wish comes true; Tamsin marches into the kitchen and announces, 'We're going now. We'll be back at eleven o'clock.'

'Where?' asks Laura, gaping as Dolly and Becca traipse in behind Tamsin wearing glistening blue and green eyeshadow, silver streaks in their hair and roller blades.

'The village disco, of course.' Tamsin leads her party out into the garden, where giggling and cursing accompanies them as they wobble out onto the road to the village. The peace, when they have gone, is palpable, but even so Laura cannot shake off the sense of being burdened. She particularly hates people feeling sorry for her; the quarrels with Dolly have been visible and audible to all, and she is sure Gina and Guy are pitying her wholeheartedly. Along with Hedley, they coax her to the pub, where her mood is aggressively cheerful. 'Isn't this wonderful?' she demands as the four of them peer through the darkness of the pub garden at their scampi and chips in baskets. 'It's such a treat to be out for supper.'

Gina, who knows full well that Inigo and Laura eat out more nights than in at home in London, raises her eyebrows. 'Is it?' she says. Both Hedley and Guy guffaw as if she is the world's greatest wit.

Laura looks at them witheringly. 'Oh, grow up!' she snaps. 'I'm so sick of pandering to teen egos, I'm not going to speak to any of you if you can't be sensible.' What she wants to know, more than anything now the children are left behind and the goat is locked up for the night, is why Guy is here on his own. Where is Celia?

She is about to ask when Guy, who is fidgeting, jumps up saying, 'I think I'll get us all another drink.'

Hedley reaches across the table, his brow quivering, and grabs his sister's hand, leaning forward conspiratorially. 'I'd better tell you before you put your foot right in it. Silly's left.'

Both Laura and Gina stare at him blankly. 'Why is he silly?' whispers Gina, who is hugely enjoying herself.

Hedley shakes his head. 'No, no, his wife Celia – we call her Silly – she left three weeks ago.'

Laura's phone trills. She longs not to answer it and to hear more of Hedley's fascinating news, but years of being at her children's beck and call make it impossible. It is Fred.

'Mum?'

'What?' If only she could train her other ear to absorb outside conversation while speaking on the phone. Hedley and Gina huddle, discussing Guy in low voices. 'Oh poor him,' Gina is murmuring. 'How could you make someone choose like that?'

Choose what? Laura wonders. It could be anything from curtain material to group sex. Fred is clamouring in her ear.

'MUM. I SAID MUM. Can you hear me?'

'Yes, unfortunately,' sighs Laura.

'MUM, have you seen my trainers?'

'No, Fred, I haven't, and I'm out at the moment so I can't look for them.'

There is a moment's puzzled silence, in which Hedley nods, saying, 'I know, and of course he's terribly shocked, poor sod.' Unlikely to be curtain material then, but quite possibly group sex.

Fred is still trying to make sense of Laura's whereabouts. 'You're out? I thought you were in the kitchen. You were there a minute ago.'

'Well, I'm not there now, and if I was, you would be much better off walking into the room to speak to me rather than frying your brains with that phone.'

There is a clunking sound as Fred moves through the house. 'Oh yeah! You're not here, are you?' he says, presumably checking in the oven for his mother. His tone is one of astonishment.

'No, I'm not. I'm trying to have supper. Don't you remember I said I was going out?'

'Did you?' Fred's interest flags, 'OK, bye Mum.'

'Bye, darling.' Laura is about to press the off button when she hears him again.

'Hey, Mum, wait – is there anything to eat?'

'Oh bloody hell. You've had supper. Yes, there are hundreds of Pot Noodles in the larder, off you go now.'

There is an aggrieved pause. 'No need to go mental,' says Fred. 'I was only asking. Bye, Mum.'

'Bye,' says Laura, maddened to see Guy returning with a tray already, and Gina and Hedley straightening and addressing their scampi with great interest. So unfair, she has missed it all.

Guy sits down next to Laura, even though Hedley is on his own on the other side of the table. Gina giggles and moves round to sit next to Hedley. They can't keep their hands off one another, and Laura is relieved when Hedley suggests a game of pool and Gina follows him into the pub.

'I'm sorry about your wife,' she blurts out.

Guy rubs his eyes and grins wryly. 'I'm sorry she's so angry,' he says. 'She thinks I'm ripping her off over her business, and it's soured everything.'

'Do you still love her?' Is it the drink, or the dark or both that is making Laura so bold and uninhibited? Guy doesn't clam up, he just looks sad as he answers.

'I don't think either of us ever loved each other. She never wanted to have children with me. I think I was a way for her to escape her family and be an independent woman.'

'What about you?' Every safety instinct Laura has is beating a warning not to ask this but she does so anyway.

Guy looks at her blankly. 'What about me?'

'You said neither of you ever loved one another.'

Guy laughs, exasperated, and stands up. 'Well, you know about me, don't you?'

Hedley and Gina, brushing their arms against one another walking side by side, appear at the table.

Guy puts his jacket on. 'Come on, let's go home, it's late.'

Back at the Gate House, the kitchen is a *Marie Celeste* wreck with a trail of cereal, spilt milk and sprinkled sugar ending in the god Zeus's basket, where he lies, snoring gently, his head resting in the sugar bowl.

'It looks as though rats have invaded,' remarks Gina, slumping in the armchair by the Rayburn, and kicking off her shoes.

'Oh, for heaven's sake, I thought pugs were too privileged to pillage.' Laura groans, automatically stooping to begin clearing up the mess. Through in the sitting room where, against Laura's wishes, Inigo had a vast television installed two days after they moved in, Fred and Shane are watching something unsuitable with blood spraying everywhere. Laura averts her eyes and forces herself to speak in a kind and loving tone.

'Hello, darlings. Are the girls back from the disco? Did you find what you wanted to eat?'

'Mmph.' Fred grunts and shifts into a more comfortable position on the sofa, but doesn't bother to look up. Shane appears to have been turned to stone on his beanbag. Screaming, followed by blood glugging like wine issues from the television and Laura closes the door, happy to return to the squalor of the kitchen if gore is the alternative. Unheeding of the dirty plates, Guy and Hedley have produced a bottle of whisky, and settled purposefully at the table. They are not going home. Guy pats the chair next to him.

'Come and have a drink, Laura.'

Gina puts a Marvin Gaye track on, and turns the overhead light off, bathing the kitchen in a pleasing rosy glow, caused by the pink T-shirt that is draped over the one lamp. She begins to dance. Hedley, swigging a gulp of his whisky, joins her. The sensible thing now would be to go to bed, but then look where being sensible gets you, thinks Laura. Guy lights a cigarette, and with a sense of leaping into the dark, Laura takes one too.

Pins and needles, a dead weight on her arm, and a thumping void behind her eyes. Laura wakes with a jolt. She is in bed with Zeus licking her cheek joyfully. She turns away and finds herself staring at a body. The head is invisible beneath a twist of sheet, but in horror Laura examines shoulders beneath a T-shirt, the ribcage rising and falling slowly. She has been sleeping with someone. Oh God. Oh hell. What is she to do? Where can she hide? Nausea, remorse and shock surge in her throat and she leaps up to rush to the loo, wishing that alcohol abuse had killed her instead of leaving her maimed and guilty, the destroyer of a happy family. Returning, only marginally purged, some minutes later to get her clothes and escape, she forces herself to look at the bed again.

'You have to confront these things, you have to face up to your wrongs,' she tells herself, and holding her breath, pulls back the sheet. A tangle of long red hair and Dolly's perfect profile greets her. Laura's relief is indescribable and eclipses her hangover for several moments. But she must have done something wrong to have the instinct of guilt, and sure enough, next to Dolly is another body. She tugs the sheet from this newly discovered form, her heart and head throbbing a vile tympany which may well kill her at any moment. It is Becca, curled up on the edge of the bed and rubbing her eyes as Zeus burrows down next to her. Relief, and the effort of dressing, pump a thousand more toxins around her body, and she totters downstairs moaning weakly, 'I need to go to hospital, I must go to hospital.'

Of all the horrible sights in the kitchen, the worst is Hedley, ashen-faced and emitting a gentle non-stop moan. His sleeves are rolled up and he is using the might of both hands to try and turn a tap on to fill the kettle. Laura takes the kettle from him, saying, 'That's the wrong tap. It doesn't work. I'll do it if you go and let the goat out.'

'Guy's done it. He's milked her too.' Hedley clutches his head with both hands as if it is a rugby ball, and staggers to the table to sit down.

'Oh, he's here too, is he?' Laura presses her hands to her cheeks so Hedley doesn't see her flush. She sips some water to practise before committing herself to tea. 'Where did you sleep?'

A spasm of alarm crosses Hedley's face. 'Err, umm. In the girls' room. They said I could, don't you remember, because they said they could easily both fit in with you.'

Laura blunders on, wielding obtuseness like a blunt instrument. 'So you and Guy shared that rickety old bed of Dolly's? God, I must have been drunk. I should have put Gina in there. I wonder how she liked the sofa? It's hellishly uncomfortable to sit on, so lying on it must be like sleeping on cobbles.'

Hedley shifts uncomfortably but is saved from answering by Gina drifting in, yawning ostentatiously and draping herself along the Rayburn. Hedley attempts a smile but just looks vacant. Laura, watching them, finally realises who slept with whom in Dolly's bed.

'I'm starving,' says Gina, shaking her hair voluptuously and throwing a speaking glance at Hedley. Guy appears in the doorway.

'Good,' he says, 'because I've found some eggs in the barn.'

'But I haven't got any hens,' Laura insists, breaking off, distracted from this mystery by the sight of Gina suddenly putting her hand out and pressing it against Hedley's chest in the v of his open shirt.

'Well, there are certainly some here, so I'd make the most of them if I were you,' says Guy, putting the eggs down.

'I've never seen anyone so keen on Hedley,' Laura whispers to Guy. 'It's a miracle.' He finds a bowl and begins cracking eggs into it.

'It's good. She's allowing her inner feelings a free rein,' he replies, referring to Gina's drunken and repetitive cry of the night before, that this new country life will help Laura become true to her inner self.

Hedley's hand circles Gina's wrist, and Laura, pushing between them to place a saucepan on the Rayburn, is suddenly struck with a pang of envy. Hurling toast into the oven, her sense of ill-usage intensifies. It is not on account of her brother and Gina's passionate liaison – no, she is thrilled about that. But she can't bear the injustice of having suffered wrenching guilt herself, as well as nearly dying of shock at the sight of a person in her bed, when in fact her existence is drearily blameless. The mists of alcohol begin to dissipate, aided by the scrupulous kitchen cleansing programme Laura is operating, and she is left with an increasing belief that a blameless existence does one no good at all. As she reaches the larder door for the second time in the walls and woodwork subsection of her housework marathon, she comes to the conclusion that she might as well have had tempestuous sex with Guy all night, as she has suffered agonising guilt for it without having any of the fun.

Polishing the greenish brass taps on the unworking sink, Laura broods. She is shocked to find herself gazing at Guy across the table when he refuses more toast, and thinking, I would have made you hungry. Really, the morning is becoming a subplot to *A Streetcar Named Desire*. She must pull herself together and think wholesome thoughts before the children come down to be corrupted.

'Mum, if your friends are going to shag all night, can you please get me some earplugs? I had to put up with you snoring as well and I'm knackered.' Dolly erupts into the room with unusual energy for the morning. She pulls a handful of soft white dough from the centre of the loaf Hedley has been slicing for toast, and swings herself onto the table chewing defiantly, her gaze not swerving for a second from her mother's face.

Laura feels herself blushing, or more likely having a hot flush. 'I don't snore,' she says sulkily. Gina giggles, Guy raises an eyebrow. It is unbearable in the kitchen with all these people. Her country idyll, her bolt-hole has turned into a doss house for the disaffected and the young. It is all wrong. Laura's phone rings. Inigo's mother, Betty, is on the other end.

'Laura, I need to talk to you.'

'Hello, Betty.' Laura gestures frantically for everyone to be quiet.

'I've been meaning to telephone you, but I've been on a cruise. Inigo sent me a ticket and I went to New York – very comfortable it was too.'

'Good.' Laura is pleased Inigo organised Betty's trip to visit him. They'd planned it as a seventieth birthday present months ago, and Laura had utterly forgotten about it. 'Did you have a nice time?' She is finding the enunciation of words very tricky this morning, but Betty doesn't seem to notice.

'Oh, Inigo is so wonderful, and he really does try to keep his feet on the ground, although I don't know how with all the attention he's getting.' She leaves an accusing pause then starts again, 'But I want to know why you don't make biscuits for him and the children.'

'What?' Betty has gone nuts, it shouldn't be a surprise, but it is. Laura clutches her head and listens.

'Yes, biscuits. The dear boy had to rush me into a private room as soon as I got there to ask for my shortbread recipe. He needed it for his show, poor lad, and he's never made a biscuit before in his life. I don't know why you haven't been helping him with this, Laura.'

'Er. Umm.' Another flush sweeps over Laura's face. It is impossible to answer Betty, there is nothing to say. In desperation Laura shouts, 'Oh Betty, we haven't seen you for so long. Come and stay when Inigo gets back.'

'No, thank you,' she says, 'I'd prefer you all to visit me. I gather it's not very comfortable where you are.'

Inigo, you treacherous creep, thinks Laura.

Shattered, she turns on her heel out of the busy kitchen and marches into the garden. Once there she slows for a moment wondering what to do, and unable to think of anything, wanders aimlessly around the garden. It is hideously abundant. Grass, tall and collapsing under its own weight, billows like the sea from the house to the apple trees where the weight of the blossom has torn a branch down, the bark peeled back to reveal a split of yellow new wood. It must have happened last week, but bindweed has already crept up the branch, coiling heart-shaped leaves among the pink blossom. Beyond the apples, nettles soar like rockets in another lagoon of grass and a breaking wave of cow parsley froths to the bottom of the wall. Everything needs doing. There is nowhere to look that does not cry out for love and attention. It is as demanding as any member of the family, and Laura is already overwhelmed. Zeus paddles towards her through the lawn, his tiny tail curled neat and crisp like a very chic black tortellino. Laura picks him up, and whispers, 'How I love to hug my pug.'

CHAPTER 16

The start of summer half-term is unsatisfactory all round. Dolly spends it in a cloud of acid-green bad temper because they haven't all gone to New York. Deaf to Laura's protests that it was never an option, Dolly becomes convinced that it is a conspiracy between her mother and Fred because they want to go to sodding Norfolk. Inigo rings plaintively from the airport and Laura remembers that she had promised to meet him with the children and had every intention of doing so until Dolly became a witch from hell.

'Oh my God, Inigo, we haven't fetched you, I'm so sorry.' She cannot think of an adequate excuse because there isn't one, she simply forgot, although she'd remembered earlier, when she had dressed in high heels and a skirt, special effect clothes chosen to show him she cared. But not enough to remember him.

'Well, I'd better get a taxi,' he says in a piqued tone. 'It'll take you an hour to get here and I'm through customs and everything. I'll see you soon.'

'Lovely,' says Laura, encompassing relief at not having to go as much as pleasure at his return.

Fred, having trawled the neighbouring streets to their house with a spatula, looking for roadkill for Vice, is red-faced and almost tearful, convinced that she will starve to death between now and the next visit to Crumbly.

'No one cares about Vice and her well-being,' he complains to the sitting room at large. 'And I've got to support her myself, and she must have red meat.' He sighs and clucks, and for the first time Laura can see Inigo in him.

'Oh shut up,' snarls Dolly. 'Go and get her a burger or something.'

Fred perks up. 'Cool, d'you think she'd eat something like that?'

'Well, maybe raw mince,' suggests Laura. 'Go down to the butcher on the high street and get some, and while you're at it, maybe a bit of chicken breast for Zeus – he's been off his food.'

Thus Inigo arrives home from too long away to find his family busy creating a feast for their pets. No one even looks up when he lets himself in, lithe and suntanned from hot weekends on the Long Island beaches, and his daily gym session. He bounces on the balls of his feet into the hall, determined to be upbeat. 'Hi, gang, how's it going?' Sunlight dances in the kitchen, and the chaos that always surrounds Laura is familiar and soft after weeks of New York. Inigo looks around; he knows now, from the cognitive group therapy classes he has been attending in

Tribeca, that meeting after absences can be challenging, and he is determined to meet the challenge on the chin. And Laura looks younger, carefree and more like Dolly's sister, laughing over that vile blot Zeus. Apart from the dog, Inigo can handle the challenge of coming home.

'Oh my God, Inigo, you're looking so well.' Laura leaps to her feet, kicking over Zeus's bowl and scattering his food across the white perfection of the floor. It's such a relief to see him and to find that she really is pleased. His smile as he kisses her still makes her heart leap, which is amazing considering the wanton direction of some of her thoughts recently.

No amount of sifting has helped her make light of her rekindled interest in Guy, and she cannot banish a growing suspicion that life would have turned out more satisfying if she'd stuck with him all those years ago, instead of taking on Inigo and his ego. Gina says it's just bored wife-manquée syndrome and it will pass, but then she would. She has been insufferably smug since coming to the Gate House and Laura has ignoble thoughts about Gina putting on five stone and Laura offering her diet recipes. But now the topic of interest is Inigo.

Fred tucks Vice hastily into his pocket before greeting his father, and is overtaken by Dolly, who has been studiously ignoring the pets and engrossed for half an hour in composing a new ringing tone for her mobile telephone.

'Dad, you're back. Listen to this, d'you recognise it?' And Dolly whirls her phone, now clad in a Barbie case with a Miss Universe bikini and sash, in front of Inigo's face. It warbles an upbeat few bars of 'Danny Boy' before subsiding into silence.

'That's great, Doll,' says Inigo. 'Now let me say hello to Mum properly.'

'You're really brown and really thin,' observes Laura, wishing she could say the same for herself. She gazes at the floor, then over Inigo's shoulder, unable to meet his gaze. Inigo's heart pounds; he has always adored Laura when she behaves elusively, and he's missed her so much. More than he could bear to tell her. He lifts her chin.

'Let me look at you.' He pulls her towards him, kissing her hard, and Laura melts and wants to cry at once. Zeus finds the intensity of the moment a bit much, and lifts his leg on Inigo's black leather luggage. It takes all the self-control Inigo has learned in ten sessions of expensive therapy to keep him holding Laura instead of kicking that ugly little black hell-pig down the stairs to the basement.

Within hours of his return Inigo is once more the centre of home and hearth, and every member of the family has cheered up. Laura is aware of this, but squashes feelings of inadequacy as a mother and provider beneath a radiant sex goddess exterior, with plans to examine her shortcomings, and Inigo's at a later date.

Having despatched the children to the delicatessen and bakery with a list and instructions not to return until both the dog and the ferret have walked off their breakfasts, Inigo walks over to Laura leaning against the cooker and puts his hands over hers on the rail. Unconsciously Laura straightens herself, and they look at one another, standing close, but not touching except their hands. Her heart is jumping, her mouth feels dry. Inigo doesn't say anything, he can't, he's suddenly too nervous, but he kisses her. Laura wants to reach up and put her arms around him but her hands are still under his. He moves his hands onto her hips, pulling her towards him, still kissing. Laura is on tiptoe, leaning every part of her against every part of him, wanting him, but distracted by being in the kitchen. Inigo undoes the first button on her shirt. She stops his fingers on the next.

'Let's go upstairs.' She is walking away as she says this, swinging her hips in her skirt. On the stairs he puts his hand under the skirt and runs it up her thigh. She grins, loving being wanted but not so consumed by desire that she doesn't look at her watch.

Oh God, how long have the children been gone? Is there time?

Laura runs up the last few steps to their room; this is better than Inigo had ever hoped for. 'What's got into you?' he laughs in the bedroom.

'You.' She unbuckles his belt, looking straight into his eyes. Inigo traces her spine with a finger through the cloth of her shirt. Following a shiver of nerves to her waist, Laura tries to banish the domestic pre-occupations which are coursing through her mind.

Is there enough Parmesan cheese or should she have told Fred to get some?

Inigo undoes the buttons on her skirt and it falls around her. She steps out, still wearing her shoes, not trainers today, but her most impractical high heels with ankle straps in honour of his return – fawn leather, beautiful, fragile and not at all mumsy. Sexy but not as sexy as boots, she thinks. Inigo's skin is smooth and smells of rain and summer. Laura runs her tongue down from his chest. His stomach contracts and he sighs her name, his hand raking her hair so it falls heavy and free like water.

What time is Lola the dog walker coming?

Inigo leads her to the bed. Laura runs her hands down his arms following the curve of the muscles and guides his hands to the buttons of her shirt. Inigo groans as her shirt falls away, and Laura undoes her bra, urgency pulsing, thrusting into her mind, blood rushing to her lips making them hot and her skin tingling, electric.

Will he mind that she has employed a dog walker once a week, or will he understand that it's such fun for Zeus to be with the whole gang that it's worth the money it costs? Perhaps he won't notice.

They fall together on the bed and the linen is cool on Laura's skin.

Oh God, she should have rung the electrician while Inigo was away.

But now he's back. He's here: he's everywhere with his hands and his mouth and his skin. She's not thinking about anything now, because she's being. She's lit up, flaring hotter, arching, yearning, reaching – and it doesn't matter that the key just turned in the front door because it's now, it's now. And it's everything.

In the kitchen Inigo rolls up his sleeves, drags the dustbin over to the fridge and throws away everything Laura has been keeping cool for the past few weeks.

'God,' he says, holding up a soup carton with purple bubbles issuing from its open spout. 'I remember you buying this borscht before I went. It shouldn't still be here – you'll get mould spores in everything.' He pours the bubbling ex-soup down the sink and turns to the cooker to stir a fragrant pan of garlic, onion and herbs. Laura, barefoot by the door, grins because he is the only one who cares about the kitchen and she is handing it back to him now – what a relief. She tears a corner from the bread and sticks it in butter while Inigo isn't looking.

Dolly frowns at her. 'Mum, you go mental if we do that,' she complains. 'Now can you move, I need to get some flour from behind you.'

Dolly has shown no interest in family life recently, and scarcely any in food unless it comes freeze dried and just needs hot water, but the force of her father's personality in the kitchen has her wrapped in an apron, breaking eggs, and peering at a recipe book, determined to add her mite and create sensuous, spoon-licking food to celebrate Inigo's return. Inigo slices tomatoes and stacks the slices with mozzarella, stuffing basil leaves in each layer until he has built a plate full of small towers, red, white and green and smelling like heaven. Dolly folds dollops of egg white into chocolate and cream and slides chocolate soufflé cake into the oven. Even Fred catches the creative fervour of the kitchen, and with maximum mess and spillage constructs four unlikely cocktails. Laura is left to lay the table, wash up after the others and surreptitiously feed Zeus again.

It's not great being the kitchen scullion, she reflects, scraping onion off the bottom of the heavy frying pan, but it is a lot better than having to cook, or worse still, think of what to cook. Inigo's return from New York has coincided with Laura's culinary repertoire shrinking to baked potatoes or boiled eggs. It isn't that she can't cook anything else, it is the determined refusal of the children to eat anything she has taken care over that has caused her to edit her repertoire so severely. There just isn't any point, and Laura is delighted to hand the apron back to Inigo, while conceding that his ability to make every meal into an event and even a celebration, is a better recipe for tempting the jaded palates of Dolly and Fred than any combination of ingredients could ever be.

Over lunch Inigo is expansive. He is feeling great despite jet lag. His libido is up where it should be, and he reckons he could match a thirty-year-old for virility, while being in no hurry to do so. His wife is pretty hot too. Oh all right, no, she isn't technically his wife, is she? Sometimes now Inigo is aware of nudging irritation at not being married. Maybe it would cheer Laura up to get married? It might stop her thinking so much about country life. But if she wanted to be married, wouldn't she have said so? Who knows with Laura? Certainly not Inigo any more. Anyway, his exhibition has been applauded by the critics, and the public are streaming in too, attracted off the street by the smell of baking. Inigo has appeared on three different talk shows and his biscuit recipe has inspired a television company to approach him for a six-part series on art and cooking. The recipe was almost Inigo's come-uppance, as he left for New York with no idea of how to make biscuit dough, having used Play-Doh for all maquettes. His cooking has always been more along Mediterranean lines with copious olive oil and capers. But within forty-eight hours he was asked for the recipe he would be using for his pastry-cutter, and to buy time he had to pretend it was embargoed for another twenty-four hours. His mind was blank, but fortunately, his next appointment was to meet his mother off the boat. She would have a recipe for sure. Betty was only too willing to help, while saying in disappointed tones, 'But I don't know why Laura hasn't been helping you with this. She should, you know.'

Inigo, who was missing Laura painfully due to the alarm of almost being caught out, maddened his mother by saying, 'She doesn't cook, she's too busy.'

Betty's shortbread recipe has gone down a storm, and several of the leading hotels in New York are serving the biscuits with a very nasty sweet sherry as the new aperitif, and calling it the Inigo Miller. While finding the drink repulsive and the combination of it and the biscuit somewhat grannyish, Inigo cannot help being flattered by becoming a bar-room name – surely just one step from entering the vernacular, where infinite fame is assured.

He allows himself a small private smirk and addresses his children. 'So Fred, Dolly. Tell me what's new at school?' Inigo is rewarded with a blank look from each of them.

'Dunno,' says Fred finally.

'Nothing,' says Dolly.

Laura sees Inigo is looking disappointed. 'It's half-term,' she reminds him, and Inigo nods and starts telling a story about a beautiful actress he met at a party last week. No one is listening. Dolly pushes her salad and the tomato and basil in her mozzarella stack to one side of her plate and leaves it, as she is on a purity binge and will only consume protein and no vegetables at all. Mysteriously, this diet allows all fizzy drinks and crisps, but Laura has learned now that the quickest way to get Dolly out of any of her obsessions is to act as though they are completely normal. Fred cuts his lunch into small cubes and posts it onto his lap, where Vice is curled content-edly, consuming whatever comes her way. Laura, having listened to the first half of the story with commendable concentration, suddenly notices a small white swelling on Zeus's ear. 'Oh you poor thing, what have you done?' she exclaims, right across the moment when the actress's boyfriend was refused entry to the night club where the actress and

Inigo were enjoying a tequila slammer as the first drink of an evening planned to return jaded New Yorkers to teenagers.

'She's got the leading role in the new Disney movie, so we'll be seeing a lot more of her,' says Inigo.

'Oh my God, Mum, it's squidgy,' squeaks Dolly from the floor where she is examining Zeus's ear. 'And I can't get it off. It's stuck, it's stuck.'

Fred drags his chair back and crouches beside his sister and Zeus, who is trembling now and licking his lips apologetically.

'Oh, rank!' exclaims Fred. 'There's a smaller one too on the inside.'

Inigo tries to continue. 'And she wants to buy one of my—'

Laura leaps to her feet and rushes to scrabble in a drawer by the cooker. 'Oh for heaven's sake! I've just remembered what they are!' she shouts. 'They're ticks. He must have got them in the garden at the Gate House last weekend. We just need a cigarette to burn them off.'

Inigo is torn between exasperation that no one wants to hear his story, surprise that there are cigarettes in the house and irritation that the bloody Gate House has contaminated his return with grey polyps. He will not even allow his gaze, never mind his thoughts to stray towards the amount of attention Zeus is getting.

'You don't smoke,' he says, frowning as Laura puffs on a cigarette to draw red heat into the end. 'Neither of us do. We gave up ages ago.'

A guilty look flashes across her face. 'They're not mine, someone left them here, but actually I quite like having one from time to time.' She inhales defiantly and at length.

'No one in New York smokes at all,' says Inigo crossly.

'So what do they do about ticks?' asks Fred, leaning over his mother as she applies the flaring tangerine heat of the cigarette to Zeus's black velvet ear.

'They don't have them,' says Inigo, trying not to sound superior as he knows it's not helpful, but rather longing to be back there, and away from the sordid elements of English pest life. 'The only reason you are smoking is that you lack self-control. Now let me put it out for you.' He reaches over to Laura, but she is beyond his reach, bending over the pug whose mouth is turned down in deepest gloom. Laura pushes Inigo away. 'Don't be silly, I'm smoking to get rid of the tick.'

'Mum, be careful, you'll burn him!' screams Dolly as Zeus yelps and scuttles under the table.

Laura drags surreptitiously on the cigarette, just to keep it alight, she assures herself. 'No, I won't. Honestly, I've done this thousands of times before and you just burn the tick. The heat hasn't touched his ear, he's just frightened.'

'Poor thing. I'll hold him,' coos Dolly, crawling after the dog. Fred and Laura watch for a second as she tries to extract Zeus from the table legs, and hearing him whimper, both crawl in too. 'Let's just do it under here,' says Laura.

Inigo is left alone at the table with half a famous actress story untold, and substantial evidence that his family prefers pest control to conversation. Nothing is going well in the greater scheme of things.

CHAPTER 17

At the studio on Sunday morning matters are worse. Dust and piled-up post greet Inigo when he opens the door and he is on the telephone to Laura immediately.

'Hello?'

'Hello?' Laura is piling supplies to pack into the car as Fred shouts through to her from the computer the meteorological predictions for the next few days at Crumbly.

'It says there's going to be an ice cap,' he announces gleefully. 'Oh, no. Sorry, that's in Antarctica. We're having flash floods and freezing cold wind.'

Dolly groans, 'Oh no. Do we have to go? I'd rather stay here and finish my project with Becca. That house is so dank when it rains. Can't we wait until tomorrow? Then we won't have to be there for so long.'

Laura, tethered to the telephone, flaps her hand at them to be quiet and continues to throw things into a basket. Matches, batteries, candles, her theme this week seems to be power; last week it was air, and she took a bag of balloons, a bicycle pump and a harmonica in her pile of essentials.

'Have you been to the studio at all while I was away?' Inigo paces in front of the windows of the studio, rolling his bicycle wheel in front of him, agitated and querulous.

'Er, yes, I think so.' Laura isn't concentrating; she is trying to open the fridge door with her toe as her arm cannot reach from within the circle of the telephone's wire.

'But it's like Sleeping Beauty land here – there's dust everywhere, and unopened post and it looks completely neglected. Manfred has left six messages about that bloody papier mâché. I finished it in such a rush to get back to you that I expect it's sodding well imploded or melted. This is the centre of operations for me. It's very important that you keep it working if I'm away.'

Laura is irritated by the tone of his outrage – it's his bloody studio after all, not hers, and if she doesn't choose to go there when he's swanning around in New York, it's her own affair.

'I've been busy,' she says silkily.

Inigo's pacing subsides next to a desk on which a large blue-bottle fly has died. This is the last straw. He spins his bicycle wheel like a coin upon his finger and yells down the line, 'Why can't you get your bloody act together and look after things properly? I get home and the fridge is full of mould, the studio is

227

thick with dust, your precious dog has got ticks and I expect the children are infested with something unspeakable, and all you do is carry more and more rubbish from home to your play house in the country. Get your act together, Laura. I've got to speak to Jack. At least my sodding agent takes care of things.'

Laura only hears the end of this tirade as the phone has slithered from her shoulder while she concentrates on filling a Tilley lamp with paraffin.

'Oh yes, I will when I've got time,' she agrees sarcastically, 'but at the moment I've got too much to do. We'll sort the studio out next week when the children are back at school, shall we? Come home so we can leave for Norfolk. You'll feel so much better out of London.' Her anger passes and automatically she soothes him, talking him down off his high horse.

He responds sulkily. 'I won't be better out of London, I hate the countryside,' he growls. 'I should really stay here and get some work done, but I suppose if I want to see you and the children, I'll have to come to that dump.'

'Yup,' agrees Laura, relieved that this conversation is on the telephone and not taking place in front of Dolly who would use it as ammunition in her stockade of sulking about going away. Laura tries to rally the sinking sensation she experiences by smoking a cigarette. It was too much to expect that Inigo's homecoming would be an unqualified success, but at least she had the sense to let him return to the studio by himself. He had wanted her to go with him and Laura had almost agreed to, indeed would have done but for the persistence of Fred who, having crawled out of bed at eleven, claimed he wanted her to help him with some homework he now refuses to look at.

Laura adds his folder to a pile of things to take to the country. With any luck Inigo will relax once he's at the Gate House. Laura, blissfully uninterested in its domestic shortcomings, can't imagine anyone not relaxing there. She and the children have been as often as possible while Inigo was away, and she is addicted to it now. Inigo can chill out and when he is ready he can help Fred with his geography project. Fred is on section six: 'Analysis of data and geographical conclusion'. Even reading the heading transports Laura straight back to the school feeling of frustration and boredom. It is, however, the sort of thing that Inigo uses in his work, minutely collaging endless maps, tufts of grass, photographs and the odd stone to create a bewildering whole; he will be quite at home with it. Just as well, as Fred certainly isn't. When Laura asks him what he is doing for his geography project, he looks at her blankly for a while as though she is speaking an exotic language.

'You know,' she says encouragingly, 'what topic or subject have you chosen? It might be something like cliff erosion, or it might be artesian basins – that must be a popular one as I seem to remember that London is one or is on one. I just wondered what you are doing your project on.' Laura sits down at the table opposite her son, propping her chin on her hands, awaiting an answer with real interest. Fred's expression changes from blankness to pain, presumably at the effort of thought. Finally he manages to drag the word, 'Dunno,' from the distant part of his brain used to operate speech. He then subsides, clearly exhausted by the effort, back into the cereal packet he was reading when Laura first approached him. The ignorance is odd, considering he claims to have reached section six of the project, and disturbing. Laura wonders if he might have contracted a hideous amnesia virus like an invaded computer, or if it is just his teen hormones manifesting themselves in sluggish contrast to Dolly's smouldering hysteria. Combine these two with Inigo's giant baby stance and Laura begins to wonder if she can stand any amount of time with them all in the cottage, and to think of the goat with sincere affection as the only sane member of the household. The linchpin.

As it turns out, Inigo can hardly see by the time they arrive at the Gate House, and remains in the car for some time after it has stopped, moaning, gasping and sneezing. 'Poor you. I'll bring you some water,' says Laura, not very sympathetically as Inigo is a difficult invalid and has been a vile passenger – Laura was forced to take the wheel on the way, so violent were his paroxysms. The hay fever began as they passed the sign announcing their arrival in Norfolk. Even through his wheezing attack, Inigo was able to point this out. The road swept out of a shaggy density of pine trees and climbed a hill to a point where two vast fields stretched away on either side to the horizon. Laura gazed out across the field on her side of the car at corn ripening and swaying, a smattering of poppies dancing crimson above the green-gold whiskers of barley, and sighed her pleasure. Inigo, on the other side, took one look at the frothing crome-yellow of acre after acre of ripe oil-seed rape and began to sneeze. Ten minutes after the first sneeze he conceded defeat and pulled into a lay-by to swap places with Laura. From there, with a soothing baby wipe laid over his eyes by Dolly, and a few puffs on Fred's inhaler, he spent the rest of the journey suffering loudly and complaining about Laura's driving.

'Oh, I feel ghastly. My head is full of snot,' he announced with relish, interrupting himself to shout, 'GO ON – you can pass that one now. I can see – I can see there's nothing coming.' Inigo slammed his hand against the dashboard as the car jerked, slowed and then accelerated, swaying wildly, past a caravan. 'Come on, Laura, we've got a lot of ground to make up with that stop.'

Laura, knuckles white, her neck muscles knotted and her jaw clenched, glanced sideways at him and was pleased to see he looked wiped out. 'Just shut your eyes and leave me to drive,' she suggested between gritted teeth.

'*Achoooo!* Oh God.' Inigo paused to blow his nose. 'I'd love to, but will we actually ever get there?' he gasped through his handkerchief.

Only by rubbing soothing lavender oil (dispensed by Dolly the pharmacist) into her wrists and turning up the Waylon Jennings tape to top volume does Laura survive the journey without assaulting Inigo. Having got him into the house and bent double over the bath where he is running cold water over his head to get rid of any pollen that might have alighted on his slicked-back hair, Laura takes herself out to the compost area pretending that she will plant some marrows there, but in fact stealing a moment of peace. Fred joins her. 'What are you doing, Mum?'

It is amazing how frequently Laura is asked this by her children. When she is hanging out washing, when she is cooking supper, when she is putting clothes away, when she is waiting for them in the car. For Dolly and Fred, these seemingly routine moments are fraught with mystery, and Laura herself is evidently a creature of strange and elusive habits.

'I am casting runes upon the compost heap and then I'm going to make some witchy spells,' she replies promptly.

'Why are you doing that? Why don't you just plant them in the ground?' Fred grabs the packet of seeds from her hand. 'Hey, these aren't runes, they're giant courgettes. Silly Mum.' He grins at her fondly and Laura laughs.

'What are you doing anyway?' she asks him. Fred is on his way to milk Grass.

'Dad's gone to lie down,' he explains. 'Dolly's making him a disgusting drink with leaves and nettles and stuff in it. It looks rank. I wouldn't drink it, but she says she looked it up in a book and it's good for his hay fever.'

In the sheds, the darkness is a cool contrast to the sunny afternoon outside, and the smell of goat and musty hay tickles Laura's nose. She sneezes and Grass leaps in alarm across her pen.

'Let's tether her in the garden and milk her later,' suggests Laura, finding herself less keen on goat work than she had anticipated. Fred leads Grass outside, her chain clanging like a convict's, and bangs the metal spike into the ground.

'Mum, you know what? I think Tamsin has got a telescope trained on our house. Whenever we come she arrives like milliseconds later.' And on cue, the gate opens and Tamsin and a small girl with a giant inflatable hammer march up the path and into the house.

'I don't think it's a telescope,' Laura tells Fred. 'It's teen semaphore – Dolly must have texted her to say we're here. I wonder who that baby person is?'

Opening the kitchen door moments later, Laura shrinks back, not wishing to interrupt the conversation between this child and Inigo. The latter, a large red spotted handkerchief mopping his nose, is sitting at the table transfixed by the small figure who has settled, legs crossed, sunglasses akimbo on her head, on the bread bin. She has had to climb onto the table to sit on the bread bin, and she is thus looking down on Inigo in the manner of a teacher. An imperious teacher.

'Do you want to know how to wash a worm? Yes or no?' Head on one side like a small bird, the child regards Inigo intently.

Inigo apparently does, since he nods. Gesticulating with small confident hands, the child elaborates.

'Well, what you do is you get a thin bowl – one you've stretched – and you square up the worm and you put it in the bowl.' This on a note of triumph. Beaming, she looks around the room, eager to embrace a larger audience. Laura and Fred remain hidden behind the half-open door.

'Anyway, then you soap the worm and dry it, and then it's ready to go back on the grass.' She gives him a measured look. 'Or you can eat it if you like. How do you like that?' The little girl jumps up and capers on the table. Inigo tries to talk her down.

'I think you should climb off there before you hurt yourself. I don't think Tamsin would like to see you on the table,' he urges.

The child throws him a mischievous look. 'No, she wouldn't,' she agrees. 'But I don't really care what Tamsin likes today.'

Recognising signs of bumptiousness, Laura decides to interrupt. She steps in and scoops the child off the table.

'You be careful, young lady,' she says lightly, not wishing to alarm her.

'I'VE ALREADY BEEN CAREFUL!' roars the child, red-faced with the ignominy of being carried by a stranger. Inigo edges away towards the stairs but is blocked by Dolly and Tamsin coming in, both self-consciously batting neon-bright eyelids.

'Oh, thanks for keeping an eye on her for me. I'd better take her home now for tea.' Tamsin squats to embrace the child. 'Hello Beauty, what have you been doing?'

The Beauty's tears vanish as if a plug has been pulled on them. She presses her hands to the sides of Tamsin's face and turns it to the light. 'Can I wear some make-up like yours?' she demands.

Dolly laughs. 'Oh Mum, isn't she cute? She belongs to some friend of Uncle Hedley's and Tamsin is looking after her for half-term. I'm going to help her.'

Laura realises that this is the child in the christening paddling pool. 'Good luck to you both,' she says with feeling, as Tamsin carries the infant out of the house, accompanied by new fury because The Beauty is not ready to depart yet.

'Is it safe?' Inigo's red handkerchief appears around the door like a flag of surrender, and behind it Inigo, his eyes still small slits in blotched red skin despite the application of camomile tea bags and more baby wipes. 'I'd forgotten what small children can be like,' he marvels, shaking his head. 'That one is diabolical. It's called The Beauty, but I've never seen anyone turn ugly so fast. She found me lying down upstairs and decided to be my nurse. I've been given three spoonfuls of neat Ribena which she insisted was Calpol, and I've had my temperature taken with a nail file. The only way I could stop her ministering was to come downstairs for a lesson in worm management. You know she keeps worms – she had about ten in a tangle of mud in her pocket.' Inigo shudders, sneezes and takes himself off to watch cricket on the television with Fred.

Laura is secretly glad he is ill; it stops him challenging her authority here, and has made him too feeble to protest at the changes wrought since his last visit. In his absence the emphasis in the Gate House has swung determinedly towards Inigo's big enemy – nostalgia.

It began with Guy's housewarming present, a copy of the *My Guy* annual in which seventeen-year-old Laura, along with Guy and Hedley, appeared as a model in one of the photo love stories. Guy brought the book round one Sunday recently, when he came to receive his orders concerning Grass – having agreed to become her babysitter during the week. Laura was crouching in front of her broad beans when Guy arrived, singing them a song of encouragement. Cally always insisted that sung-to plants performed better, and although she could hardly be classed an expert as she only possessed two urban window boxes, Laura was so desperate for bean success that she would follow any lead.

'Here, Laura, I've been doing some clearing out and I thought you might like this.' Guy waved the book, and laughing, Laura took it from him.

'Let's have a look, Mum.' Fred, Laura's reluctant garden assistant, thrust between his mother and the book, snorting mirth which turned to stunned silence when he reached the page starring Laura. There she was, riding piggy-back on Guy who, pale and etiolated as he then was, looked about to collapse with the strain. 'Girls On Top,' read the caption. 'How to get your boyfriend where you want him and keep him there.' Fred blinks and turns the page, still not speaking.

Imagining his silence to be respectful, awestruck even, Laura leaned over Fred's shoulder and said mistily, 'It was such fun. Do you remember the one where I had to pretend that plank of wood was my boyfriend and you came and challenged it to a fight?'

'WHAT? You mean you did more of these love stories? Was Guy actually your boyfriend then?' Fred dropped the annual onto the struggling broad beans and looked between his mother and Guy, his mouth slack with disbelief. Taking their silence as confirmation, he staggered back in mock alarm. 'That is the saddest thing I've ever heard. I hope you didn't tell Dad – he might divorce you when he gets back from America, it's so lame.' Fred's tone was withering. Laura turned pink and glanced at Guy then away fast because he was looking at her.

'Um, yes,' confessed Guy, looking hunted. 'Once in the dim mists of time Laura was my girlfriend.'

'He can't divorce me because we aren't married, are we?' Laura retorted, brushing earth and leaves off her annual and hugging it to her.

'Aren't you?' asked Guy, raising his eyebrows in surprise.

'Er, no,' said Laura, somehow wishing she hadn't disclosed this information. And then, to change the subject, 'Have you got any more? I'd love to get hold of the others and stick all the pictures in the loo or somewhere.'

Fred groaned faintly. 'I can't believe you're actually going to have these where people can see them,' he complained. 'I've got to tell Dolly, she'll go mental.'

He wandered away, shaking his head and muttering, clearly much moved.

'I should still have the others somewhere,' said Guy. 'I'll have a look.' He dug his hands into the pocket of his jeans and looked at the ground. 'Celia has been going through everything and taking all her stuff away, so I'm left with heaps of chaos I can't really bear to sort.'

He looked so bewildered and so bravely bereft with the elbow of his jersey worn to a hole and his tall frame hollowed with shock, that Laura felt a lurch of compassion and smiled warmly. 'I'll help, if you like. I'm good at other people's disorder – it's just my own I can't deal with.'

CHAPTER 18

Inigo's hay fever is little more than a memory and a sodden handkerchief the next morning, which is maddening as Laura has planned to go and finish Guy's sorting for him. The vigour with which Inigo yells, 'What the hell is that pile of suburban shite?' at the hissing and chiming of the Goblin Teasmade, leaves Laura in no doubt as to his mood. Admittedly it is seven in the morning, but Laura is always delighted to be served tea whatever the hour, and especially since finding this domestic classic in the attic at Guy's house and making it her own. Inigo wraps a pillow tightly around his head and turns his back on Laura and the open window behind her, through which silver birdsong wafts in snatches and a whip of rose stem scrambles. Laura sips her tea, soaking up tranquillity and chatting to the silent Inigo. He's not asleep, no one could be asleep with their hands almost knotted around a pillow wedged over their head, but he probably can't hear her. Still,

239

chatting in bed in the morning is the sort of thing couples should do, so Laura does it.

'I've been helping this old friend Guy – you know, the one who looks after the goat for us – to clear his junk out.' Inigo makes no response, Laura nudges him. 'Well, I was helping him a couple of weeks ago anyway, although I never finished it, so I ought to do that.' It is good to make it sound like a chore, Laura thinks. 'And I've got to go to the village later this morning to sort out the table-top sale we've organised for next weekend, so will you be OK here with Doll and Fred?' She looks hopefully at Inigo's back. It quivers. 'The sale is to raise money for the church, and I can't believe how friendly and helpful people are being here about it. It would be a good opportunity to promote Guy's organic business too, so I thought I'd make some leaflets—'

Laura stops, interrupted by a spine-chilling groaning sound from beneath the pillow and a tiny, muffled voice saying, 'This is like a nightmare. When I went to New York you were my dream woman, sexy, clever, sharp, maternal – everything I ever wanted. All right, so you're a bit clumsy and you don't always remember useful things, but you were everything I loved.'

Well, you never bloody said so, did you? Laura thinks, biting her lip to stop herself yelling, 'You are a sexist pig!' as Inigo bursts from under the pillow, red in the face, and leaps out of bed, striding about stark naked, intent on his message.

'And now look what's happened. You've got this hovel here like a chutney Mary, and you've become a lesbian dog-lover type with Women's Institute written all over your face and Do Gooder stamped on your bottom. I can't stand it. You've probably got hairy legs. Now you listen to me.' Inigo pauses and points his forefinger at her accusingly. 'The only table-top stall you're doing is an Allen Jones Private View for me in this bedroom and that's that.'

Laura rolls her eyes and looks at the ceiling. Allen Jones, with his pneumatic rubber doll goddesses, has always been Inigo's favourite artist when he's annoyed with her. It's not great listening to this sexist diatribe, although it's quite funny watching Inigo marching up and down. If men want to be taken seriously then they must wear something, but this is not the moment to remind Inigo he has nothing on. There is a screech of brakes outside as the postman stops by the box at the gate. Inigo grabs a towel and wraps it around himself.

'And who *is* this guy Guy? Fred showed me that *My Guy* annual.' He stops, and says with feeling, '*My Guy*, for Christ's sake. You could have done *Penthouse* or something decent.' He glares at Laura again and restarts his pacing. 'I know perfectly well that Guy is that bloody farmer from your past you used to go misty-eyed over. What are you doing minding his business for him when my studio is covered in dust and you haven't asked one single question about the show in New York? That hideous dog of yours is more interested in my work than you are. At least he walked around my portfolio. You just bloody tripped over it. You'd better watch out or you'll be so dug into Norfolk mud that you can't get out.'

It isn't helpful, but Laura begins to laugh. Inigo in his bath towel, ranting his way around the room, throwing the odd look of loathing at the Teasmade, is so very comical. Laura has never found his tantrums particularly threatening. She is used to men with mood swings, and in fact, she is increasingly sure that the energy of Inigo's temper is the energy he harnesses for work.

She runs through the list of things she wants to achieve this weekend, trying to find something for Inigo to do which will take his mind off the affront of Guy's table-top sale. Tying up the roses? No, Fred is doing that; he promised because he kicked a football into the most overblown one and it collapsed on top of him, and Laura feels it is important that he should be the one to put it right again. Looking after Grass? Well, that's supposed to be Dolly's job, time-shared now with Guy who leaves notes with cartoon drawings of himself pushing Grass up the hill to his farm, or messages purported to be written by Grass complaining about the facilities in his yard. This chore was forced on Guy a few weeks ago by Hedley's behaviour. Bored with banging in fence posts for her field when he wanted to be off with Gina, up for the weekend to stay with him, Hedley announced one Sunday afternoon, 'Actually, I don't want to be responsible for this goat any more when you're not here. I'm going to have Grass butchered.'

'You can't,' protested Laura.

Dolly burst into tears and rushed from the room screaming, 'You're a heartless bastard, Uncle Hedley, and I'm going to become a vegetarian from now on.'

Fred, hearing her as he came in, shook his head in amazement, and held up his ferret until he was looking into her glistening black eyes.

'Don't worry, Vice, I won't let that crazy veggie anywhere near you. She might spike your roadkill with tofu mix.'

Laura, forced out of her most enjoyable perusal of a plant catalogue by Dolly's slamming and sobbing, sighed, steeled herself and rang Guy to ask if he knew a goat sanctuary Grass could be sent to. Guy's suggestion that he could time-share the goat himself was one of rare nobility. 'And if we get bored of each other I can put her in that paddock Hedley made you,' he had pointed out.

It is hard, Laura admits to herself, dressing without speaking and carrying the Teasmade past the glowering Inigo, to keep him on the pedestal he likes to occupy, when others are acting with so much more generosity of spirit.

By the time Laura has given everyone breakfast, and helped Dolly make an outdoor milking parlour for Grass, the morning is half over. Guy telephones.

'Hi, Laura, I've finished sorting the junk; I thought you were probably a bit too busy to fit it in. I've been up all night making plans.'

He sounds brittle and not himself. Laura takes her phone upstairs and looks out of the window at her vegetable plot bright with marigolds, borage and vivid green pyramids of peas, trophies from a plant sale for a neighbouring church.

'What's the matter, Guy?' She notices she hasn't removed the labels, and wanders out into the garden, still on the phone.

He laughs wildly. 'Oh, Celia has won. She wanted to keep the name of the business – my business – for her disgusting sugar-beet potions. She's done what she hoped to – she's taken something that matters hugely to me, just out of spite. I've got to find a new name and frankly, I'd like to jack it all in.' He sighs, miserable and bitter.

'I'm sorry,' says Laura, and something inside her deflates, leaving a sense of loss that makes her want to sob.

'Anyway, I'm going out to Greece for a bit to look at some farms there. I'll see you in a few weeks. I'll miss you, Laura.'

Laura switches off the phone, and walks back to the house, not liking the gloom that has settled on her with this call. What should she do now? She's been pretending it's fun to be useful, organising this table-top stall, when in fact it's been fun to hang around with Guy. If only Inigo would take more of an interest in what she has done here. Guy understands; and Guy is leaving. Inigo just doesn't care about the Gate House as a place. Nothing exists for Inigo unless it's related to his work. With a pang of guilt she recalls his cry that she isn't interested in his work any more. Keen to make up for this, Laura sets off down the road to find him. He has been gone for some time, armed with a digital camera and a notebook. She meets him on his way back; Inigo is bouncing with good humour.

'This is good,' he shouts to Laura. 'The village is so primitive. The inhabitants are so friendly.'

Laura winces. 'You could just call them people,' she suggests.

'Oh, don't be so ridiculous and politically correct,' he roars. 'Now then, let me have a look at this milking business.' He marches over to Dolly, who is browning her back in a purple halter neck while Grass stands in the shade of a large silver canopy. 'That's my light reflector,' protests Inigo.

'I know, it's really good for getting a suntan,' grins Dolly.

Instead of making a fuss, Inigo crouches to film Dolly's hands as they flex around the long hot udder. 'God, it looks like a pair of those bloody sweet potatoes, or maybe brown parsnips,' he mutters. 'It's the weirdest shape I've ever seen.'

'Poor Grass, don't listen,' says Dolly, who has entered a halcyon phase with Grass since she stopped being shut in her shed and became a free, laidback goat with a field.

Later, Inigo finds Laura harvesting a row of salad leaves and dreaming of opening a salad bar in the village with Guy.

'It's great,' he says, stepping over her neatly edged beds to hug her, all the fury of the morning forgotten now. 'I've got a new project. It's called *Nanny State* and it's opening with the milking shots really close up. I'm going to explore udders, breasts and milk.'

'Oh are you? Great!' says Laura, speaking enthusiastically to hide her guilt, and actually thinking it sounds a bit kinky at this early stage.

'Yes. It will be my entry for the National Academy Award this year. Where's Hedley? I need him to take me to look at some cows' udders.'

CHAPTER 19

Thrusting her feet into a teetering pair of heels, Laura winces. It would appear that her feet have put on weight during the summer. She wriggles her toes and, for good measure, her bottom, and stands on tiptoe in front of the mirror, leaning forwards to try and see her whole reflection. The top bit, her face, is fine, but Laura is uneasy about everything else. The black chiffon dress she has chosen is meant to wrap over, leaving a delectable cleavage and the occasional flash of leg, but no amount of wrapping in either direction achieves the desired effect; Laura is either entirely exposed as if she is wearing a porn star's nightdress, or hidden up to her chin with suffocating fabric.

How can this be? Last time she wore it, it worked. That was the summer evening she and Inigo drove to London for dinner with Manfred. Laura was reluctant on that occasion because she was discovering the joy of jam-making, a form of cooking which seemed so different from creating meals that she lost her inhibitions and entered into it with gusto and success. That success has clearly not rolled over into dressing, Laura thinks crossly now. Pulling the ties, turning herself sideways, holding her stomach in, she observes her reflection critically. It's no use, the dress, chosen because it is her celebration outfit, has sensed her doubt. It will not fall into place for this party and persists in making her look like a folded pancake.

Inigo's selection as Artist of the Year by the National Academy will be announced this evening at a party in an old test-tube factory in East London. Inigo already knows the result because Jack, his agent, had a mole in the selection committee, and has used this knowledge to ensure television coverage of the announcement and the beginnings of a sponsorship contract for Inigo with a rubber company. Even now, Inigo is sitting in a limousine hired by Jack, heading for the party along with Carl the rubber magnate and his long-legged blonde assistant who, now Laura comes to think of it, was wearing a successfully draped wrap-around dress with tassels falling provocatively across her thighs as she wriggled up to make room for Inigo in the car. Laura wonders, belatedly, what they do with their rubber.

Inigo, suave in his giant fly dark glasses, managed to shake hands and appear urbane climbing into the cream leather interior of the car, despite Zeus, who escaped from the house and hurtled to the car to join his master in keen pursuit of fun and adventure. However, Zeus failed to achieve the necessary momentum to get him into the car, and could only stand on his hind legs, tongue lolling, pleading to be lifted in. Laura, in her dressing gown getting ready, ran out to fetch him, biting the inside of her cheek hard to stop herself giggling at the absurd spectacle of so much power confounded by so little a dog. Inigo and his entourage drove off with much back-slapping and the clamping of large wet mouths (Carl's and Jack's) around cigars. Laura is very glad to be travelling separately and hopes to be able to find the announcement of Inigo's triumph properly thrilling by the time she gets there.

To be frank, the news that Inigo has won a giant silver-plated painter's palette and a lifetime's free entry to any of the Academy's shows doesn't thrill her to the soul. It is not, after all, the first time that Inigo has received this particular accolade; indeed, the palette from his previous success ten years ago would still be cluttering up the basement had Fred not added it to the jumble of items at the table-top sale a few weeks ago in Norfolk. Venetia Summers's mother Araminta bought it, as far as Laura remembers, for one pound fifty, to give to her friend the vicar.

'Rev Trev will love this,' she had enthused, handing over her money to Fred. 'It's like a communion plate but bigger. I think there could be a chance that he'll use it for the collection on busy Sundays. I don't suppose you've got a lovely goblet to go with it, have you? So nice for a drop of wine now and then.'

Laura smiles at the memory and has to force herself back to the present and Inigo's big celebration. With every new success, the gulf between them is widening. Inigo's world is his work, and it is no longer Laura's. He was always going to be extremely success- ful, and Laura thought that was all she wanted. For a while, Inigo's work defined her as much as it did him. But now satisfaction is increasingly to be found in her vegetable garden. She is even beginning to enjoy cooking; it creates such a good send-off for the things she has grown to be praised and then eaten. Inigo himself admits that Laura's broad bean soup is peerless.

She peels off the wrap dress and wriggles into a plunging, saucy milkmaid outfit with a low-cut bodice and frills around the hem. Made of bright yellow and pink floral crepe, it is jaunty and rustic-looking. Inigo loathes it because it is not streamlined and elegant; Laura loves it because it is cheerful and makes her feel curvaceous, like Betty Boop. The addition of a coat should stop Inigo making unpleasant comments.

Leaning into the mirror, Laura drags a crimson- dipped brush across her bottom lip and closes her mouth to stain the top lip too. She can summon little enthusiasm for the evening ahead; it would be a lot more fun to be going to the pub in Crumbly with Guy and Hedley and having a game of pool. Probably with Araminta and the vicar. Laura blinks at her reflection, and picks up her bag from the small chair beneath the window. There is a thump on the bathroom door and muffled cursing; it is Dolly.

'Mum, Mum, Fred's hogging the computer look- ing up ferret rubbish. He's been doing it for hours – can you come and get him off?'

In the tiny pause where Dolly draws breath, Laura answers, 'No, I can't. I'm going out.'

Dolly doesn't for a moment slip from thinking about herself to noticing what her mother has said. 'And I can't find my pink T-shirt, and I've looked everywhere, and you said we would take Zeus to dog training tonight. Just you and me on our own.'

The self-centredness of teenagers is truly breath-taking. Laura opens the bathroom door, not for Dolly, but because she is now running late and must leave. Dolly is there on the threshold, tall now, so she is eyeball to eyeball with her mother. Draping a friendly but demanding arm around her neck, Dolly accompanies her down the stairs, leaning into her, whispering pleas. 'Fred won't mind being left here on his own while you and I go to dog training. I just think it ought to be two of us not three, but can we just look for my T-shirt? I think it might be—'

'Dolly, DOLLY.' Laura turns to face her at the bottom of the stairs, disentangling herself from the tentacled grasp, waving an exasperated hand in front of her face. 'I'm going out! Look! I'm wearing lipstick and party clothes. I'm going with Dad to a party. We can't go to dog training tonight, I'm sorry.'

Breathing shallow and fast Laura shrugs her coat on. Trying to ignore the gloom gathering on Dolly's face, in the droop of her shoulders, the slump of her body against the banisters, Laura kisses her briskly. 'Come on, darling, I did tell you days ago that I had to go to this thing.'

Dolly shakes her head. 'No, you didn't. You never tell me anything.' She gives her mother an evil look. 'You just aren't interested in anything any more that isn't to do with your stupid life in Norfolk.'

Laura sighs. Dolly is showing all the signs of working herself up into a hysterical frenzy and the party will be in full swing by now. Laura should be there. She pats Dolly's head, flashes an instant smile and picks up her keys, ready to depart. She looks at her watch and suggests soothingly, 'Watch a movie in my bedroom, and have a look in the ironing pile. I think I might have seen your pink T-shirt there this morning. Bye, darling. Look after Fred.'

Retching sounds issue from the sitting room, faintly accompanied by Fred's indignant voice. 'Don't be so sad, Mum! I'll puke if she tries to look after me. I can do it myself, thanks.'

Fuelled by guilt and a strong sense of inadequacy as a mother, Laura reaches the mystifying address in the East End. 'X Building, Work House Street, Hoxton' reads the invitation. Laura is convinced that the only reason the National Academy chose this place was its name; and locking her car, this conviction grows. It is a damp September evening and the slice of sky Laura can see is bruised purple above the yellow glow of the city. The street she is in has the empty silence of a film set – few cars parked along its narrow length, no lights in the dirty windows of five floors of warehousing in front of her, and at the end of the building, a grey block that must be the factory.

Regretting her choice of the yellow milkmaid dress when black, no matter how badly wrapped, would have been so much less conspicuous, Laura crosses to the factory and walks its length looking for a door. There isn't one, nor is anyone else arriving. A car alarm throbs in the distance but Laura can hear no voices, no footsteps, no music. Nervously, she reaches into her bag to check the address on the invitation, and on the *A to Z*, in case she has gone mad. Looking up again, she notices a ramp beyond the end of the building. It would be so much more enjoyable to get back into the car and drive home at this point, but it isn't even worth considering. Laura turns the corner and walks down the ramp towards a pair of big brown metal doors, one of which has a small opening like an up-ended letter box flooding light onto the ramp. A constellation of fairy lights Laura recognises as The Bear because she has seen it labelled as such in the National Academy shop, twinkles above the narrow doorway. Evidently, she has arrived.

Two photographers, both swarthy and wearing leather jackets, hear the click of her heels before they see her, and throw the lit remains of their cigarettes into the gutter. They lurch forwards, unbalanced beneath a battery of cameras and flash guns. Laura grits her teeth and raises her chin, knowing what will come next. The younger one almost hoists a camera to his face, and begins to shout out, 'Come on love, give us a—' but a whispered word from the other and he turns away, fumbling in his pocket for another cigarette, not wanting to catch her eye now he's been told she is no one they need to photograph. Laura flashes a tight smile at them and steps in over the threshold. It would be so much better for morale if they could just pretend to take a picture of you at these parties, she thinks. No need to waste film, anyone would fall for the tungsten gulp of a flashbulb, but that lit-up moment of being wanted, glamorised for a white bright second, would be as good as a drink for creating a small cushion of confidence with which to greet the party.

The room is colossal, ill-lit and loud when Laura walks in. There is no one she knows and no one she wants to know, and not for the first time at a party, she wishes she had worn dark glasses like Inigo, so she could hide the nervous sweep of her gaze around the crowd. There are hundreds of people here, all impossibly thin, striking poses with hips thrust forward and shoulders back or spines curved over a pointed toe to give an impression of angles and concavities.

A girl wearing almost nothing except a criss-cross of belts offers Laura a glass from one of the belt's pouches. 'Here, have a shot. I've got vodka, tequila or absinthe.'

God, what a choice. Laura teeters between living dangerously and diving into a bohemian abyss of drunkenness, and chooses the middle way – tequila. The alcohol burns a path into her stomach, and lighting a cigarette Laura nods at the bottle, signifying her enthusiasm for a second one. The tequila girl shrugs her indifference and refills Laura's glass, then moves on through the room. Feeling very much braver, Laura stares at the crowd, craning on tiptoe for a glance of a familiar face. Remembering her mother's somewhat redundant maxim that, 'At a party you should always have a talking point handy – how the room is heated, for example, or the many uses one can find for a ball of string,' Laura takes a deep breath and plunges into the crowd in search of Inigo and another, less challenging drink. She finds neither, but a warm hand clasps the back of her neck and Jack Smack presses a really horrible soft kiss on her cheek and a second, worse still, on her mouth.

'Laura, what a pretty dress!' His amused gaze travels slowly up her person, making her long to punch him on the nose, the patronising git. Smiling sweetly she steps back from him.

'Hello Jack. Where's Inigo? Have I missed the awards?'

Jack's attention span has never been impressive, but with her first words he has already lost interest, and his eyes move restlessly past her as he answers, 'Er, Inigo? Inigo? Can't tell you that, m'dear, but I do know you haven't missed any awards and,' he grips her by the elbows and swings her forcibly to one side, 'just stay there a minute,' he murmurs. 'There's the chairman. I must just catch him, we've been trying to have a word all evening.'

Jack dives back into the throng, his now realistic-looking bottle-brush hair sailing for a moment above the surface of strange figures before sinking with him into a fawning greeting. Laura is relieved to have got away so lightly from him. Peering round a man wearing a white velvet suit who is gazing silently, but passionately at a small electric fire which is dangling from a socket next to a label saying Hang Fire, Laura at last sees Inigo. She jumps up and down and waves, suppressing an urge to shout, 'Yoo Hoo!' because she would only be doing it to annoy him. Inigo raises one eyebrow to acknowledge her approach, but continues to nod and gesture to his companion, a figure draped in black feathers and lace and looking more like a shuttlecock than a person.

'Are you an exhibit?' Laura asks with polite interest, having kissed Inigo on the cheek and rubbed off the lipstick she inadvertently smeared on his face. Inigo laughs lightly while shooting Laura a venomous glance.

'Now darling, you must know Mabel Babel-Bentley? She's with the *Daily News* and, I think I'm right in saying, she is our most feared and revered art critic.' The pleading note in Inigo's voice is not lost on Laura. What fun. She puts her head on one side and scrutinises the pile of lace in front of her, deciphering a large, vigorously powdered nose and a bloodshot eye behind the filigree. She shakes her head regretfully. 'No. I'm sorry, I don't think I've had the pleasure,' she says, enjoying herself hugely. 'But then it's so hard to tell. People tend to blur into one after a few years of going to these parties.'

There is a snort from within the Babel-Bentley outfit and a muttered outpouring which Inigo bends his head to decipher. Laura's memory stirs, with the recollection of a children's programme she used to watch in which a creature looking very similar to Mabel Babel-Bentley had a walk-on part.

'Do you remember Michael Bentine's *Potty Time*?' she asks no one in particular. 'It was on when I was little anyway and – Ow! Don't do that, Inigo, I'll fall!'

Laura is thrust forwards and away from the lacy lunatic by a firm hand between her shoulder blades. Suddenly she is sandwiched between the wall and an ironing board with a Barbie Doll strapped down on it in front of a tiny toy train. Inigo stands over her, a black expression on his face.

'You bloody idiot,' he hisses. 'That woman is incredibly important. What were you playing at?'

'Well, she looks ridiculous. I can't take this nonsense seriously any more. I mean, look at this.' Laura pings the rubber band holding Barbie down and it flips away. Inigo slaps his hand down over the doll, as if protecting her modesty. Laura pulls his hand up, and holding it in both of hers, looks at him beseechingly. 'This is real crap, and it was shortlisted with your stuff. I think it's undermining, Inigo. You shouldn't be doing this any more, we're too old to play these games.'

Inigo's eyes are opaque with rage. He grips her arm and steers her away from the throb of noise in the party to a shadowy doorway.

'This is not crap.' He leans towards her mouth. Laura closes her eyes. Surely he can't be about to kiss her? She rather likes the swoony savagery of a snog in the middle of a row. Mmmm. Why not be a little depraved? However, Inigo merely sniffs her breath and steps back again.

'You're drunk,' he says accusingly, adding in a special slow voice for halfwits and drunken wife figures, 'Now listen to me, Laura. This is the art world and it pays for our lives. I have a reputation in it, and a place in it, and so do you, so pull yourself together and play the game, because if you don't we're on the streets.'

Laura pulls free, rubbing her arm, exhausted now, the alcohol flush already burned out and the truth of his words hanging in the air between them. Hot tears sting and fall on her cheeks, and her bravado landslides to dust.

'I'm sorry, Inigo. I didn't expect to feel like this. I can't play this game any more. I don't believe in it. I'm going home.' She squeezes Inigo's hand, then pats the back of it and walks away, biting her lip to stem the falling tears.

At home, she unlocks the front door and treads as silently as possible across the hall, wanting to reach her bedroom and not be seen by the children. However, the click of her key in the lock, the creak of a floorboard and the pug Zeus is at her side, the tip of his tongue peeping out, absurdly pink in the wrinkled anxiety of his face. Laura scoops him into her arms and runs up to her bedroom, where, placing Zeus gently on the bed, she takes off the milkmaid dress and pulls on jeans and a shirt. Grabbing a small bag, she flings in socks and jerseys, books and underwear, overtaken by the momentum of her own actions now. Zeus finds her behaviour upsetting, and climbs into the bag, burrowing into the pyjamas Laura flings towards him.

'Good, that's enough.' Laura looks round the room, slides shut all her drawers to hide the chaos within them, and picks up the Zeus-heavy bag, groaning a little at its weight. She opens it to reassure him before hoisting it onto her shoulder, and gazes in fondly. 'Don't worry, I won't leave you,' she says. Dear God, if Inigo could see her now, talking to a bag, he'd say she's gone nuts. Lucky he can't then. Laura glances at the clock on her bedside – it is only nine-thirty; she will be there before midnight if she goes now.

The children blink astonishment and yawn when she floods on the lights in the sitting room where they are watching television.

'Whaddryoudoin?' groans Fred, ducking beneath a cushion. 'Turn it off, Mum, I'm trying to watch something.'

Laura marches into the room and stands in front of the television. She keeps experiencing moments of panic when she is sure she shouldn't be doing this, but before she can change her mind and unpack the dog and her pyjamas, she finds she has done something to push herself further along the path towards going.

She tells the children, 'I'm going to Crumbly. I've got things that I need to do there and I'm taking Zeus. You two can come with Daddy at the weekend as usual if you want to, but I won't be back for a bit.'

'What do you mean "a bit"?' Dolly asks suspiciously. Fred, however, accepts Laura's behaviour without a blink.

'Cool. Mum, can you take my ferret with you? She much prefers it there.'

Dolly jumps up and stands facing her mother in the middle of the room. 'Does Dad know you're going?' she asks, her hands on her hips.

'Er, no.' Laura tries a competent brisk grin. 'But you can tell him if you like.'

Dolly's face collapses. She presses her hands to her cheeks and stares wide-eyed and shocked at Laura.

'You're leaving,' she gasps.

Rolling her eyes, Laura adjusts her bag on her shoulder. 'Yes – I mean no, I'm not leaving, I'm just going to Crumbly. I've got a lot to do there and I thought if I went up early this week I could get it all done for you at the weekend.'

Dolly continues to look stricken; Fred finally catches on to the existence of a scene taking place and hurls himself at his mother, lagging his whole weight on her waist. 'Mum, please take me with you. I can't stay here, I won't go to school. We could say I had flu, no one would know.'

By now Laura is regretting not just the way this evening has gone, but almost everything that has ever occurred in her life, with special reference to motherhood and the fact that her children are huge now, and so are still up at nine-thirty at night being obstacles to her escape instead of tiny angels tucked up in their beds sleeping innocently.

'Oh bloody hell,' she shrieks, stamping her foot in frustration. 'This is a sodding nightmare from hell.'

Dolly and Fred leap away as if they have been electrocuted. Dolly unzips Laura's bag and grabs Zeus, holding him high for a moment as if he is a football trophy.

'Stress-yyyy,' whispers Fred under his breath, and departs, muttering, 'I'll just get Vice and my stuff. Hang on, Mum.'

'You sh-sh-shouldn't swear,' sobs Dolly, now heaving with tears, hugging Zeus close to her chest and watching her mother with imploring eyes.

Laura is cornered and outwitted. For a moment she stands poised for flight, glancing wildly at the door, her bag clenched in one fist, the car keys in the other, panting slightly. Fred comes back, and both children stare at her apprehensively. Fred attempts a brave, reassuring smile and suddenly all the hysteric energy she has been relying on deserts her, and she drops bag and keys and slumps onto the sofa, her head in her hands.

'All right then, I won't go!' she exclaims, half-waiting for protestations of joy from her offspring.

'Why not?' Dolly leans solicitously over her, all tears gone now, a soothing nurse-like calm attending her every word and movement. 'You must go if you want to, Mum. We'll be all right.'

Fred drops a duffel bag on his mother's feet. It contains a trail of clothing and emerging from the pocket is the bushy and electrically smug-looking tail of Vice the ferret.

'I won't be all right,' announces Fred. 'I want to come with you and I don't want to stay here. Come on, Mum. Let's go before Dad gets back and tries to stop us.' Fred's eyes glitter with excitement, he is clearly enacting a scene from some ghastly Hollywood teen movie; Laura has played unwittingly into his hands and is now too confused and depressed to see a way out at all. Dolly's nurse-like references are more obscure, but Laura has no doubt that self-interest is fuelling her new enthusiasm for this departure.

'Why don't we all just go to bed?' she suggests feebly.

'No way,' chorus the children.

'Come on, you'll feel better when you get there,' soothes the new, weirdly kind Dolly. 'Here, let me take the keys. Come on, it'll all be fine, and look . . . we're by the car now.'

And somehow Dolly and Fred have martialled Laura across the hall, out of the front door and down the street to the car. Orange street-lighting throws a Haliborange glow on all their skin, and has turned the car dank pond green, its dials bleeping and flashing as Dolly leans in to put the keys in the ignition. Laura protests once more that Fred should stay behind and go to school, but no one pays any attention, least of all Fred who is strapping himself into the passenger seat, making a little bed for Zeus at his feet with a jersey and reminding Dolly to tell his friend Shane that he's gone away for a bit and doesn't know when he'll be back.

'I will. Byeee! Byee, Mummy, see you soon!' Dolly waves them off, and Laura finds that she is indicating, drawing out of the parking bay and setting off up the street towards Norfolk.

Fred settles back in his seat, twists the volume on the car sound system to high and in the pause before the beat begins, grins at her and says, 'This is so cool, Mum, I love it.'

'Oh God,' says Laura. 'Oh well, what the hell, we're doing it now.' And she grins back at Fred and attempts to sing along to his favourite rap anthem.

CHAPTER 20

A real, working weekday in the country is very different from being there on holiday. This is instantly noticeable when Laura walks into the village to buy breakfast for herself and the still-sleeping Fred. There is a bustling structure to everything, from the roar of tractors passing on the road to the clockwork charm of the village. Even the sun seems to be shining purposefully, glittering in through windows, forcing people out and on with the business of the day. Crossing the stream, Laura pauses on the bridge to watch the mist rising off the water, evaporating in the soft morning air. A lady in a red coat cycles past with a small terrier in her basket. Zeus watches with barely contained wrath as the terrier skims by, paws up on the front of the basket, ears floating behind, nose set high for autumnal scents and a pleased smile playing across his mouth.

'Good morning,' flutes the lady, her own nose high above a cheery smile, inclining her head graciously towards Laura.

'Good morning,' parrots Laura, amazed that this Ealing Comedy village life is really happening. On towards the shop, and all around, she sees people doing proper things; there is the milkman, beaming as he rattles and jerks down the street in his float, leaping out to place a bottle or two on a doorstep; he waves a greeting at an open window, trills a few whistled notes and blithely performs his ritualised slow dance around the village. In the small front garden of a cottage a young woman pegs her washing on a line slung between two laden apple trees. At her feet a toddler brooms a lorry across the mown grass, crawling to reach windfalls which he places in the lorry's trailer. Two doors down, the postman opens the gate and rings the bell, balancing a parcel and a handful of envelopes in one hand so he can pat the fat Labrador which appears when the door is opened. Over by the post office a bus idles, and a slow trio of pensioners embark upon the climb up its three steps, assisted by walking sticks and hindered by pull-along trolleys. Their labours are surveyed with sleepy amusement by a black cat sitting in the sun on top of the letter box. There is a loud clopping sound and Laura turns to see a shaggy horse trotting past the shop with a red-faced girl bouncing in the saddle. This is the last straw for Zeus; to him it is not an Ealing Comedy, but is in fact *Invasion of the Body Snatchers*, and he erupts into tinny, unrealistic barking. The horse screeches to a halt, puts its head down and starts snorting, regarding Zeus with spellbound fascination.

'I'm sorry, I'm so sorry,' says Laura, automatically expecting blame from the rider for being here at all.

'Oh, don't worry,' smiles the girl. 'I don't think she's ever seen a pug before and—' The rest of the sentence is left unsaid as the horse squeals, whips round and begins to trot away in the direction it came from. Hot with shame, Laura tries to bundle Zeus under her coat. The girl's voice floats back to her from beyond the last house of the village. 'PLEASE DON'T TAKE THIS PERSONALLY, WE THINK PUGS ARE GREAT.' With a sigh of relief, Laura puts Zeus down again, and tying him to a post, enters the shop.

Laura and Fred quickly establish a routine for their days which owes nothing to the dreary repetitiveness of the school run. Having always assumed that anything that is routine must by its nature be dreary, Laura doesn't really dare to admit that she is enjoying herself, and lives, as much as is possible for a separate human being, through Fred's pleasure. Fred is quite unable to believe his luck. He has been allowed a mammoth skive, and his daylight hours are filled with knife sharpening and mass destruction – to mention but two of his top pursuits. He has even received money – a twenty pound note from Betty and a cryptic message recommending him to study hard and ignore adults. Laura, taking this to mean her, is furious, and is only diverted from telephoning Inigo to complain about his mother's interfering ways when news reaches her that Grass the goat has escaped and invaded the village shop. By the time she and the now very fat goat return, Betty's iniquities have paled to nothing besides those of Grass. In a sixty-second raid, Grass, in common with those who win a minute to go wild with a trolley, managed to eat four packets of cheese slices, two boxes of doughnuts, an ice lolly, some crisps and a lettuce. She was just starting on a box of tissues when Laura caught her.

Fred, assiduous in his desire to be helpful and good, seizes one of Laura's many dithering moments and sets himself the Herculean labour of clearing the front garden.

'It'll be really good when we have enough flat grass in front of the house to make a football goal,' he observes, sitting down to lunch with Laura, goose-grass balls and leaves adorning his hair like his sister's multi-coloured accessories. 'I reckon it will be some time this year,' he says serenely, gazing across the bramble explosion that is the area in question, so far only theoretically changed by his hours of exertion.

'Do you?' Laura is impressed by his optimism.

As if they have always done it, Fred and Laura divide the dog walking and wood gathering, fire lighting and hanging out of laundry duties without any of the intransigence or martyrdom the family usually specialises in. However, should these useful qualities go unremembered, the telephone rings frequently with messages of stubborn saintliness from Inigo and Dolly.

'It was Fred's school's parents' evening last night. I went in your place. They said they were having trouble communicating with him. I gave them this telephone number but I had to admit he's a closed book to me. I blame that ferret,' is left by Inigo.

Dolly's are more to the point, and all in texted shorthand Fred has to translate for his mother. TELL DAD I ALWAYS GET MONEY FOR LUNCH NOT SODDING LUNCH ITSELF is followed by SINCE WHEN HAVE I BEEN ON A 9 O'CLOCK BLOODY CURFEW? WOT IS THIS – THE STONE AGE?

A pithy DAD IS A TOTAL S*** is the last message from Dolly for a day or two.

Although it is September, the summer is determined not to end, and each morning Laura is woken by low sunbeams slanting into her room, filling it with amber warmth. Grass is in full milk as usual and a fit of housewifery assails Laura. She spends a depressing evening decanting sour milk into various plastic containers, and is finally rewarded, in the small hours, by the beginnings of a pot of yoghurt. The next morning she phones Hedley.

'Come to breakfast in the garden, and bring Tamsin before school. I have created some yoghurt.'

'Christ, you'll be wearing sandals and growing hairs on your legs next,' Hedley replies, unconsciously echoing Inigo.

Laura gathers a plate of blackberries, admiring their shoe-shine black gleam as she places them next to the yoghurt in the middle of the table outside. To mark the importance of the occasion, the ferret Vice is wearing a purple ribbon, and Zeus, looking not unlike a giant blackberry himself, has been plumply deposited on a large pink velvet cushion Laura bought at a car boot sale for him.

Hedley arrives alone, and has entered the foraging spirit of the occasion by bringing with him a dead hare. He waves it at his sister, who recoils and edges away, not wishing to kiss either Hedley or the hare.

'I thought you could make that amazing pasta thing with hare,' he says hopefully, draping the corpse over the fence.

'I couldn't, but Inigo could. Let's ask him to do it if he comes,' says Laura.

Hedley looks around uneasily. 'He's not coming now, is he? I was hoping for a peaceful breakfast. Especially as Tamsin wouldn't come. She said she had to meet someone to get a lift with them to school. It must be a boy – she had so much make-up on she could hardly see to get out of the door.'

Fred ambles over. 'Mum, can we start, I'm starving.' He reaches across and grabs a fistful of blackberries.

Hedley frowns. 'You should stop him doing that kind of thing, Laura,' he scolds.

His sister raises her eyebrows. 'Why? It doesn't bother me, and anyway, I've had enough of telling people what to do. They never pay any attention and it makes me miserable. I've turned over a new leaf and I just don't care.'

A slow clap behind her and Laura turns to find Guy also laden with provender, grinning. 'Bravo. You tell them, Laura,' he says, and holds out a basket full of brown oozing mushrooms.

'What are you doing here?' Laura is shocked – she hasn't seen him for weeks. 'You're brown,' she adds accusingly.

'Sorry, Hedley told me he was coming, and I wanted to see you – and taste the yoghurt.'

Laura glares, caught offguard, sure he is laughing at her but not sure exactly why.

'I brought a few different mushrooms because I didn't know what you liked.'

Hedley interrupts. 'I didn't say you could come though,' he points out, not best pleased that Guy, who is a bit wild at the moment, is already hanging round his sister, and he's only been back from Greece for a few days.

The pot of yoghurt, always on the small side, seems particularly forlorn when everyone sits down, crowding over it around the small table. Hedley, Guy and Fred stare at it, then as one, all put their spoons down.

'I think Guy should fry a few mushrooms as an opener,' suggests Hedley, and Guy jumps up so quickly that he knocks his chair over. Fred picks it up and follows him into the house, intrigued by the sinister appearance of breakfast.

'Are any of them poisonous?' he asks Guy.

'No, not these ones.'

Fred prods at them with a wooden spoon. 'Oh, that's a pity. D'you think we could get some poisonous ones later?'

Left outside at the table with Hedley, Laura leans back in her chair and closes her eyes, seeking the sun's warmth as it melts onto her.

Hedley coughs and says conspiratorially, 'Laura, we should talk.'

She opens her eyes to find him leaning towards her across the table, concern and embarrassment expressed in the darting of his eyes and the attention he is giving to the sugar spoon.

'Are you staying here?' he says.

'What does it look like?' Laura retorts, rude because she is rattled and doesn't know what she is going to say.

He sighs. 'You know what I mean. Are you staying for good, you and Fred? And what about Inigo and Dolly and your life in London?' Hedley gives her a sharp look. 'You can't keep the boy out of school forever, you know. You've got to face the music some time.'

'But we've only been here a few days,' Laura protests. 'I needed some space and I decided to find it here. The weather's beautiful and I'm having a nice time. What's wrong with that?'

'Nothing,' Hedley replies, keeping his voice down because Guy and Fred are coming back now with a plate of fried mushrooms and a loaf of bread. 'But it would be a mistake to think this is the real thing. It's an Indian summer and they never last.'

Hedley does his best to outstay Guy, and would have sat all day, bristling like a guard dog, but Gina and her mother are arriving for the weekend, so he has a lot to do.

'I hope she likes crab,' he mutters as he departs. 'I can't cook anything else.'

Guy and Fred are talking about music as Hedley leaves, or rather Guy is listening, while Fred explains what is acceptable now.

'You can't really listen to that stuff any more,' he says. 'And it's usually true to say that if Mum likes it, it's sad.'

'Fred,' Laura protests. Her son holds up his hand. 'But Dad has good taste. I can lend you a tape he made me. It's good, it'll give you a new load of stuff to get to know.'

Guy nods. 'Good, I could do with catching up.'

Laura laughs at him. 'But you've never been into this kind of thing, have you?'

'No, but it's never too late to start.' His determined expression surprises her, but stops her teasing him further.

Hanging out the washing that afternoon, Laura reaches the final sock and feels the first drops of rain on her face as the leaves on the plum tree crackle with the whip of the wind. The golden morning has fled and a soupy grey light covers the sky. Unpegging the line of damp laundry again, Laura discovers a philosophical calm has come upon her. In the usual scheme of things, it would be infuriating to have to waste her precious time undoing the chore she had just done, but yoghurt-making-country-dwelling Laura seems able to smile to herself and muse that really it's no more time-wasting than the usual process of hanging it out wet, bringing it in dry, putting it away, waiting for Fred to cake it in filth or Dolly to scrumple it up and chuck it on the floor before Laura (and it is always her, no one else) scoops it up and puts it back in the washing machine. In fact, she could just put all the clothes back in the machine now and save herself and Fred the bother of wearing them.

A crack of thunder breaks Laura's reverie and she runs to fetch Grass in from the bank where she is tethered, yanking her chain so she trots fast to her shed where rain drums on the tin roof like tiny hooves. Leaving her with hay and a snatched handful of hog weed, Laura heads for the house to shut all the windows. She is guiltily aware that Fred is watching football on television, but comforts herself with the thought that it is Friday afternoon, so even if he was at school it would be almost time to go home now anyway.

There have been no messages from Inigo or Dolly, but Laura's close inspection of her mobile phone shows that the battery is flat; as Zeus has eaten through the charger there is nothing she can do about it. Trying not to think about the telephone box in the village, she begins cooking a chicken casserole from a recipe on the back of the salt packet. This will put her in a win/win position, she thinks, as Inigo will be impressed with her domestic skills if he comes, and if he doesn't, there will be enough for her and Fred to eat until they go back on Sunday.

'We're going back on Sunday.' She tries saying it out loud to make it real, but Fred is immersed in a goal replay, and doesn't hear her; Laura is not convinced that talking to yourself counts as real.

By evening she is almost climbing the walls with anxiety. What will she say and do if they come? What should she think if they don't? And what on earth will chicken casserole from the back of the salt packet taste like? The rain pours steadily, creating a dimension of claustrophobia for the evening. Laura cannot sit down; she paces the length of the small kitchen. A car idles in the lane and stops by her gate. Craning out of the window Laura can see nothing but the glare of headlights and a silhouetted cloaked figure running up the path, head bowed in the driving rain. It is the wrong height for Inigo, and anyway, there's no Dolly, not that she would dream of running anyway. Perhaps it's an axe man? Unlikely, but Laura's grasp on reasoned argument is slender enough for her to consider this option carefully before dismissing it because there is no sign of an axe. She breaks into slightly hysterical laughter when Guy bursts in through the kitchen door wearing a stiff oilskin cape in which he somehow manages to look like a rakish Mexican bandit rather than ET. He pushes the hood back and finding her manic laughter odd, glances covertly at her mug on the kitchen table, presumably expecting it to contain gin.

'It's tea,' Laura tells him. 'Would you like some?'

'No, thanks, I've got to go,' he replies. 'I need to check the ditches in my field by the stream. The water levels are rising ridiculously and I've got sheep in there.' He kisses her on the cheek and his face is cold and hard. She is horrified by how erotic she finds this

274

moment with him standing there in his oilskins. She had thought she had passed through her crush on Guy and was out the other side now. He hands her a small bouquet. 'Here, these are the herbs you'll need for cooking the hare. I thought I'd drop them off now as I won't be here this weekend, I'm going to a farm management conference in Kent.'

Disappointment lurches through her. 'Oh,' is all she manages to say.

'I should be back on Monday, so I'll see you then.' Steam begins to rise from Guy's dripping cape. 'I'd better go. I'm soaking your house. Your supper smells good.' Laura nods, her throat tight, eyes smarting because she won't be here on Monday. It is ridiculous to be this worked up about going home. Anyone would think she was never coming back.

She mumbles, 'Yes, I know, I have high hopes for it. Next week would be nice,' and she waves Guy off down the white-lit path of his headlights.

'Who was that, Mum?' Fred's sangfroid in the face of his father and sister's possible and imminent arrival is commendable. Laura cannot suppress a small squeak of alarm when he puts a hand on her shoulder as she sits, perusing the classified advertisements in today's paper.

'Oooh! You made me jump.'

Fred laughs. 'You're mad, Mummy,' he says affectionately. 'What's for supper?'

'Well, it's a sort of casserole,' Laura explains doubtfully. 'But I think we should wait until the others come.'

'Are they definitely coming?' Fred peers into the cast-iron stewing pot, his voice muffled as he sniffs his mother's culinary effort. 'Blimey, it smells quite nice,' he adds.

'No need to sound so surprised. I followed a recipe,' says Laura defensively, pinging off the walls almost literally, as she searches for a cigarette she knows Hedley left here a few days ago. 'It will help, it will help if only I can find it,' she mutters.

Fred lolls against the table, watching her rummage in the drawers, reach up to the high mantle above the Rayburn, then run her hand along the windowsill.

'What are you doing, Mum?' he asks eventually.

'I'm trying to find the cigarette Hedley left here.' Laura is on her hands and knees with the torch now, craning her head to see behind the kitchen cupboard.

'I've smoked it,' says Fred.

Laura reaches beneath the cupboard with the broom handle, sweeping it along and creating a small storm of dust and cobwebs which billows out in her face. 'I can't see it, but it must be here – you've WHAT?'

Suddenly she is on her feet facing him, her heart thumping, legs turned to jelly. Fred has admitted to smoking a cigarette. Her cigarette. Actually Hedley's. He's pinched a cigarette and smoked it all on his own without peer pressure. Oh God – if he can tell her this, what deeper iniquities might he be hiding?

Laura feels a chasm open in front of her and Fred speed away on the other side of it. She has no idea what to say. Does it matter? Is it true? Did he like it?

Why didn't he tell her? Why did he tell her? What does it mean? Is she angry? Should she be?

Laura does not ask any of the hundred questions which have popped into her mind. None of them seems the right thing to say. What is the right thing to say?

'Have you got any more?' Damn! Hell's Bells. Definitely not the right thing to say. No, no and no again. It just escaped. How wonderful life would be if you could unsay things you should never have said.

Fred reaches in his pocket, and passes Laura half a cigarette. 'I didn't like it much so I put it out. You can have the rest if you like.'

Laura can't help feeling that he is handling this scene much better than she is. Wordlessly, and shamefully, she lights the fag end, narrowing her eyes as the match flares close to her hair. She exhales and glances sideways at Fred. There is no point in telling him not to smoke. There is no point in being angry, and anyway, she simply isn't angry. Laura tries to be self-aware, and decides that she is amazed that he told her, and honoured. Beyond that she can't see a need to react.

'Oh well,' she says.

Fred pulls his Game Boy from his pocket and begins twiddling his thumbs on the controls. 'Why aren't you cross?' he asks, after a few moments where the only sound in the room is the sprightly electronic jangle of his game.

Still feeling her way through this peculiar situation, Laura hesitates. 'Er, I'm just not,' she says, flailing for her next words. Luckily, there is no need to grapple far for them, as Zeus suddenly hurls himself at the door, barking his toy dog bark.

'Hooray, they're here,' shouts Fred, rushing out to greet Inigo and Dolly.

Humming like someone in a gravy commercial, Laura ladles chicken onto plates and wishes she was wearing curlers and a pinny to complete the homely effect. Dolly staggers in carrying several spilling bags of books and wearing a huge pink and black rugby shirt, ostentatiously inside out and even more ostentatiously marked with a name tape saying Luke Johnson.

'That smells nice,' says Dolly, caught off her guard by the domestic scene Laura has created. Laura hugs her, her heart leaping perversely, as Dolly reverts to her customary scowling; she has clearly remembered that it is never a good thing to be enthusiastic.

'Who's Luke Johnson?' Laura asks casually, but Dolly fields her effortlessly. 'Oh, just a friend at school.'

'He's her boyfriend and he's really lame. He likes crud music and— Owww!' Fred comes out of the sitting room to be thwacked by Dolly, and retreats again sniggering.

Inigo had expected at best a chilly cheek to kiss on arriving, and at worst a locked door, particularly when none of his messages were answered today or yesterday. To be greeted by Laura smiling and cooking – well, it surpasses not only his expectation but also what he deserves. Inigo is cravenly aware of his mission this weekend, and finds himself wishing Laura didn't look so happy and relaxed. She is laughing now, at Dolly's impersonation of Gina (who had been outraged to discover Laura had gone to Norfolk without telling her). Better by far that Laura should have greeted him with sullen rage. Then he would have had something to bargain with. There seems no good moment to begin the conversation, but Inigo does vigorous penance in advance all evening, washing up, putting away, admiring the chipped china Laura has collected from junk shops, and consciously holding back from his customary overbearing behaviour.

It is curiously restful, taking the secondary role in the kitchen. Taking time to look properly at Laura, Inigo sees her as if for the first time in years. She is dressed differently now, in jeans and an old, frayed shirt, and her hair is wild, coiled around a pencil to hold it up on her head. On the floor, leaning against Dolly's chair, her arms wrapped around her knees, Laura looks young, and carefree in the firelight. She leans forwards to push a log further onto the fire, and he sees the back of her neck as he saw it the day they met, and he wants to cry out with the rawness of how he feels.

Fred yanks his sleeve. 'Look, Dad, I've made this,' he says, and passes him a stick he has carved a handle for. This is unbelievable. Fred doesn't make things, he breaks them. That's how it works in this family. Inigo is absurdly moved, and impressed by the detail of the carving.

'What did you use?' he asks.

'Oh, Guy lent me his knife. It's a really good one, and I tried to model what I was doing on some of the Red Indian symbols. He showed me them in this book.' Fred reaches behind to the windowsill and passes his father a book.

Bloody Guy again, thinks Inigo, but forces himself to say, 'That's great, what an interesting book.'

Dolly, kicking the chair as she beeps her way through a series of quickly executed messages on her phone, gazes around the room. 'Urgh, this is so boring,' she groans, sliding down in her chair until her head disappears beneath a cushion. 'There is nothing to do here. Can I go to Tamsin's and stay with her tonight?'

'No.' Inigo hardly looks up from Fred's stick, and Laura hears a storm mounting with Dolly's fast intake of breath and the clamp of her teeth as she grits them for battle. Laura jumps up.

'I know, let's all go for a walk,' she says brightly.

'It's bloody raining,' hisses Dolly. 'And it's the middle of the night. You're mental, Mum.'

'Oh all right, we won't then.' It is fine that the idea was a non-starter because Dolly is smiling now; the storm has passed.

A glance at her watch tells Laura it is almost nine o'clock. What on earth can they do for the rest of the evening? It is hard to remember supposedly normal evenings in the bosom of her family because they are so few and far between. In London she and Inigo are often out at Private Views, and if they aren't, Inigo returns late from the studio, cooks supper and then balances a few domestic items or he fiddles around on the computer. There has to be a major family crisis or the smell of fantastic food for Fred to unplug himself from the television, while Dolly is always obsessively texting, bathing or talking on the telephone, according to her mood swing. All four of them sitting gazing into the fire suddenly strikes her as being absurd, and very sweet. It is as if they have become other long-ago people. It isn't a good idea to smile though; Dolly might see and it will make her furious. Of course it can't last. It doesn't. Inigo spoils it.

'Why are all your clothes too small?' Inigo asks, out of the blue and without preamble. 'Have they shrunk or are they meant to be like that?' Thinking he must be talking to Dolly, Laura turns to defend her, and finds he is staring at her. His tone is perfectly friendly; he clearly doesn't realise how cutting the remarks are.

'They aren't too small, they're supposed to be like this and it's meant to be flattering.' Almost subconsciously she pulls her stomach in to stop it lolling against the waistband of her jeans. Inigo has not finished.

'But it isn't flattering unless you're twenty-five,' he insists. 'And if they're meant to be like that, why are you the only person who wears them?'

'What do you mean?' Laura tries to maintain detached interest, as if she and Inigo are having a non-personal debate, but he is not interested in this technique.

'Well you don't see Gina going around with a too-small shirt on and those jeans that make your bottom look square,' he says, folding his arms as if that is the end of the conversation. Exasperated, Laura turns back to the fire. It isn't going to become a row, it would be crazy to argue about clothes. She keeps her voice steady and sensible, soothing even.

'Well, if I had another shirt I'd wear it, but this is the one I brought with me here, and this is what I'm wearing. If you don't like it, don't look at me.'

He is unable to let her have the last word. 'I don't see why you're getting aggressive, Laura. No one has to wear that teenage stuff except teenagers. You're too old for it now.'

'What are you trying to say?' Laura asks, bewildered.

'I'm saying grow up and get real about your life,' he replies promptly. 'You are not a child of nature living under a blackberry leaf, you are a mother, you are nearly forty and you are a partner in a conceptual art company.' He stands up, thrusting his hands in his pockets and begins pacing.

Laura stares into the fire. There's no reason to cry, there really isn't. It's just such an odd feeling being told you look horrible when you were thinking about cosy family life at the fireside. But there is no such thing after all. And he's not getting the last word in.

'Thanks, Inigo,' she murmurs, and with forced sprightliness, she scrambles to her feet. 'I think I'll go to bed now.'

It's only half past nine, but there is no way she can keep going this evening with Inigo here. He delves into the log basket and begins piling logs in neat pyramids along one wall of the sitting room. He works quickly, his lips pursed, and doesn't look up when Fred sighs, 'Oh Dad, do we have to have balancing here?'

Brushing her teeth, Laura notices the mattress behind the bathroom door from the summer weekend when the house was full to exploding point. If she puts it down on the bathroom floor, with sheets and an inviting brand new blanket, maybe Inigo will get the message and sleep there. There is a malicious joy in imagining him snuggling down next to the avocado green of the panelled bath, the drip of the loo as it finishes all its flushing and babbling and settles for the night. Laura rinses her face and the water feels good – earthy and gentle, fresh as a stream. A child of nature living under a blackberry leaf? Should she go outside and snuggle down in the hedge? No, it's not worth sinking to guerrilla warfare herself, it will simply upset everyone.

On the way upstairs, she grips the banister. Her legs are heavy, weighted solid as if they are filled with flour, and weariness trickles and seeps through her skin and into her bones. Getting into bed she groans aloud with the pleasure of lying down, and settles back against the pillows with the latest weepalong novel, recommended by the morning chat show she and Fred watched when they first arrived.

Opening the book, Laura gazes instead at the wall beyond her bed. Despite Inigo, or better still completely ignoring Inigo, there have been real improvements in her life recently, and it's important to take stock of them, so as not to be too downcast by his unpleasantness. There is the small joy of each physical achievement she has experienced in learning how to put up shelves, cultivate a vegetable plot and nurture a nanny goat. Laura had never imagined that practical skills could be so rewarding, but now the idea of returning to London and the cerebral challenges of the studio, and Inigo's brilliant career, is unappealing when set against the reclamation of the garden and the weirdly satisfying pickling and jam-making programme she has planned under Guy's supervision. As someone who has never been interested in food beyond fuel, Laura is bemused by her own newfound enthusiasm for making things. She finds herself jotting a note on the dust jacket of *Thief of My Heart* to remind herself to try the rosehip and crab apple jelly recipe she was given by the lady in the village shop today.

The latch clicks, and automatically Laura hides the book under her pillow.

'Are you all right?' Inigo keeps his head bowed even now he is through the low doorway.

Laura nods, turning her face away, furious to find that a tear has slipped out and down her nose. Inigo sits on the bed. Nothing about him belongs there – his green jacket instantly attracts a small puff of feathers from a hole in Laura's flowery quilt, and his oiled hair is slick and almost menacing in the rosy light which dances through a raspberry lace shade

Laura created from an old petticoat. He sneezes; she passes him her handkerchief.

'I didn't mean to upset you.' He sneezes again. Laura sighs. She doesn't want to have a painful, raking conversation now, she is tired. And he's got hay fever.

'I'm not upset, I'm tired.' She picks up her book.

'Chirst, you haven't started reading that rubbish again, have you?' Inigo looks at the book with so much disgust that Laura wonders if he has mistaken the cover illustration for something specifically offensive to him – a naff cartoon character or a fast food outlet, for example.

'Mind your own sodding business, I'll read what I like.' She turns over and lies down, hoping to signal that the conversation is over.

Inigo moves nearer, emanating anxiety and smelling faintly of woodsmoke. 'Laura, there are things we need to talk about,' he says, sniffing as dust motes rise in the room, disturbed when he moved the lampshade a trifle to see her better. 'I think we've reached the end of the road in London.'

Laura's heart thumps in her neck. She's looking at him now; her mouth is dry and her hands are clenched fists on the pulled-up sheet. It's like a warped scene from *Red Riding Hood*. She flings the covers back and sits up so she is next to Inigo. Both of them stare at the floor.

'What are you saying?' she asks, and it's like falling in a dream because she can't go back now they're talking like this, and she doesn't know how she would choose her life to change if she could.

Inigo's arms are folded across his chest, his elbows crunched on his knees as if he has been winded. 'I think we should move out. Rent the house for a bit,' he says. 'I want to give New York a go. The opportunities are there for me and my work and we can have a great life there together – like we did when we met, remember?' Even the way he's worded it is selfish. Laura's eyes smart.

He looks at her, hoping, willing her to say, 'Yes, of course, let's do it,' but she can't. Laura thumps the mattress, her jaw set, and speaks through gritted teeth. 'You know we can't do that. It's the wrong time. And anyway, as you've pointed out, we've done it already. I want to move on, not go backwards. That's what we should all be doing now, Inigo.'

'It isn't backwards for me.' His voice is so low it's a whisper. 'And I don't know what else we can do together.'

There is nothing to lose in suggesting her own idea. Laura shuts her eyes.

'We could all come and live here and the children could go to school with Tamsin and—'

'HERE?' Inigo is gob-smacked. 'But I can't stand this place,' he says, so shocked that he cannot keep his guard or any pretences up at all. 'This isn't a place to live. This is the middle of nowhere. It's quaint. It's an experience, not a way of life you know, Laura.'

'Don't be patronising, and don't be so narrow-minded,' she hisses, pulling the covers back around her as protection. 'I think it would save us from all becoming strangers.' He might relate to a bit of therapy speak. 'The countryside is grounding. I've found being here so healing.'

'You've been reading too many self-help books,' Inigo snarls, uncurling from his pleading position to stand scornfully, hands dug into his pockets, looking down at Laura in her bed.

She bounces up onto her knees, hair awry, eyes blazing fury. 'And you've been resting on your laurels so comfortably you've forgotten how to behave within a family. Now go away and leave me alone. You can sleep on the bathroom floor.'

'Oh good. Nice and reasonable,' mutters Inigo. 'There is no way I'm sleeping in the bathroom, I'd catch typhoid from that pit. I shall sleep in the sitting room tonight. Tomorrow we shall tell the children.'

'What are we telling them?' Laura yells to no avail. He has closed the door behind him and gone. It is only mildly satisfying for Laura to hurl the weepalong novel at the door and to burst into angry sobs.

CHAPTER 21

Waking early, Laura wavers between continuing her attempts at tweaking home and hearth by making pancakes for breakfast, and following her own inclination, which is to go for a walk. The rain of the previous night has departed, leaving a sky so blue it almost sings above the sparkling waterlogged landscape. Opting for virtue and pancakes, Laura finds that the reward is built in – batter as illustrated in her very easy children's recipe book only takes a moment to construct, and soon she is walking down the lane, an emancipated woman with a pug at her heels. However, being alone with her thoughts is more than Laura can bear, and she finds herself approaching Hedley's house, hoping her brother will be up and able to divert her mind.

She hears Hedley before she sees him. 'Get over. GET OFF. I said GET OFF, you little bastard.' Following his voice, Laura discovers him in a small field, glaring at a very small black pony. The pony,

288

which is wider than it is tall, has one miniature hoof placed on Hedley's foot, and ignoring his fury, is devouring the contents of the bucket Hedley holds in his hand.

'God, how I loathe horses. You WILL get off my sodding foot now.' With supreme strength, Hedley pushes the pony off his boot and limps over to Laura. 'It belongs to Venetia – it's for the children, but it's a surprise so I've got it for a few weeks until the unveiling.'

'That was kind of you.' Laura strokes the pony's nose. Hedley grunts.

'Mmm. Well, it was Tamsin. She's been doing a lot of baby-sitting for them and she encouraged them to get a pony and she's going to help teach them to ride it. I thought that as she was doing something positive rather than just lying around with the curtains drawn watching television, I should support her. Not that she's pleased with me,' he sighs. 'She seems more removed than ever now Gina's around, and I thought they'd get on so well.' He looks suspiciously at his sister. 'Why are you here? I hope you're not trying to palm that goat off on me again.'

Laura's face crumples.

'No, no. It's not that. But I don't know what to do,' she wails. Hedley's jaw drops, but he pulls himself together and pats her on the back.

'Come on now,' he says heartily. 'Nothing is ever that bad, is it?'

Laura does not return to the Gate House until much later in the morning. Both she and Zeus are liberally

289

covered in mud from the long walk with Hedley across the marshes. She is restored though, and able to face Inigo without crumpling into indecision. She finds him in the shed, where he has set up a projector and is running through slides of his work with Grass as his silent audience. Laura opens the door as the lecture ends:

'So, as illustrated by the loop which runs through all my work, there is a universal truth, and that truth is that there is no end, just continual progress towards the future.' He glances round at Laura, and adds quickly, 'Let's get there together,' but she doesn't hear.

'Where are Dolly and Fred? I think we need to talk to them,' says Laura.

'Aah yes,' says Inigo. 'Well, if it's all right with you I suggest that—'

'No.' Laura raises her hand, speaking fast to get her point in first. 'It's not all right with me. I will say what I am doing now. I've made my decisions and I don't want to be steam-rollered by you any more.'

Tears pour down her cheeks; she presses her fingers into her eyes to try and stop them flowing but they swell hot from her eyes and drip down her hands instead. She sniffs and wipes her sleeve across her nose. 'I don't want to hear what you think any more. I have decided what I am doing. I shall stay in London in the week until the end of this term and then I am coming to live here with Dolly and Fred. I know Dolly won't like it, but at least she's got Tamsin, and I don't think it will ruin her life as she doesn't like anything much anyway. You must do what you must do, but I have to do this.'

Panting slightly, Laura buries her hot face in Grass's pungent neck. The goatiness is too much to stay like that for long. Laura rises, pats Grass and begins hanging buckets on hooks, anything to occupy her hands and the direction of her gaze.

'Very well, Laura.' Inigo has retreated behind a wall of icy disappointment. 'You do as you please, and I'll go to New York and earn some goddamn money to pay for everything.'

'Please don't pretend you're being hard done by,' Laura flashes back at him. 'It's what you want. You hate it here. You said so.'

Inigo's ice wall melts for a moment. He flushes and puts out a hand to Laura but she doesn't see because she's folding paper sacks in the corner. Grass's shed has never been so tidy. Unremarked, Grass placidly chews at the jacket Inigo hung on her door.

'I didn't mean it when I said that, Laura, you know I didn't. It's just – it's just –' He waves imploringly. 'Well, you know. I'm a town type. This is a culture shock for me. All this business with animals and mud and picking fruit just gets in the way of life.'

Laura's voice is small and sad, and makes Inigo want to weep when she replies, 'But to me it *is* the way of life, or it could be. You just haven't given it a chance.'

Inigo reaches for his jacket. 'I can't now – JESUS H CHRIST! Where's my sodding sleeve? Look! Look, Laura! This hell fiend has eaten the whole sleeve. I tell you, goats are Satan's children and if I have to, I'll—'

'Oh, for goodness sake shut up, it's only a stupid jacket,' snaps Laura. 'You liked the goat fine when you were using her for art.'

'That was the only thing she will ever do that is worthwhile in her whole life,' snarls Inigo, hurling the jacket at Grass's feet and marching out of the shed with his slides and his projector.

Laura and Grass look at one another. Grass takes another bite out of the jacket. 'Since when are goats supposed to be worthwhile?' asks Laura crossly.

Inigo vents his temper by shutting himself in the kitchen for the rest of the morning with an earsplitting Eastern European opera at full volume and all the lids and doors of the Rayburn open to create a satisfactory fug in which to cook. The evisceration and jointing of the hare provides the outlet his battered pride needs, and by the time he clamps the lid on for the meat to braise, much of his usual aplomb is restored. Humming, he turns the music up, trilling along to Janáček, and one of Janufa's mother's blood-chilling arias. Laying the table with a red checked cloth, plonking yellowed half-melted candles on it and a vase of golden leaves and rose hips picked by Dolly, Inigo sings a burst of opera and thinks how nice it would be to have a parallel existence as a bistro owner in a small town in France or Italy where food is appreciated and even talked about.

He puts the food on the table and calls his family to sit down, pouring himself a large glass of red wine and gulping it down in one, as they appear in the kitchen and arrange themselves around the table. Laura tries to smile at him across the table, but is met with an impenetrable stare, so turns to Dolly, who has scraped all the meat sauce off her pasta and is fastidiously picking out the tomatoes from the salad.

'This is horrendous, I'm a vegetarian,' she wails. 'And I had to have meat last night with that stew Mum cooked and now this. You're trying to starve me. Can't I just go and get a Pot Noodle?'

Laura winces, expecting Inigo to erupt at the mention of Pot Noodle, but he ignores Dolly's rudeness and simply says, 'If that's what you want,' before leaning back to put the kettle on for her.

Fred drops his fork in melodramatic mock amazement, and whispers to Laura, 'Can I have one too? I liked that hare, but it wasn't enough, and I don't want seconds of it, I want something else.'

Wondering whether any conversation about their family will penetrate the skin of self-absorption each child displays, Laura nods, then coughs, and closes her eyes as she speaks.

'You two need to know our plans, I think.'

Dolly groans, 'Oh God, you're getting divorced. I might have known it. This is what happened to Becca and she got really bad acne the next day just before the school disco and it ruined all her chances with Luke Johnson.'

'I thought Luke Johnson was *your* boyfriend,' says Laura.

Dolly throws her a withering look. 'He is now,' she says patiently, 'but he used to be Becca's.'

'Oh, I see.'

Fred passes Dolly her Pot Noodle, and Laura blinks and inhales the plastic sweet smell of monosodium glutamate.

'They can't get divorced because they aren't married,' Fred points out.

Inigo stands up and begins circling the table, a knife twirling on the back of his hand. He pauses and arranges three oranges so they sit on top of one another on the windowsill. He tries for a fourth but the stack collapses, oranges squidging onto the floor. He bends to find them and tries again. He does not speak or look at the children.

'We're not getting divorced or whatever the non-married version is,' Laura says. 'But—'

'Oh, I know what "But" means.' Dolly pushes her Pot Noodle away and sits, arms folded, hair pinched back from her face, strumming her fingers on her arms, her gaze darting between her parents. 'Come on then, tell us what's wrong.'

'Nothing is wrong, nothing will really change now,' Laura soothes, 'but next holidays we might come and try living here for a bit while Dad's in New York.'

Dolly's skin turns chalk white; her mouth wobbles. Laura gabbles to try and protect her from her shock. 'It should be great fun and Zeus will love it,' she finds herself saying.

Without a word, Dolly pushes her chair back and leaves the room.

'Cool,' says Fred, reaching for Dolly's Pot Noodle now his own is finished. 'Can I have another ferret then?'

Laura looks helplessly at Inigo. His mouth is set in a grim line as he pours himself more wine. Laura starts clearing the table, reflecting wryly as she washes the pasta saucepan that she will miss his culinary expertise. A tear plops into the washing up, but she blinks others away, reminding herself that she is becoming a domestic success herself.

'I'm going to make blackberry jam this afternoon,' she announces with this in mind. No one pays any attention. Fred is bombarding Inigo with questions he cannot answer. 'Will I leave my school?'

'I don't know, I suppose so.'

'Where will I go instead? The same one as Tamsin?'

'Er, I don't know, I suppose so.'

'Will you come and live here when you get back from New York?'

'Umm. Mmm. I don't know.'

'But you suppose so.' Fred nudges him, grinning. Inigo gets up from his chair and moves over to the sink next to Laura. She gives him a clipped little smile.

'Come on, let's all go and pick some blackberries,' she says brightly. 'We need fresh air. I'll go and call Dolly.'

Coaxing Dolly out of her room is slow work. Inigo and Fred set off across the stubble field behind the house, and are out of earshot by the time Dolly is ready, wrapped as if for the tundra in three fleeces, two hats (one a hood, the other a stripy egg-cosy type knitted by Laura when the children were tiny) and two pairs of socks inside her pink trainers, but with several inches of midriff exposed between the bottom of her fleeces and the top of her studded jeans. The long shadows of the afternoon are shot with bright sunbeams and Dolly winces when she steps out of the door, but recovers and sets off leaning on Laura's arm. Laura decides that this invalidish behaviour is entirely acceptable, and hugs her close as they march in pursuit of the others up the cropped golden field.

The soothing quality of being out of doors is palpable, and Dolly is able to greet Inigo with a genuine smile when they catch up with him and Fred skimming stones on a pond in a derelict farmyard. She clamours for a go. Laura moves away to watch the sun as it spills liquid flame across the soft grey of a distant wood; a pheasant screeches and flies up, rewarding Zeus's scrabbling at the bottom of a hedge; a damp scent of leaves hangs in the air. It is impossible not to feel happy in this moment.

CHAPTER 22

By Tuesday, however, Laura fears that it is unlikely that she can ever be happy again. London is damp and fog-ridden, Inigo is leaving for New York in two days, and Jack Smack is in the house from before breakfast, chivvying him and missing no opportunity to gloat. For no good reason as far as Laura can see, he elects to travel with them to the studio today, and announces that he will spend the morning there helping them.

'We've got a lot to get through,' he says with relish, when they reach the building. Flinging his telephone on the red Formica table he draws up a chair and reaches into his pocket for a pen and notebook. 'We won't put the house on the market yet,' he mutters almost to himself. 'We'll see what you find in New York before we burn our boats here.'

Laura, going through the post on the desk next to him, slams her fist on the surface before Inigo has a chance to reply.

'Jack, this is between me and Inigo, not you. Our house is not going on the market. This whole thing is nothing to do with you. Do you understand?'

Jack rolls his eyes and says, 'Don't you think it's time you faced facts, Laura? You and Inigo are history. You want different things in different places and neither of you is prepared to compromise. My job is to make this whole situation easier for you both.'

'Oh come on Jack,' says Inigo. 'That is total crap. You are bloody nosy, that's why you're here and I wish you'd sod off and do something useful.'

Crestfallen for a moment or two, Jack takes out a large handkerchief and wipes his face. Refreshed, he delivers a cheesy grin and tips back on his chair, one hand in the pocket of his tight black jeans, silently watching Laura. So as not to slap him, she has to clasp her hands tightly behind her back. She stands up and walks over to the door, holding it open. 'No. You're out, Jack. I'd like you to leave now, please.'

Raising his eyebrows, Jack looks over to Inigo for support; he does not look up from his computer screen. Jack stands up and gives Laura a squeeze on the arm. His brittle hand softly dents the fabric of her jacket and she shudders, disgusted.

Jack mistakes this for hysteria. 'I can see you're taking it hard,' he says, his eyes treacle dark, glooping fake sympathy. 'I'll take a rain check. Inigo, I'll call you.'

Laura watches from the window as Jack appears on the street below, weaves across the traffic and sets off on the opposite side of the road at a brisk pace.

'Why did I never do that before?' she marvels.

Inigo, who keeps expecting her to capitulate, and who is looking on the internet for large houses to rent in New York for his family to follow him out to, gives her an uneasy look. 'I don't know. You seem to have become very assertive. Maybe you're having a mid-life crisis. I deal with Jack, you don't.'

'Well, I'm sick of his shadow in our lives, and I don't have to put up with it any more,' replies Laura. 'I've never liked him, and he's never liked me much either. He'll be glad to see the back of me.'

The telephone rings. It is Hedley, his voice strained and high-pitched with anxiety. 'I don't know what to do. Tamsin's run away from home. She went this morning. She's left a note saying she's not coming back and she's not alone. I just don't know what to do.'

Shock thuds at the back of Laura's throat; she strains to keep her voice steady. 'Oh Hedley, stay calm. I'm sure she's fine, she's probably gone to stay with a friend.'

He groans. 'I don't think so. She isn't at school – I went there first thing, and none of her friends have seen her. Do you think Dolly might know something?'

'I'll ask her when she comes home. I'm sure she hadn't heard from her this morning, but they did spend the whole of Sunday lying on the bed in Dolly's room talking, so she might have some idea of what's going on. Did you try calling her?'

'Yes, but her phone's switched off or she's screening calls from me because it just rings and then I get

299

her answering message. Shall I call the police, Laura? Gina says to wait but what do you think?'

The anguish in her brother's voice surprises Laura; Hedley is not a man to show any emotion, unless it's irritation.

She tries to calm him down. 'No, I don't think so. She's left a note, so she hasn't been abducted. I'm sure she's fine and she'll be back soon. Try not to worry too much.'

Laura puts the phone down, then, thinking out loud, says, 'Actually, I'll go to the school now and ask Dolly. It's never a good idea to hang around with this sort of thing.'

Inigo does not look up from his computer. 'Bye,' he says absently. 'Hope she turns up.'

As if she's a missing letter, Laura thinks savagely, flouncing out of the studio. She finds Dolly sitting on a radiator eating crisps in the school front hall. Her response is reassuringly Dollyish.

'Oh yeah. I knew she was doing that. She's gone with Dan, her boyfriend. Hedley doesn't know him. I think she wants to go and find her mum.'

Resisting the desire to scream, 'OhforGodsake-teenagersareanightmare,' Laura arranges her face into an expression of polite but non-pressuring inter-est, as if she were asking Dolly about her favourite nail polish.

'So do you know where she is at all?'

Dolly looks shifty. 'No, I don't think I do,' she says cautiously. Deciding it's best not to push her, Laura returns home to speak to Hedley. As she dials his number she reflects briefly how utterly this new crisis has eclipsed her own, and is trying to unravel her thoughts about Inigo when the telephone is answered by a male voice.

'Hello?'

'Hedley?'

'No, this is Guy, you've got the wrong number. Is that you, Laura?'

His voice is warm, and, Laura finds herself thinking, very sexy. Absently she runs her fingers through her hair. 'Oh sorry, yes it is. It's me. I meant to ring Hedley, you see. I'd better get on with it. How was your trip?'

'Oh, it was great. I'll tell you all about it next time I see you. But what's the matter, Laura, you sound upset?'

No one ever notices when Laura's upset, or if they do, they don't say so. Grateful tears spill onto her cheeks, and she sighs shakily. 'Oh, it's a long story. I'll explain another time. But I'm OK, honestly.'

'Are you sure? Is there anything I can do?'

'I'll let you know if there is. Thanks, Guy.' Laura puts the phone down; her cheeks are flushed, and she smiles, staring out the window for an instant before dialling Hedley's number.

By evening, Tamsin and her boyfriend have been found. Or rather, the bell rings at Laura's house and she opens the door to find two pale, bedraggled individuals, both carrying backpacks, their trousers dark with wet from the knees down. Their faces are shrouded by their hooded tops; one is tall with a hacking cough, the other jogs about impatiently on the doorstep, long empty-ended sleeves flapping at its sides. In their grey hoods in the street-lit evening they look sinister and other-worldly. The sight of them gives Laura a nasty shock.

'Ugh!' she shrieks involuntarily.

The smaller one hastily pulls down its hood. 'Aunt Laura, it's me, Tamsin. Look!' it shouts. 'And this is Dan. We're back. We didn't know where to go because Dan's friend wasn't there, so we thought we'd come here. Is that all right?'

Laura gapes at them for a moment before nodding, words rushing as she ushers Tamsin and Dan into the house.

'Of course it is. How sensible of you to come here. Oh Tamsin, thank God you're all right, Hedley has been so worried. I must call him right now. Or maybe you should.'

She herds them into the hall and yells up the stairs, 'Dolly, Tamsin's here! She needs some dry clothes.'

Dan unzips his sweatshirt and peels it off and, like a frog prince, suddenly a boy with floppy hair and gentle brown eyes appears in place of the creepy alien he was a minute ago. He edges to the door of the sitting room where Inigo and Fred are immersed in football on the television and peers in.

'Hi,' says Fred, sensing rather than seeing him, as he is unable to look away from the television. 'Come and watch this. It's a brilliant match.'

302

'What's the score?' mumbles Dan, glancing at Laura as if for permission.

Laura, wondering if she should be cross, but dismissing the thought as it really isn't her concern, and anyway, she isn't cross, she's glad they're here, simply says, 'Have you called your mother?'

Dan nods sheepishly. 'Yup. I said we were coming here. She's going to call you, I think.' He slides on to the sofa next to Fred. 'What's the score?' he whispers again, removing the next damp layer of his clothing and dropping it on the floor in front of him.

'Three-one,' says Inigo, leaning to pick up the sweatshirt. 'Shall we dry this for you?'

'Yes please,' says Dan, settling back in the sofa with a speaking sigh. Tamsin, almost prone in Dolly's arms, drags herself up the stairs. Laura longs to know what prompted the flight and the somewhat precipitate return, but no confidences are coming her way, so she has to content herself with draping fugitive clothes along radiators.

It's important for a mother to know her place, she reflects, listening out as Dolly and Tamsin head for the bathroom. But all she hears is Tamsin blurting, 'Oh Dolly, it's been such a pain running away, I can't be bothered with it any more,' before the door is closed on her curiosity.

Laura decides she will drive Tamsin and Dan back to Norfolk the next morning, partly to get away from Inigo and his packing, and partly out of sisterly duty to Hedley, who is anxious that Tamsin should not be allowed out of an adult's sight for more than a moment.

'It's all right for you to let her go to the loo on her own,' he agrees, when Laura telephones to tell him her plans. 'But hide her shoes.'

Laura is incredulous. 'Why?'

Hedley groans. 'So she can't do it again, of course. I saw it in a film about the Second World War.'

'Just keep quiet about things like that and I'm sure she won't do it again.'

'Hmmmph,' says Hedley, making Laura glad for Tamsin's sake that she will be present at their reunion.

It is not until she, Tamsin and Dan are in the car and heading for the motorway that Laura realises she hasn't said goodbye to Inigo. When she returns tomorrow, he will have left for New York and their life together will cease. Or will it? The situation over the past weeks has been so difficult and ambivalent that Laura is not sure what is really happening. Inigo is going to New York, but is he moving out? Is he removing his belongings from the house? Is Laura supposed to take her things out of the studio? Or is she still working there? Instead of pain, Laura finds she is experiencing disbelief.

Tamsin leans forward from the back of the car into Laura's thoughts. 'Can we have some music on, please?' She waves a disc, and grateful for the curtain of sound to hide behind, Laura turns the volume higher and gives herself up to introspection.

The teenagers shuffle closer together and surreptitiously hold hands in the back. Glancing in the rearview mirror, Laura notices Dan wink and grin at

Tamsin as the track on the sound system changes to a song from the genre Laura thinks of as: 'Cut the bitch up and stuff her in the boot' songs. It is possible they have a shorter, more user-friendly classification, but no one has told Laura yet. Fred, who likes this music, generally ushers his mother out of the room when he is listening to it, saying, 'It's not your sort of thing, Mum, it's a bit difficult to get into,' as if she is only fit for the Eurovision Song Contest. He has a point; Laura's taste is moving steadily towards the rocking chair of easy listening, and she can no longer hide her preference for Radio Two because it is the only station tuned in on the car radio. Dolly loathes this nose-dive out of coolness, and as a reaction has moved on to tinkly, and sometimes moany Moroccan-based music. Laura is not sure which she dislikes more, but knows that in order not to alienate herself from her children she must try to pretend to appreciate both. Maybe Tamsin will report back how much Laura is enjoying the car music. She turns it up a bit and pretends to hum a note or two. The song however, descends into fast and filthy rap and Laura is left way behind mouthing, 'Oh baby.' If Inigo were here he would love it. He is always prepared to give all music a chance, and positively relishes listening to Fred and Dolly's latest favourites. He likes to put them on in the car at full volume and drive. Aching sadness cuts through Laura's thoughts, and she has to take deep breaths and concentrate on the rapper, who has now tied up his baby and left her in a bedsit, to prevent herself from U-turning the car and heading back to London to beg Inigo to stay.

At Crumbly, Hedley bounds out to greet them, his enthusiasm only just eclipsed by that of the Labrador Diver, who sticks his nose up Laura's skirt as she fumbles in the car for Tamsin and Dan's backpacks. Behind her she hears Hedley's voice, faltering, 'Tamsin. Hello. It's nice to see you.'

'For God's sake give the girl a hug.' Laura spins around to see Guy is here too. He pushes Hedley towards Tamsin, as she stands awkwardly, pale and numb by the car. Tamsin reddens and falls into Hedley's arms, sobbing.

'I'm really sorry, I've been so stupid and I realised it was a mistake. I quite like Gina, in fact and I don't really want to go and live with Mum in her women's camp, and Dan . . .' Hedley, finding his shoulder damp already, thrusts a handkerchief at her. Tamsin blows her nose gratefully. '. . . And Dan was brilliant because he came to take care of me and he didn't want to because he had to miss kick boxing and he knew his Mum would blow him out.'

She subsides into Hedley's arms, and he, stroking her hair, leads her towards the house, saying, 'Come on, Tamsin, you need to sit down and tell me everything when you feel a bit better. Dan, you come too, we'll sort everything out.'

Laura leans against the car, arms folded, amazed at her brother's transformation into a caring and sensitive listener, a responsive and loving stepfather. She turns to Guy, rushing over her words. 'I think you must have been working on him. I was so worried that he'd shout at her.'

Guy shrugs and digs his hands into his pockets, rolling a stone under his shoe and not looking at Laura. 'No. I just told him to hug her. The rest comes from him. He's been so worried, and since he knew she was with you, he's done a lot of thinking.' He looks up, straight at Laura. 'It looks like Hedley's finally had to grow up.'

Flustered, Laura suddenly wants to be on her own.

'I must get to the Gate House,' she says, jumping into the car. 'Say goodbye to Hedley for me.' Rap music floods out, drowning anything else she was going to say. Guy laughs and waves, mouthing something Laura can't hear.

CHAPTER 23

Autumn has come to the Gate House. Walking up the damp path to the door, Laura steps over windfall apples amid a tapestry of gold and green leaves. The roses by the porch are still flowering sparsely, and delicate pink petals drift against the wet red-brick of the wall above a few straggling lavender heads. The grass, grown long once again, Laura notices in despair, is covered by curling oak leaves and half-open chestnut shells, and an impromptu pond, a silver disc with tufts of green bristling at the edges, has formed in the middle of the lawn, nowhere near the official pond.

Inside the house, the chill in the air tells her as she opens the door that the Rayburn is out, but even so, Laura moves instinctively towards it, her hands outstretched, anticipating warmth she knows is not here. Collecting kindling and newspaper to light it, she wonders why it is that fires which are out leave a room so much colder than fires which are never lit. It must be to do with expectation, or more mundanely, flues, she decides, putting her coat back on now she has lit the stove, and stamping her feet to try and warm them up. It's no good, it's freezing. The only way to get warm is to go to bed. Laura does so, and inevitably falls asleep, waking with a heavy drugged feeling, and no idea where she is.

Her phone rings. It is Fred. 'Hi Mum, I've borrowed Shane's mobile to call you. I'm on the way home from school. We had curry for lunch today.' He pauses expectantly.

'Good,' says Laura encouragingly. 'It's lovely to speak to you. I've seen Hedley and—'

'The thing is, Mum, the curry's reminded me that Vice needs some more roadkill really badly and—' background sounds of: 'Wicked, Fred. Whaddyamean roadkill? Is it like, dead bodies?' interrupt him, but Laura knows what is coming next.

'So seeing as there isn't much in South End Green, do you think you could possibly go and find some today?'

'I suppose so.' Laura realises how ungracious she sounds. 'I mean, yes of course I will, if I really have to.'

'Thanks, Mum. Get a rabbit if you can. I hate plucking pheasants.'

Laura tries to divert him. 'Don't you think Vice might like some bacon or something to keep her meat-eating instincts alive until you next come here?'

Fred shouts back, 'NO, and make sure it isn't too splatted. GOT TO GO. BYE, MUM.' More background appreciation from Fred's ghoulish friends and the line goes dead.

Ah good, Laura thinks wryly, now the rest of the day is taken care of. No time to start feeling sad again; this is not the moment to sit down and make plans for life or the garden, nor to sweep dead leaves. It's time to get up, get dressed and hit the road with a spatula. Laura wishes, not for the first time, that she had known more about the private lives of ferrets before agreeing so blithely to Fred having one. The thing to remember now is that he is bound to want another one, and it is important to be vigilant in preventing this. Any slacking and Fred will have a whole ferret farm. What a hideous prospect. Laura makes a big attempt to do positive thinking and after a struggle, finds it in herself to be pleased that Fred is being responsible about his pet's diet. Even though the hunter-gathering is palmed off on his mother, Fred has been thinking of someone or rather something other than himself, and that is a good thing. Armed with this uplifting thought, she removes the spatula and, not wishing to be under-equipped, the fish slice from the drawer, and heads out to the car.

What had been a fine day when she went into the house at midday has now become spiteful and nasty. A lowering pewter sky, with blacker patches of rain on the horizon, greets Laura, and a vigorous gust of wind whips her hair across her mouth and bites through her clothes so she shivers as she runs to the car.

A future of scraping flattened rabbits off the tarmac to a constant background noise of Radio One is a bleak one, and scanning the lane ahead, Laura tries to imagine anyone sane turning down a comfortable life in New York with pavements and underfloor heating to have this privilege. For her though, there is no choice; the impulse to move forwards and to make her own decisions has taken over.

There is a clap of thunder, the wind rises and rain begins to pour, loud and metallic, on the roof of the car. The wipers flick back and forth across the windscreen, but do not increase Laura's visibility. Beyond the car a veil of rain sweeps in every direction, fogging the fields and the road ahead. Laura stops the car, unable to see to drive on. Cocooned in muffled safety, she winds down her window to hear the rain. The steady thud begins to slow a little, and other sounds filter into the car; a distant engine explodes into life, there is the startled crack and strangled shriek of a pheasant soaring to roost, and more persistently, a mournful bleating. Laura listens vaguely for a few moments, gradually becoming aware that the bleating is sounding increasingly desperate. Something, a sheep probably, needs help.

I am a countrywoman now and a sheep needs help, thinks Laura, and looks around in search of more convincing, perhaps more professional help. But there is not a soul, nor a building in sight, not a tractor in a field, not a car on the road. Laura will have to perform a Pet Rescue operation alone. Dolly's boots – silver with big pink daisies on them, are in the car. She puts them on and scrabbles under the seats and among the layers of sweet papers and old magazines for a hat. All she can find is a pink sequinned straw stetson left over from the summer, mangled and damaged, but better than nothing. She puts it on, but can find no form of coat, not even a plastic bag to convert. Resigned to saturation, Laura climbs over the gate and into the field beyond.

The scene within is not what Laura had expected at all. Where there should have been a charming flock of sheep grazing on an idyllic green sward beneath an ancient oak, there is a vast mud-brown lake stretching to woodland. Along the middle, and parting around the ancient oak, a current flows vigorously, suggesting that a stream or ditch lies beneath. On the other side of this fast-flowing rip, half a dozen sheep stand looking foolish and frightened, next to a small black pony. They are already submerged up to their knees, and as the rain continues unabated, Laura imagines they will soon be swimming. She must go and find someone. A tractor and then perhaps a small boat will be needed. It is just like Noah's Ark. Farmers with lifeboat skills, that's who she needs. There must be some; after all, the sea is only a few miles away. Laura turns to climb back over the gate to the car and her telephone. She should ring Hedley. He will know what to do, and who to inform. Laura has a feeling she has seen the pony before, but where?

Peering towards the animals again, Laura gasps. One of the sheep has slid from its vantage point with the others and plopped heavily into the racing current. Its legs flail pitifully, its mouth is open as it twirls and bobs along, vanishing beneath brown water. Laura sees the fleece, heavier as it absorbs water, dragging the sheep down. A moment later another sheep, bleating and struggling, slides in too. The pony heaves itself backwards, snorting. The bank the animals are standing on is giving way and none of them can see where to move to in order to save themselves. Horrified, Laura realises that the first sheep is no longer struggling; its legs stick straight out from the scribbled blob of its fleece as it is borne onward along the stream towards the fence.

Laura swings off the gate and runs towards the stricken animals. After a few strides the water is too deep to run in, and she slows down, wading as fast as she can, plunging deep to her thighs where there is a hollow in the field, then shallower, to her knees again. Her boots fill with swirling water; she kicks them off and wades on.

The pony has plunged into the deep water now, and is swimming, trying to gain purchase with his feet on the bank. Another sheep struggles on the edge. Laura's breath comes in rough gasps; she loses balance and falls shuddering with shock and cold under the water. She has stumbled into a deeper part now, and the current pulls her so she is half-swimming towards the pony and his remaining companions. She manages to put her hands out and stop herself being swept past, and she stands up, crouched to protect herself from the hooves and weight of the scrambling pony.

'Don't worry, whoa, boy,' she says, stretching up to grasp the pony's head collar.

'WAIT, I'M COMING. DON'T MOVE, FOR CHRIST'S SAKE DON'T MOVE!'

Above the rush of the stream, the hiss of rain, the snorting of the terrified pony and the constant tragic wail of the sheep, Laura can hardly believe she had heard a voice. Over at the gate, yellow lights flash on the roof of a vehicle, and through the dusk a dripping figure approaches, beaming a torch at her face, splashing and wading towards her.

'Are you all right? What are you doing in here? Can you get out?' It is Guy, reaching down to pull her up from the deep water where she's standing. These must be his sheep, and the pony is the one Hedley was looking after. Knowing the animals personally makes the situation worse. Laura's teeth chatter, and she grips the pony's head collar more tightly, her hands slipping in the fabric as more rain slides down the pony's face and through her frozen fingers.

'Yes, yes, I'm fine. But look, over there – one of the sheep is being swept away towards that fence and I think another has drowned.'

Guy tries to see where she is pointing; his expression is grim. 'Can you try to draw the others away from this dyke? Take the pony first. If you go up to the corner, there is a way across and you can lead it up to the gate.' It is almost dark now, and the rain falls unabated. Guy gestures in the twilight towards the hedge and hurries downstream to the sheep, which has pulled itself out of the flowing current and has collapsed in shallow water, still bleating. Laura scrambles up until she is standing level with the pony and slowly begins to lead it along the edge of the ditch, stumbling in the floodwater. A gunshot echoes across the water. Laura bites her tongue in shock, almost grateful for the throb of pain because it's warm in her mouth and the rest of her is wrapped in ice by her drenched clothes. The pony, and the sheep following, shy away in fright. The pony flings back its head, its eyes rolling white and terrified. Laura clings to it with both hands, afraid that it might turn and bolt back towards the treacherous dyke.

'Sorry about the shot.' Guy's voice floats to her out of darkness, somewhere above the bobbing torch. 'The ewe's leg was broken, she was in agony. I'm going after the others, just keep going with that pony.'

Absurdly, tears trickle down Laura's face as she leads the hesitant pony slowly along the ditch towards the looming blackness of the hedge, small rivulets of warmth running down her chin and her nose. Having reached the hedge, Laura knows she is meant to turn and cross the ditch and from there it is just a few steps to the gate. The car headlamps pour light into the field, the bars of the gate burning a black grid into the white beam. The illumination almost reaches Laura, and adjusting her eyes to the eddying flood, she notices the stillness of a width of water ahead of her, beyond which the current pours fast again. It must be the bridge. Treading slowly, sliding her feet one in front of the other, she begins to wade into the still stretch of water, the pony stepping slowly after her, huffing and snorting in alarm. Sure enough, the ground remains solid beneath her, and holding her breath, she reaches the other side. Immediately the height of the floodwater drops and Laura and the pony are on dry land in front of the gate. From Guy's truck, above the roar of the weather, Laura can hear a throbbing beat and she grins shakily. He is listening to the music Fred lent him.

'Laura, how are you feeling?' Guy, looking remarkably cheerful for someone who has just had to shoot a sheep, appears out of the darkness, trailed by indeterminate woolly lumps which Laura assumes must be the rest of the sheep. His dog skims the group, trotting back and forth just beyond the beam of torchlight.

'Fine, thanks.' She nods, and this vigorous movement is too much for the sodden brim of her straw hat. It drops flat over her eyes like a pair of blinkers. Laura removes the hat. 'What shall we do with them all?'

Guy unlocks the gate and marches out towards the back end of his truck. 'We need to get this lot dry. If you wait while I get the sheep in the back, could you drive them back to my place and I'll lead the pony? I won't be far behind you. It's only a mile or so.' Laura nods, hoping he can't see the degree to which her heart has sunk. She is frozen, soaked and shocked. All she wants is a hot bath and an anaesthetising drink, and instead she's going to spend the next part of the evening driving sheep around.

'You can leave your car here and I'll bring you back to fetch it later,' says Guy, throwing her the keys of his. Laura catches them and climbs stiffly into the driver's seat. She is secretly impressed by Guy's handling of the situation. He seems able to keep his head in a crisis, which Laura, who invariably weeps or laughs, while Inigo shouts, finds enviable and attractive.

Guy appears by her door. 'I'll soak your seat.' She searches on the floor for something to sit on, but there is nothing. Guy reaches in and stretches his hand over hers on the steering wheel. Laura looks at their touching hands and says nothing.

'Christ, you're frozen.' Guy takes off his coat and tucks it over her legs. 'Get going and when you get there, drive into the big barn and open the back of the truck. There's loads of hay in there and the sheep will be fine until I get back. Then go into the house and have a bath.' Laura raises her eyebrows as she starts the engine.

Guy grins. 'Please,' he says. 'Sorry, I shouldn't be shouting orders at you,' and he leans across the steering wheel and kisses her. On the mouth. Without thinking, Laura kisses him back and warmth floods through her veins again. The music pounds in her head. Her skin is so numb she wouldn't have thought she could feel anything, but Guy's arm is around her waist and she shudders, leaning towards him, her hands holding his face. Guy is half in the car now. Laura is breathless and electric. His hand is under her shirt, Laura gasps and lets her head roll back. As she does so, the music stops with a click as the tape ends. Laura wrenches herself to reality. Cold, wet reality.

'I must go.' She pushes Guy away and slams the door, her cheeks flaming as she grates the gears and manoeuvres the truck away from the flooded field.

Her instinct is to put her foot down, get the sheep back and get out, but she hasn't got her car, or indeed her keys as they are in her car, back at the field, and anyway, the sheep would probably break if she went more than twenty miles an hour. Determinedly not thinking about anything except sheep, Laura crawls back to Guy's house and drives in the barn. Now what? She could sit in the truck in the dark until Guy and the pony arrive, or she could go into the house and have a bath.

In the bath, Laura lies back in scented water, relieved that it is orange blossom, and not sugar beet extract. She shuts her eyes and slides down until all of her except her face is underwater. It is calming, but her thoughts are still tumbling out:

'Unbelievable. What do I think I'm doing? How can this have happened now, when I thought it couldn't. It wouldn't. I thought this would never happen. I mean, I never thought this would happen. Actually, I'm overreacting. Nothing has happened, just a kiss, that's all. No one will ever know about that.' She sits up and reaches for a sponge, trickling water down the centre of her face with it. 'I shouldn't be in the bath in this house. Mind you, it smells amazing, Guy ought to be producing this stuff.'

She picks up the bottle and reads the label. 'Celia's making it. Clever her, it's blissful. I wonder if she's been back here? Oh God, I heard something. He's back now and I'm still in the bath. I look as if I'm leading him on. I feel as if I am too. I should go back outside and be in the barn, but it's too late, I can hear him on the stairs now. The door isn't locked. That's provocative. Mind you, I couldn't lock the door because there isn't a lock. Anyway, he hasn't come in. Why hasn't he come in? He started it. Now what's going to happen?'

Laura gets out of the bath and looks with disfavour at the pile of sodden clothes she was wearing. She'll have to borrow something. Once she has the dry clothes she can go home and life will return to its normal equilibrium. Except it hasn't got one. Normal has gone. Not that life with Inigo is normal by many people's standards, but to Laura and the children it is. Perched on the edge of the bath, her ability to move diminishes. She has pulled the plug out, and the last drops gurgle away as she sits, now dry, and still warm in her towel, staring at the dirty clothes in the corner, not wanting to put them on.

Guy knocks at the door. 'Hello?'

'Hello.'

'I thought you might need some dry clothes.'

'That's exactly what I thought.'

'Well, they're here, outside the door. Shall I pass them to you?'

Feeling that the conversation is labouring, and anxious to dispel this self-consciousness, Laura flings open the door, holding her towel up.

'Thanks,' she smiles, reaching for the clothes. Guy takes a step towards her, and in reflex she raises the towel higher. Startled, Guy backs away again; he swallows nervously.

'I'm not coming in,' he says.

'Certainly not,' agrees Laura with dignity. She turns on her heel and goes back into the bathroom. Shutting the door, she glimpses her back view in the mirror. The towel in no way covers her bottom. This is a pity. Laura looks again: actually, it is a *big* pity.

She dresses quickly, much enjoying the sense of exciting thinness brought about by being lent jeans and a shirt that are far too big. Even the socks flop off her feet, reminding her of the high-heeled moment when she had thought her feet had put on weight. Just thinking about high heels and urban clothes makes her stomach flip. Everything is so complicated. It would be so nice to sit by the fire here and to have someone to talk to. Gloomily she remembers that the Rayburn hadn't got going properly before she left – it will have gone out again now. And she didn't get any roadkill for Vice. Damn.

Laura bundles her wet clothes into a bag and goes downstairs. Guy is crouched in the fireplace, blowing a smoking wigwam of kindling. He stands up to pour Laura a drink, touching her fingers as he passes her the glass.

'It's a Whisky Mac. It's the most warming drink I could think of.'

Laura takes a gulp and coughs, as the strong sweetness catches in her throat. 'It's delicious,' she says hoarsely.

'I'm glad I bumped into you,' says Guy conversationally, as if they have just met at the shop in the village. 'I wanted to talk to you about Greece. I'm thinking of buying a farm there.'

Laura perches on the arm of the chair by the fire and looks at Guy, a suspicion beating in her head. He stands, one foot on the fender, leaning his shoulders against the mantlepiece, looking down into the fire. He is still wearing jeans with mud caked around the hem, and his hair is standing on end. He looks up, half-smiling, feeling Laura's gaze.

'What?' he says.

'Nothing,' she replies, and suddenly it has gone. All the confusion and yearning, wanting and wishing is past. Inside, Laura is just empty, rattling sadness. 'I'm sorry, Guy. I'll always be sorry.'

Bewildered, he moves towards her. 'Sorry about what? You have nothing to be sorry for. Do you?' There is panic in his voice. 'Please can you stop looking like that, Laura.' He is crouching by her chair now. She puts her glass down and holds his hands.

'I wasn't the right person for you a long time ago, and I'm still not. I can't lead the life you want. I never could. But I thought I might be able to. Recently.' She stands up and moves to the door, feeling on the hooks for her coat, her vision blurred with tears. 'I need to go now please, Guy.'

He is beside her, holding her coat for her, raking his hands through his hair in anxiety. 'But I wasn't even talking about that – wasn't thinking of now. Why are you rushing on, Laura?'

She picks up her bag of clothes. 'I know you weren't, you probably haven't been thinking about it at all, but I have been, and it's wrong,' she says baldly.

321

The music in the truck is still Fred's tape. A haunting ballad, not typical of his taste, but one of Inigo's favourites, begins to play. Laura turns up the volume and gazes out at the starlit sky, so miserable, self-absorbed and lonely she can almost relate to teenagers again. Neither she nor Guy speaks until they reach her car in the mud-churned gateway of the flooded field.

'Thanks,' she says and slams the truck door on the lamenting voice of lost love. In her own car she switches on her phone, but the battery is flat, so she can't call the children. She'll go to the pub and do it when she's been home and lit the fire.

Alone in the car, she tries to pull herself together and be rational. It's so easy to wish someone is here when they aren't. Look how she built up a whole fairy-tale around Guy. And all of it evaporated with a kiss. Now she can admit to herself how keen she had been. How she built her snatched weekend life at the Gate House on Guy's foundations. How the grass seemed greener in the country. But it isn't. None of it was ever real, never could be, but it's sad and empty to wake up to that just now. And Laura is alone.

It's so easy to wish someone is here when they aren't. Particularly when they are departing for another continent; of course, there is the intransigence, the overbearing bossiness, the control freakery. It's nice not having that around. But Laura's not thinking about that. She's got the apron he wears for cooking on her mind. It's hanging on the back of the kitchen door. And the flowers he buys all the time, lilies usually, which fill the house with luxurious scent. It's silly to be remembering these small things and to forget the big picture. The big picture where she can't see herself because she's invisible in it. There, but invisible. It's silly, but in Laura's mind, Inigo is looking at her, intent and utterly focused and they're kissing. She's not just visible, she's reflected in his eyes. It's only in her own that she's invisible.

Cold creeps through Laura from her feet; running into her heart. 'I've blown it. I've blown it,' she whispers. She stops the car on the road outside the Gate House. The lights are on in every room. Before she can think that she's sure she didn't leave them on earlier, the door opens and Zeus zooms down the path, puffing delight at seeing her. Laura's heart leaps in her throat as she reaches the door. The children are here – Gina said she might bring them. Everything suddenly becomes less bleak.

'Hello!' she shouts, grinning as she walks in. There is no one in the kitchen; a bucket stands on the table, crammed with lilies, their scent riding on the warm air, making the lodge sybaritic and delicious instead of spartan.

'Oh, how lovely,' she says, leaning into them, calling through to the sitting room. 'They always remind me of Dad. How clever of you to bring them now he's gone. Let's leave him a message, shall we?'

'What will you say?'

Laura twists round and Inigo, who should be on a plane, is behind her balancing a ring on the tip of his finger.

'Inigo,' Laura gasps. 'What are you doing here?'

He takes her hand and puts the ring in her palm, then presses his hand on top.

'I couldn't leave you behind. I'm staying, I want to be with you, wherever you want to be, and I'm going down on one knee right now, with no cameras or agents or art galleries anywhere near, to ask you to marry me. I thought we could keep it a secret, just our secret. But only if you say yes.'

He strokes Laura's hair. She nods, and he pulls her towards him to kiss her.

'But I don't want it to be a secret,' she says.

Inigo is on his knee now, pushing the ring onto her finger. He looks up, relieved, as she says this, then grins wickedly.

'That's lucky, because I've already given an interview to the radio and I've begun work on a piece called *My Wife, My Life*.'

He stands up and wraps his arms around her. She clasps her hands behind his neck and whispers, 'So what's it like?'

He bends to kiss her. 'It's incredibly high maintenance, and it starts like this . . .'

SUMMERTIME

After one year of being 'buffered from single-motherhood' by her boyfriend, David, Venetia Summers suddenly finds her life unravelling as he is sent to the Brazilian jungle and she is left alone in Norfolk. As chaos reigns in her home and her three children run wilder than ever she finds her life further complicated by a bad-mouthed green parrot, a burgeoning fashion career designing demented cardigans and her brother's outrageous wedding. As emails languish unanswered, phone lines cut out and her long-distance relationship proves both vexing and bewildering, life and love take some very unexpected turns.

A PERFECT LIFE

The Stone family live a fairy-tale existence in their home in rural Norfolk, complete with adorable children, glamorous parents and postcard-perfect seaside picnics. Nick, Angel and their family lead a charmed life. And yet beneath the surface all is not as it seems.

Why is Nick away so often? Where's the laughter? And what is happening to the children?

We all want a perfect life, but at what price?

POPPYLAND

On a freezing cold night in an unfamiliar city, a man meets a woman. The encounter lasts just moments, they part barely knowing one another's names, they make no plans to meet again. But both are left breathless.

Five years on they live thousands of miles apart and live totally separate lives, except that they both still think about that night. So when they meet again it seems clear that they will do all they can to try and stay together. But can it be that easy? Will they be able to escape their past? Will they be able to take the risk they know they should?

BLOOMSBURY

FROM A DISTANCE

April, 1946. Michael, a soldier, returns to Southampton on a troop ship. Brutalised and in shock, he cannot face the life that awaits him at home. Impulsively he boards a train to the western tip of Cornwall, where his life is shaped by his heart and the fragmented Britain he has come back to.

More than half a century later, Kit, an enigmatic stranger, arrives in Norfolk to take up an inheritance he doesn't want – a decommissioned lighthouse, half hidden in the shadows of the past, now sweeping its beam forward through time. According to Kit, his life is complete, and he doesn't wish to see anything the lighthouse's glare exposes. But the choice is out of his hands.

Luisa, a second generation Italian, has so far lived through her children and has reached a point of invisibility. The constant push and pull of family life has turned like the tide, and she is suspended, without direction. Kit and Luisa meet and neither can escape the inevitability of Michael's split-second decision at the Southampton docks.

Moving between the post-war artists' colony around St Ives in Cornwall and present-day Norfolk, Raffaella Barker's new novel explores the secrets and flaws that shape our interactions across generations. *From a Distance* is a tender and compelling story of human connection and the yearning desire we have to belong.

'I love Raffaella Barker's books – so funny and acerbic'
MAGGIE O'FARRELL

BLOOMSBURY